The Fountain

Suzy Vadori

*For Patience,
May all your
wishes come
true!
Sy Vadori*

EVIL ALTER EGO PRESS

www.evilalteregopress.wordpress.com

Evil Alter Ego Press

www.evilalteregopress.wordpress.com

Published by Evil Alter Ego Press, 869 Citadel Drive NW, Calgary, AB T3G 4B8, Canada

The Fountain, Copyright © 2015 by Suzy Vadori.

Edited by Jeffrey A. Hite and Julayne Hughes.

Cover by Jeff Minkevics, copyright © 2015 by Jeff Minkevics.

Interior design and layout by Michell Plested.

Print version set in Cambria; titles in Cambria, byline in Cambria.

Published in Canada

Library and Archives Canada Cataloguing in Publication

Vadori, Suzy, 1975-, author

The Fountain / Suzy Vadori.

Prix Aurora Edition (2016)

Electronic monograph issued in EPUB and print format.

ISBN 978-1-988361-07-9 (pbk.).
ISBN 978-0-9947266-5-0 (epub).

CONTENTS

CHAPTER ONE

The Fountain

"I'm *terrified* of expulsion," Ava hissed at Ethan, "but this isn't negotiable. Go back if you're scared. I never asked you to come."

Ava turned her back, blinking to clear his cowed expression from her sight. She pushed deeper into the dark of the West Woods, walking as quickly as she dared, pushing branches aside that blocked the path as she went. The fountain waited out there, and it was getting late. The sooner she undid her wish, the sooner everything could go back to the way it was supposed to be.

She could tell by the sound of footsteps that Ethan followed, though he seemed to be keeping his distance. Gritting her teeth, she wished she'd brought her phone. The thin beam from Ethan's flashlight, shining from behind, wasn't strong enough to show the roots that lay ahead in her path. Turning toward him, she waited. Despite his teasing, she was really glad he was here.

She looked at him smiling awkwardly at her through the gloom as he approached. Her own thin smile felt forced. They'd be missed by now. The New England wind found the holes in the weave of her sweater, sending a chill up her back.

I wish to undo the wish I made here on September 14th that made Courtney disappear.

I wish to undo the wish I made here on September 14th that

The Fountain

made Courtney disappear.

Ava fiddled with the coin in her sweater pocket, shivering against the cold. The fountain had already granted her one wish. She needed it to work again.

She watched as Ethan sidestepped the roots at his feet. His ball cap hid the coal-black shock of hair she'd grown used to. His dark eyes met hers from beneath the veil of his cap. Did he want to believe her story as much as she wanted him to?

Averting her eyes to watch her feet, she continued along the path. Ethan walked easily beside her. Ava heard her own breath rise and fall. Ethan's hand nearly brushed hers as they walked, the narrow path pushing them together. Ava flexed her fingers, toward the heat of his hand. One slight move and she could clasp the security that he offered. Could it really be that simple?

"We're almost there," Ava announced, her voice breaking a little.

She cleared her throat and took a small step sideways, away from him on the path.

She noticed him withdraw, stuffing the hand she'd almost grabbed into his jeans pocket.

Ava felt a sinking feeling. She couldn't leave St. Augustus yet. There was so much she needed to explore.

She'd managed to lead Ethan right into the clearing. The beam from his flashlight shone before them in a wide arc.

Ava dropped the coin she'd been fiddling with, her hand hanging slack at her side. The coin sank into the long grass at her feet without making a sound. The clearing blurred in front of her. She felt Ethan move quickly, his warm arm suddenly pressed against her waist, keeping her from collapsing onto the ground.

Ava reeled. This was definitely the clearing where she'd made her wish.

So, where was the fountain?

CHAPTER TWO

St. Augustus

The room Ava had been assigned was smaller than she'd expected from the photos she'd seen. The shared closet wasn't even big enough for her roommate's wardrobe, which dwarfed Ava's own school uniforms and the sparse outfits she'd managed to shove onto the end of the rack.

One of the beds had clearly been slept in, its covers tangled atop the mattress. Ava reached over instinctively and pulled the offending blankets up neatly. A moment later she thought better of it and tossed them back more or less the way they'd been. The other bed must be hers. Ava frowned slightly at the stacks of clothes on top. From the looks of it, her roommate had been using it like an extended closet. The pillow looked inviting. Ava gingerly moved the stacks over to the desks. How many clothes did her roommate need, anyway? Maybe Ava could ask her when she arrived. At any rate, she'd probably figured that since Ava had missed the first day of school, she might not be coming at all. Ava hoped her new roomie wouldn't be too disappointed about sharing.

Catching sight of her own reflection in a mirror hanging on the closet door, Ava took a step closer. Her face puckered at the navy track pants that clung to her hips in an unflattering way. Her hair, usually the color of wet sand, had taken on a grayish hue in the fluorescent light of the dorm. Ava wrinkled her nose as she tucked a limp strand behind one ear.

Ava sighed as she looked back over at the shared closet. She'd hoped her roommate would be a friend. All the visions she'd had of finally being here included a confidante. She and this girl weren't going to have much in common.

Feeling the hairs prickle on the back of her neck, Ava turned to see a girl in a too-short kilt standing in the doorway, looking at Ava with a strange expression on her face. The girl looked stylish, even in her St. Augustus uniform – though an almost indecent amount of her caramel-colored legs showed between her white knee socks and the hem of her skirt. More surprising, a dark bra was clearly visible under her starched white blouse.

"Can I help you?" Ava's new roommate asked. Her long ponytail swung over her shoulder as she breezed into the room, landing in the middle of her back in straight black licorice strands. A fringe of glossy bangs bounced as she moved, settling each time in a ruler-straight line across her forehead.

"I'm Ava Marshall, your new roommate."

After a moment's pause, the girl wheeled around and surprised Ava with an enthusiastic embrace.

"So nice to meet you!" the girl gushed, releasing Ava. "You're from California, right? I'm so sorry about using your dresser. I thought you weren't coming after all. I'm Jules."

Ava looked over at the dresser standing at the foot of her bed. She hadn't looked in it yet.

Jules moved toward the closet as she talked, casually peeling off her plaid kilt and dropping it in a heap on the floor, followed by her blouse. Wearing only a deep pink bra and matching panties, Jules stretched her bare limbs to reach a pair of jeans on the top shelf of the closet.

Ava looked at the ground as Jules bent over to step into the jeans, her shapely rear pointed in Ava's direction. Hurrying over to the open door, Ava dragged her own suitcases away, letting the door swing shut. Maybe Jules hadn't realized that the door was wide open. Ava stole a curious look at the other girl, who shimmied her skinny jeans up over hot pink panties and zipped them up. White rhinestones lined the pockets on the rear of her jeans in a zigzag pattern. She lifted a soft-looking purple top over her head and pulled her long ponytail out from the back, letting her hair ripple down over her shirt like dark satin. Ava stared. Jules looked as if she was heading out to a nightclub. Ava's hands moved to smooth down her own track pants, which crackled with static.

"I'll pack some of my clothes away to make some space," Jules said.

She turned to face Ava then frowned. Jules stared at the two small suitcases beside Ava's feet.

"Where are all your things?" Jules asked. She looked back at Ava's few items hanging at the edge of the closet. Her frown deepened.

"This is all I brought," Ava replied, with a weak smile.

The look on Jules' face told Ava this was not good news. A few moments went by while the two girls sized each other up.

"Well then, we'll have to do some shopping," Jules finally said, her face breaking into a smile. "Lucky for you, there's no homework yet, so I have lots of time to show you around before dinner. Did you go to classes today?"

Jules opened the door to the hallway, holding it for Ava.

"Nope," Ava replied, feeling lightheaded as she stepped into the hall. "My Aunt Mia couldn't get away from work until last night. I thought I'd make at least my last class, but everything took forever. We took the red-eye flight into Boston this morning. My dad wouldn't let me make the trip alone. He's working overseas, in Malaysia."

Jules nodded, as if in sympathy. Ava wondered if Jules missed her own parents as much as Ava missed her dad - and her mom. Tilting her head to one side, Jules put her hand on the doorknob of the room directly across the hall and opened the door confidently.

Ava hesitated, unsure if she should follow Jules into someone else's room. She looked around, not wanting to be left in the hall by herself.

"C'mon in," Jules urged. She nodded her head toward the open door. "Come meet Kelly and Kiera."

Ava took a deep breath and entered.

Amidst hugs and high-pitched squeals, Ava was introduced to brunette twins who roomed there. Their constant giggle was contagious and Ava felt herself actually grinning as she and Jules said their goodbyes and headed back into the hall.

"All the juniors and seniors live on this floor," said Jules, after they'd left the twins' room. "The younger girls' rooms are upstairs and the boys' dorm is on the other side of the main building. Can you believe boys used to room on this floor? That changed a while back, though. The school was smaller then."

"Yeah," Ava replied, following Jules down the hall. "My aunt and my parents came to St. Augustus, so I've heard some stories." Very few stories, she reminded herself.

"Oh, you're an alumni kid," Jules declared. "That explains the trip across the country."

"What did you call me?" Ava asked her, stopping in her tracks. Whatever it was sounded pretentious.

"An alumni kid," Jules repeated. "You know, kids with family connections to the school."

"Oh," Ava replied, flatly, "my family isn't really involved anymore, though my gran lives close to campus. My mom and my aunt never even lived in the dorm."

"Where did you do your freshman and sophomore years, then?" Jules asked, as they approached the next door down the hall.

"Public school," Ava replied, "near my house in San Francisco."

"Oh, interesting," Jules replied, although her tone suggested that it wasn't.

Jules breezed from one room to the next without bothering to knock, interrupting girls in various stages of undress. Ava trailed behind, picking at her sweatpants. The noisy dorm was a far cry from the quiet house she'd shared with her dad. The wagging tongues around her put her senses on overload. She didn't hope to remember all the names, though she had to admit they'd all been nice.

Her boyfriend Lucas had been the only frequent visitor to their house in San Francisco. He was a fixture, really. She smiled slightly, knowing how he'd roll his eyes at all these gossiping girls. They'd been best friends since they were kids. Even in the middle of this sea of new faces, Ava suddenly realized she was alone for the first time that she could remember.

Jules knocked gently on the door to the last room on the floor. A girl with a fiery mane of red hair swung open the door. Ava took a step back without meaning to. School had ended almost an hour ago, but this girl had not changed out of her uniform. There were other girls in the room, also still wearing their blouses and kilts. They crowded together on the room's two small beds. The girl at the door leaned her arm across the doorframe, preventing Ava and Jules from stepping inside.

"Courtney, this is Ava Marshall," Jules announced, gesturing toward Ava in an uncharacteristically stiff manner. "She's my new roommate."

Ava looked sideways at Jules. She hadn't used Ava's last name before now. The warmth in Jules' voice that Ava had gotten to know over the past hour was gone.

"I've heard you're a swimmer," the girl replied, her green eyes unblinking. "Rumor has it you're pretty fast, for a public school girl."

Courtney's gaze traveled from Ava's flyaway hair, down to her well-worn tracksuit and back up again to meet Ava's eyes. Ava looked at Jules. Why had they stopped at this room? This girl clearly didn't want to chat. Behind her, the room was cramped with visitors.

Ava's stomach flip-flopped. Was this girl on the swim team? She craned her neck a little to see past Courtney into the room. The other girls in the room sat silently, not looking at Ava.

"We'll see," Courtney said, still leaning against the door frame.

"Well, okay then," said Jules, her voice tight. "Come on Ava, we've still got lots to see."

She touched Ava's arm lightly, guiding her down the hall.

"Oh, and Ava," Courtney called after them as they walked away down the hall, "swim practice is at 7:30 tomorrow morning. Coach Laurel asked me to tell you."

"Uh, thanks," replied Ava, turning back to see Courtney's thin smile.

"So I guess you think your mom's history guarantees you a spot on the team?" Courtney said loudly.

"Excuse me?" replied Ava, taken aback.

"Your mom," Courtney replied, flatly. "Just because she swam here doesn't mean you'll get to."

"I, uh, I know that." Ava stammered, staring at Courtney. Of course she knew that.

Ava pushed down the urge to run down the hall and out onto the lawn. How did Courtney know about her mother? Ava looked over at Jules for help, but Jules looked away, twirling her hair with her pinky.

"Good," said Courtney, closing the door without saying goodbye.

Ava numbly stared at the wrought iron numbers hanging on the door. She'd lost her mom when she'd been ten. It had been a car accident. Swimming was something they'd had in common. Her mom had wanted her to come to this school. Ava squeezed her hands into fists at her sides. She felt off-balance somehow.

Jules' hearty laugh snapped Ava back to reality. Jules dragged her by the arm, out the side door and onto the lawn.

"That was Courtney Wallis," explained Jules, once they were outside. She made a face. "Her parents paid extra this year to get her *that* room. She doesn't even have a roommate."

"No roommate?" asked Ava. There had been two beds in the room, same as the other rooms on the floor. "Who were the girls in her room?"

The campus lawn stretched several hundred yards toward the West Woods, beyond which was Gran's house. Jules led Ava in the opposite direction, toward the main building.

"I overheard Courtney telling someone it's so that her friends can come and go as they want," replied Jules, with a small laugh. "But my guess is that none of them would want to live with her. I try to stay on Courtney's good side and that's my advice for you, too. She could make things difficult for you if she felt like it. So, you swim? Are you good? She's pretty good."

"I'm okay," mumbled Ava, thinking of every California state championship meet she'd been at since the seventh grade. "Difficult how? She looked at me like I was already on her bad side."

"Last year," Jules said, dropping her voice, "there was this girl Rhoda who was in our year. Nice girl, though I didn't know her that well. Rhoda transferred schools. People say it was because of Courtney."

They were almost at the main building now. Ava hadn't been prepared for how she'd feel, finally being on this campus. The knot in her chest she'd felt when she'd been in the hallway with Courtney released a little. She'd seen the ivy-covered spires of the main building plenty of times as a kid from the edge of the woods, although up close she could see the intricate carvings on its brownstone walls.

"It takes a while to get used to," said Jules, interrupting Ava's thoughts.

"What does?" Ava asked, following Jules' gaze in the direction of the main building. Courtney faded from her mind. She was here.

"Some of the students call it a castle," Jules replied, gesturing at the building, "but I find I don't notice its gaudiness anymore. The classrooms inside are actually quite plain. They say the founder of St. Augustus was an eccentric."

Ava nodded, stepping onto the broad stone steps.

"What did you mean by *that* room?" Ava asked, as they climbed toward the heavy black double doors. "You mean, room sixty-five? Courtney's room?"

"Honestly, Ava," Jules replied with a sigh, stopping with her hands on her hips in front of Ava on the stairs. "Alumni kids usually show up for their first week of school bragging how much they know about its silly superstitions."

"Well, my dad doesn't exactly like to talk about St. Augustus," Ava explained, meekly. "I guess it brings up painful memories of my mom. She, uh... died."

Ava felt suddenly exposed, standing on the stone steps with students passing by them on all sides. A strong breeze blew Ava's stringy hair into her face. She reached up to tuck it behind her ears. A long moment passed between them before Jules spoke.

"Oh, sorry," said Jules, scrunching her tiny nose.

"It's okay," Ava replied, with a shrug. "I was ten."

It really was okay. One of the reasons Ava had pushed so hard to come to St. Augustus was to feel closer to her mom. Talking about her was an important step in that direction. There hadn't been much talking about the past with her dad.

"Well, if you don't know, then I'll tell you," said Jules, huddling close to Ava against the stone railing of the steps.

The scent of Jules' shampoo tickled Ava's nose.

"Room sixty-five is supposed to be lucky." Jules told her. "School legends say whoever lives there has good fortune. Have you ever heard anything so ridiculous?"

"Wait," said Ava, tilting her head to one side, "is Courtney's dad Jim Wallis?"

"Yep," replied Jules, with a chuckle. "State Senator Jim Wallis. Why do you think all those girls hang out with her? They seem to think Courtney can get them all internships in DC when they graduate."

"Oh, I didn't realize he was a senator," said Ava, feeling sheepish. "It's just that my dad knows him. I think they went to St. Augustus at the same time."

"See?" Jules said with a laugh, "you're an alumni kid, whether you know it or not."

Turning and climbing the last two steps, Jules tugged on the solid door to the main building and held it open for Ava. Ava paused for a beat before following her inside and steeling herself against the busy foyer. Maybe Jules would turn out to be a friend, after all.

CHAPTER THREE

On the Verge

Ava's stomach fluttered as she walked toward her first St. Augustus swim practice the next morning. She couldn't wait to meet her new coach. The morning air was refreshing. Her backpack was full of her swim gear, towel, and uniform.

It had been pretty considerate of the coach to have Courtney invite her to the practice. It was one less thing she'd had to worry about as she got used to her new surroundings. Courtney's words ran through Ava's mind. Ava had been the fastest girl on her team last year, but she knew that didn't guarantee her a spot. The St. Augustus girls' team was one of the best in the country.

The oversized windows on the sports complex gleamed against its gray stone as Ava approached. Ava had only seen this building in brochures - it was only a few years old. She'd been to the old pool a few times - the one that her mom had swum in. She and her mom had snuck in on a few of their visits to watch the teams practice. Ava hadn't been to campus, or even the town of Evergreen to visit Gran since her mom had died.

Entering the building, she looked around for the pool entrance and saw a door to one of the gyms propped open with a basketball. She poked her head in to investigate the sound of squeaky shoes against the wood floor. A tall, dark-haired boy practiced free throws inside, wearing a basketball uniform. His calf muscles flexed and his arms rose above his head fluidly as he set up for each throw.

The boy's dark eyebrows knit together while he lined up his shot - rising in anticipation as he watched the arc of his ball sail toward the net. Ava craned her neck to follow. Toss after toss dropped right into the basket. He was pretty good. In between throws, he jogged after the ball, coal-colored hair flopping over his forehead in a playful way each time he bent down to retrieve it. On one of his return rounds to the free-throw line, he looked over at the door where Ava was standing, flashing a dazzling smile. As he caught her eye, Ava clumsily stepped away from the door, feeling color rise into her cheeks.

Taking a deep breath, she peeked back into the gym, where the boy stood watching the door with an amused look on his face.

He ran backward in a curved motion, going for a three-point shot while smiling in her direction.

Ava rolled her eyes dramatically. His ball missed. She stifled a giggle.

Voices approached in the hall behind her, Ava looked back to see two more ball players heading toward the gym, dressed in St. Augustus green and silver. The boy had gone back to his free throws. Ava pulled her phone out of her backpack to check the time as she made her way down the hallway toward where the ball players had come from. On her phone, there was a text from Lucas from the night before, making sure she'd arrived.

She quickly typed "YES! xox," hit send, and stuffed the phone back into her pack. It was still pretty early on the West Coast - he wouldn't be awake for a few hours yet.

Finding the girls' locker room at the far end of the hall, Ava stepped inside. The metal door clanged shut behind her, ringing an echo into the empty room. She listened for a moment. Something was wrong. The locker room should be full of girls by now. Ava felt her stomach drop as noises reached her from the direction of the pool. The team was already here.

Mumbling under her breath, Ava found an empty locker. She slammed it open with a bang. Of course she should have checked the swim practice time herself. No wonder Courtney had been so quick to tell her about it. Well, if making her late for practice was the best Courtney could do, so be it. Ava squared her jaw. She could take a little hazing. She yanked her towel and gear out of her backpack. In fact, giving her the wrong time for practice was downright unoriginal, she thought, fumbling into her swimsuit. Ava shoved her backpack and uniform into the empty locker and snapped on her swim cap, stuffing her fly-away ponytail inside.

A noise came from the restroom off the main locker area. Ava looked up to see Courtney emerge from one of the toilet stalls and walk toward her. Ava narrowed her eyes as she took in Courtney's wet navy swimsuit and matching Owls swim cap. Courtney had a white towel draped over her shoulders.

Ava looked toward the entrance to the pool, then back at Courtney. She hated being late.

"Oh, Ava," Courtney said with mock surprise, tossing her damp towel down casually on the bench. "It's nice of you to join us."

"So, Courtney," Ava asked drily, her foot tapping involuntarily, "does the team warm up before practice?"

"Well, some do," Courtney answered in the sweet, measured tone Ava had heard the night before, "but practice started at 7:00. Coach Laurel wasn't impressed that you weren't here. I'd think you'd *want* to make a good impression, what with it being your first day and all."

Ava's temples throbbed. She could almost feel steam pour out of her ears as she glared at her new teammate. She wanted to wipe the sickening smile off of Courtney's face. Did she think Ava would just pack up and go home?

Courtney picked up her towel from the bench with a swooping motion and headed off toward the pool, leaving Ava fuming in front of the row of lockers. Scowling, Ava hastily grabbed her combination lock sitting open on the bench and wiped it on her leg. It was slippery from being under Courtney's damp towel. She turned toward the locker she'd filled and snapped the lock shut.

Ava rinsed quickly under the shower before heading out onto the pool deck. She knew she was late, but she needed a moment to collect her thoughts. Could she tell her new coach that Courtney had made her late on purpose? Ava stuck her head under the steady shower stream, feeling the warm water splash off of her cap. Hot water landed on her shoulders and ran down her back. The coach wouldn't want to hear that. The warmth of the water spread across her purple swimsuit, slowly soaking in until her skin underneath warmed. She'd just tell the coach that she'd made a mistake, being new to the campus. Ava knew she'd not be late again.

She shut off the shower and grabbed her towel. Taking a deep breath, she stepped out onto the pool deck. Familiar airborne chlorine burned her nostrils.

Ava gave a shallow gasp at how many heads bobbed in the swimming lanes. There were at least twice as many girls here as could make the team. Ava squinted at the moving bodies in the pool. It was hard to judge how fast they were swimming, though the technique she saw was good. Ava cleared her throat. Her best would have to be enough.

Usually, Ava stretched before she swam, but she hesitated. She was already late. Maybe she should just get in the pool. Undecided, she looked around for someone in charge. Instead of spotting her new coach, she saw Courtney standing on the pool deck nearby, watching her with a smug expression on her face.

Ava clenched her teeth. What had she ever done to Courtney?

"Ava Marshall?"

The barking voice came from a heavy-set woman that headed toward her on the pool deck. After flashing Courtney a brief look that would kill flowers, Ava found a smile to paste on. She couldn't afford to be distracted by Courtney right now. The last thing on her mind was to start a war. Maybe Courtney would be satisfied with Ava starting off on the wrong foot and back off.

"I'm Coach Laurel," the woman said, rearing up in front of Ava.

The coach wore a green and silver tracksuit that stretched over her thick, muscular frame. Her husky voice carried an air of authority.

"Ava Marshall," said Ava, extending her hand to her new coach. "So sorry I was ..."

Coach Laurel held her hand up. "I don't know what the rules are in California, but the St. Augustus Owls don't tolerate tardiness. Practice starts at 7 a.m. sharp. You'd also do well to remember that I pick this team. Bragging to your teammates about who your mother is, or was, will not influence my decision. Your status with the school's alumni does not interest me in the least. Only your hard work can impress me."

Ava felt her whole body flush as she dropped her outstretched hand to her side. Her mind raced. Courtney had brought up Ava's mom the night before. What did the coach know about her mom? Ava had come to St. Augustus in hopes of weaving a connection to her mother, but she hadn't shared that with anyone. Not even her dad or Aunt Mia. She looked around, but Courtney no longer stood on the pool deck. Ava opened her mouth to reply to the coach, but nothing came out.

"What are you waiting for?" asked Coach Laurel, pointing to the full swimming lanes in the pool beside her. "Get in and earn your spot."

All Ava could think to do was nod her head and make her way to the starting blocks, her stomach tightening in a way that might make it tricky to swim. She tried to relax, knowing that her deep, guttural breaths made her stomach protrude from her swimsuit. She looked down at the stretchy fabric. She'd been so happy to find this suit on the rack at Macy's this summer. It was purple with light blue stripes down the sides. Racing stripes, she'd thought. Most of the other girls here wore plain green suits, with the St. Augustus Owl silk screened neatly in silver on the breast. Ava's suit practically screamed outsider - or at least freshman.

Stepping up onto the block at the head of the closest swim lane, Ava took three deep breaths. One-Mississippi, two-Mississippi, three-Mississippi. Hearing a sharp peal of laughter ring out over the echo of the swimmers, Ava squinted in its direction to see Courtney, now standing on the deck at the far end of the pool. Ava felt invisible. Courtney leaned in to whisper something to a girl standing next to her. A shock of Courtney's red hair stuck out from under her swim cap. Ava's steadied herself against the tremble that rocked through her body.

"All I have to do is swim," Ava told herself, repeating her breathing exercise. "I can do this."

She stretched her arms above her head and looked around for a time clock. Taking note of the second hand, Ava dove into the pool, feeling the cold slap of the water shake her out of her funk. Gliding out into her lane, automatic strokes took over. As her head moved in and out of the water with her front crawl, sound faded. Ava homed in on the slice of her own limbs hitting the pool. Courtney and her hectic morning were pushed from her awareness, replaced by the rhythm of her practiced strokes.

When Ava reached the end of the pool, she missed a beat on the turn, popping her head up to see if Courtney was still there. She wasn't. Her former scowl melted into the water as she remembered Courtney's hair sticking out from her cap, thinking how much it looked like devil's horns.

Ava hadn't counted her laps, though she guessed she'd swum nearly fifty when she started to tire. As she flipped her body over in the water to do a few lengths of back-crawl, her strokes bounced vacantly against the water. Looking around, she found herself alone in the pool. Gliding up to the starting blocks, she reached for the edge and looked up, seeing Coach Laurel standing near her on the deck.

"I like your spunk," Coach Laurel told her. "Time trials are on Saturday morning at eleven. If you swim as well as you did today, there'll be a spot for you on my team."

"Thank you, coach," Ava replied, treading water and feeling light. "I'll be here on time."

Coach Laurel gave a curt nod and walked away, disappearing behind a door in the opposite direction of the change rooms.

Ava nearly hopped out of the pool then walked quickly toward the locker room. Hot rain from the shower felt good on her skin, each drop seeming to wash her frustration down the drain. It was going to be okay. Ava ducked her face under the stream of water and slowly peeled her swimsuit down over her calves and onto the floor.

Turning off the shower, she immediately noticed the silence in the locker room, much like it'd been when she'd arrived. She was alone. But this time, she was glad. First picking up her soaked suit off the shower floor, she tiptoed nude to grab her towel. Her shoulders relaxed as she dried off and moved toward the wall of blue lockers. Her combination lock was the only one left hanging in the row.

She'd been on campus less than twenty-four hours. None of it had been as she'd expected. Spinning her combination on the lock, she pulled, but the lock didn't open. Frowning, she wrapped her towel around her body and tried her combination for a second time. Ava took a step back and looked at the wall of lockers. She'd been flustered when she'd put her things in the locker. Had she forgotten which one was hers? She'd had the same lock for years, so she knew she hadn't forgotten its combination. She distinctly remembered retrieving it from the bench where it had gotten damp with Courtney's towel thrown on top. Peeking in through holes in the metal door, she saw her own backpack hanging inside the locker. Her school loafers sat neatly on the bottom of the metal box. This was definitely it. She held the weight of the lock in her hand and tugged again. Could a lock break? It was old, after all. She studied it closely. This lock didn't look old. It was black with white numbers, somehow shinier than she'd remembered. Ava shook her head at the locker.

An overhead fan spewed a cold breeze onto her, spreading gooseflesh down her damp arms. She pulled her towel tighter against her shoulders and considered her options. She could go find Coach Laurel. Ava shook her head. The coach already thought Ava was disorganized. Besides, what could the coach do about a lock that wouldn't open?

Ava felt like she'd been turned upside down, aware that the clock on the wall ticked the minutes by as she stood there. If she made it to the dorm quickly, Jules might still be in their room. Her dorm keys were in the locker. Her phone was in the locker. Classes were starting soon and she'd have to do something fast if she wanted to be there. She wanted to be there. Turning toward the mirrored wall beside her, she looked at herself for a moment. Her summer tan had faded to just a shadow on her pale skin. The towel wrapped around her shoulders gaped in front, not quite covering her small breasts, navel and more down below.

Taking her wet swimsuit in her hands, she wrung it out, dripping excess water onto the locker room floor. Gasping as the cold, wet, purple fabric touched her now dry skin, Ava shimmied back into the suit. She wished she'd chosen one with less color. She stuffed the corners of the towel under the skinny shoulder straps of the swimsuit, fashioning a makeshift toga. Ava frowned at her reflection. The towel covered her swimsuit, but not much else, giving the illusion that she was naked underneath. She looked herself over, feeling utterly miserable. If she walked quickly, she thought hopefully, she might not see too many students on her way back to the dorm.

Squaring her shoulders, Ava moved toward the door to the hallway and opened it, listening for sounds of life. When she heard nothing, she timidly took a step into the corridor, feeling the grit on the floor under her bare feet. It was still possible to make it to her class on time, even stopping to change at the dorm. Wasn't it?

"I can do this," she told herself, under her breath. "It's no different than walking across the pool deck in my swimsuit. I do that all the time. It's no big deal."

She'd only gone a few steps down the hallway when rowdy voices and laughter reached her ears. Ava groaned. She'd forgotten about the boys' basketball practice. A low whistle sounded from the sweaty mass of teenage boys that materialized in front of her in the hall. She stepped toward the wall to let them pass, crossing her arms tightly across the towel wrapped around her chest. A hot blush sent heat down her neck and shoulders. She reminded herself that she wasn't actually naked underneath. But it didn't stop her gut from churning.

Ava lifted her chin. Looking forward as she marched ahead, Ava noticed the ball player she'd seen practicing in the gym walking in the middle of the group. His dark eyebrows rose, a hint of a smile seeming to dance on his lips.

Ava thought he looked vaguely sympathetic and gave him what she hoped was a pleading look amidst catcalls from the other boys. His lips parted in a smile, as he bowed his head slightly at her.

"C'mon guys, leave her alone," he said, as he nudged his teammates down the hall, toward the locker room.

Ava stood pressed against the wall as they passed, her eyes studying the floor. When the last ball player had disappeared into the boys' locker room, Ava turned toward the exit and ran, holding her towel around her tightly. Bursting out onto the campus lawn, the morning air smelled sweet and she drank in deep breaths. This corner of the campus was thankfully deserted. With one hand on her flapping towel as she ran, Ava sprinted barefoot over the damp carpet of grass. Panting, she tugged open the door to the main building and stepped into the foyer, crowded with students. She made a beeline through the main building to the front door, keenly aware of the smirks as she passed. She was thankful she didn't know many people yet. Maybe they wouldn't notice her, either, she thought. Once she left the main building, it was only a few quick moments across the lawn until she reached the security of the girls' dorm. Slowing to a walk and gasping for air, Ava pulled her towel off her body and wrapped it around her soggy hair. Down at the other end of the dorm hall, she spotted Jules coming out of their room.

"Ava, what are you wearing?" Jules gasped, her mouth hanging open as Ava approached. She gaped at Ava's bare feet.

"I'll fill you in later," Ava mumbled. "Can you please just let me into our room? My keys are still at the pool."

"Sure," replied Jules, still looking astonished as she opened their door.

"Did anybody actually see you walking around like that?" Jules asked, incredulously, as Ava brushed past her into their room.

Ava frantically pulled off her swimsuit and threw on the bra and panties she'd worn the night before that she'd tucked under the bed. She then grabbed another kilt and blouse from her uniforms hung in the closet. Tugging white knee socks on over her calves, Ava fumbled deeper under the bed for her suitcase, which she pulled out to retrieve a pair of shoes.

"Yep," Ava replied, stepping into the shoes she'd found. "People definitely saw me."

Fully dressed in only a few moments, Ava squeezed back past Jules into the hall, her damp hair now flopping up and down in its ponytail as she walked. A wet trail led from the nape of her neck down the back of her blouse.

"Ava," said Jules, barring the way with her arm, and staring now at Ava's shoes, "you have to wear your loafers to class."

"I don't think I can get my stuff back before school starts," replied Ava, shrugging helplessly.

"Headmistress Valentine will be livid. Those shoes have sequins!" Jules said, giggling. "But they actually have style."

Aunt Mia had insisted on buying her the low-heeled sequined shoes for her last birthday. Ava would have left them behind in California if Mia hadn't added them to her suitcase. At least they were mostly black, though the sequins shimmered with a silver gleam. The only other shoes she'd brought were her new running shoes – too bright white, with fluorescent orange soles.

Ava and Jules walked together toward the foyer. Ava's heart raced as she remembered the brief interactions she'd had with Courtney since the night before.

"Jules," said Ava, glowering as they passed room sixty-five, "what can you tell me about Courtney? Like, why she might want me off the swim team and just how far she might go?"

"Ava," Jules asked, her tone guarded, "does Courtney have anything to do with you walking around campus like a drowned rat?"

"Yes," Ava answered darkly. "I'd be willing to bet she does."

CHAPTER FOUR

Ethan

Well, here's the office," said Jules, indicating a heavy wooden door. "Miss Samantha's desk is just inside; she'll be able to print you a new class schedule."

Ava didn't have much time to get to class. Being late for practice had been bad enough. If there was a way to get to her first class on time, she had to try. But first, she had to figure out where she should be.

"Thanks," said Ava as she grabbed the wooden door's brass handle.

"How did you say you got locked out of your locker?" Jules asked.

"Uh," Ava replied absently. She stared at the middle aged woman with puffy hair sitting at a large desk in the office. "I think I must've gotten my lock mixed up with someone else's."

"Oh," Jules replied, not looking convinced. "Well, I haven't had breakfast yet and I'm starving. I've got to hit the cafeteria before I go to class. Will you be all right here?"

"Sure," mumbled Ava.

"Well then, good luck," said Jules.

Ava barely registered Jules' apprehensive wave as she walked away.

Ava entered the school office. Sitting at her desk in the center of the room, the puffy-haired lady sat engrossed in a phone conversation. She must be Miss Samantha.

Ava hung back near the door, shifting her weight from foot to foot. The clock on the wall seemed to tick the seconds by quickly. Miss Samantha still hadn't hung up the phone. Ava now had only ten minutes to get to her first class. She looked around. Dark woodwork set against deep burgundy walls made the room dim. A large wooden door behind Miss Samantha's desk had HEADMISTRESS MOIRA VALENTINE on its brass nameplate.

"Ahem," Ava cleared her throat, hoping to get Miss Samantha's attention.

Miss Samantha held up one hand without looking up at Ava. Ava checked the clock again. Nine minutes.

"Yes, Mr. Wallis," Miss Samantha said in a sing-song voice. "The homecoming football game is on the Sunday, and we expect a good alumni turnout this year. Your speech will be directly before the game."

Ava started at the mention of Courtney's father. He was going to be at the homecoming game. Her school back home had homecoming too, but Ava had never paid much attention. Their football team hadn't been very good. She listened keenly, wondering if Jim Wallis was anything like his daughter.

Eight minutes.

"May I help you?" Miss Samantha asked, hanging up the phone and looking over to Ava, who still stood by the door.

"I... uh," Ava stammered, almost forgetting why she was there. "I left my class schedule at swim practice this morning. Would you be able to print me a new copy?"

"Sure thing," Miss Samantha replied, clicking away at her keyboard. "What's your name, dear?"

"Ava Marshall."

"Oh, Ava, so nice to meet you," Miss Samantha gushed, her whole face breaking into a broad smile. "How was your journey here? I've spoken to your aunt a few times on the phone. Too bad you missed a day of classes already.

"Let's get your schedule here and make sure you don't miss another one. Anything else I can help you with, dear?"

Six minutes.

"I also need to get into my locker at the pool," Ava replied, after pausing for a moment. She needed to get her phone and her books. "The, uh, combination isn't working."

"Oh, that *is* a problem," said Miss Samantha, frowning sympathetically. "I think Giles our custodian was in the hall a little while ago fixing the water cooler. Take a look and see if he's still there. He can help you with your locker."

"Sure," Ava said, studying the printout in her hands. "Could you please tell me where can I find Room 202?"

Four minutes.

"It's on the second floor of the West Building," Miss Samantha said, nodding her head in the appropriate direction. "Go out of the front doors and follow the pathway to the left and it's straight ahead."

"Thanks," replied Ava, turning quickly to go.

"Oh, and Ava," said Miss Samantha, as she peered over her reading glasses toward Ava's feet. "The St. Augustus dress code doesn't allow sequined shoes. If Headmistress Valentine sees you she'll insist that you go back to your room to change."

"Oh, right," Ava acknowledged, backing out of the office, clutching her schedule to her chest. "Thanks."

Out in the hall, Ava looked around for Giles. There were only a few students in the hall now still making their way to class. The late bell would ring any moment. Ava saw a stout man crouched beside a water cooler with a wrench in his hand and a large toolbox sitting at his feet and walked hurriedly toward him.

After a brief explanation of her situation, she arranged to meet Giles and his bolt cutters at the locker room after school.

Calling her thanks to Giles over her shoulder, Ava turned and jogged down the hall in the direction Miss Samantha had pointed just as the late bell buzzed through the halls. Ava couldn't remember ever being late for a class before, but today had definitely been a day for firsts. She picked up her pace across the lawn and entered the silent halls of the West Building. Miss Samantha had said room 202 was on the second floor. A wide wooden staircase lay straight ahead and Ava took the stairs two at a time, each tread creaking loudly under her feet as she climbed.

Reaching the top, she turned left to find herself staring at the closed door of her English class. Ava stopped outside, straining to hear, though she couldn't make out what the teacher was saying. Smoothing down her rumpled blouse and kilt, Ava slowly turned the doorknob, wincing as the door opened with a loud groan. Painfully aware of her disheveled uniform and still-wet pony-tail, Ava felt thankful that at least she wasn't still in her swimsuit. She scanned the room quickly, feeling all eyes on her. Her heart sank as she saw Courtney, sitting near the back. Ava looked away quickly. Courtney's irritating smile never seemed to fade.

"Ms. Krick?" Ava said. "I'm Ava. Sorry I'm late."

Shaking off her self-doubt, Ava edged quickly into the classroom to find an empty seat. She kept her eyes focused on the floor, well aware that her glittering shoes tapped loudly on the floor with each step she took. To Ava's surprise, she looked up to see Ms. Krick's slight frame positioned in Ava's path, blocking her way.

"Yes, your mother was often late for class as well," said Ms. Krick, with an icy smile. "And I always sent her to the headmistress' office for a late slip, just as I will do for you now."

Ms. Krick's lips twitched, almost forming a sneer as she pointed toward the classroom door.

Ava's cheeks burned as she turned and walked from the

classroom, hugging her class schedule to her chest. *What was this teacher's problem? Couldn't she see that this was her first day?* Choking back sobs, she walked back across the lawn to the main building. She took a few deep breaths as she walked, fighting back the urge to scream.

"Breathe, Ava," she told herself.

Reaching into her pocket for her phone, she remembered that it was still in her locker. She didn't have time to call Lucas anyway, though it would be nice to hear his voice. He always knew how to calm her down. He wouldn't mind that she'd woken him up.

Ms. Krick had taught her mother. It was obvious to Ava that Mariam hadn't been her favorite student. She wondered what her mother had done to earn Ms. Krick's distaste. Something told Ava she shouldn't come right out and ask her new English teacher.

When Ava arrived back at the school office, she was happy to see a friendly face.

"Ah yes, Ms. Krick," said Miss Samantha. "She does insist on following school rules. I should have thought to send a late slip with you earlier."

Miss Samantha busied herself filling out a small slip of pink paper with a blue ball point pen.

Behind Miss Samantha's desk, the door to the headmistress' office opened and a sharply dressed woman stepped out. Ava drew in a breath and casually stepped behind a trash can, effectively hiding her shoes from the headmistress' view.

"Headmistress Valentine," Miss Samantha said. "This is Ava Marshall, our new junior."

"Oh, hello Ava," said Headmistress Valentine, smiling at Ava politely. "I hear you are quite the swimmer. We look forward to winning even more championships this year with you on the team. Have you met Courtney Wallis yet? She's a lovely girl. She's the favorite for captain of the girls' swim team this year and only a junior! I'm sure that you two will be the best of friends."

Ava remained behind the trash can hiding her feet, trying to paint a smile on her face. She wasn't quite sure how to respond to the headmistress' suggestion that she and Courtney would get along.

"Oh, I'm sorry Ava, I didn't mean to offend you," the headmistress said. "I'm sure Coach Laurel would consider you for the captain position too, if it's something that you want. It's just that leadership comes naturally to Courtney. She's always looking out for her teammates. She won an awful lot of medals for the Owls last year."

Ava realized that her attempt to smile had been unconvincing. She'd never considered being team captain, though the thought of Courtney being in charge of the team was unsettling.

"There you go, dear," Miss Samantha said, winking as she handed Ava the pink slip she'd finished filling in. "You just give this to Ms. Krick and you'll be fine."

"Thanks," Ava replied, taking the piece of paper and giving Miss Samantha a grateful smile.

"Nice to meet you, Ava," said Headmistress Valentine with a small wave. "You should be getting back to class, though."

"Yes, of course," replied Ava meekly, turning to go.

She crossed the floor to the door as lightly as she could, willing her shoes to not draw attention to themselves. Slipping noiselessly out the door into the hallway, she let herself relax.

Headmistress Valentine wanted Ava and Courtney to get along. Ava frowned as she started back toward the West Building. She felt sure it had been Courtney who'd switched her lock. Nobody else had been in the locker room when she'd arrived.

Taking the stairs at a more leisurely pace this time, she found herself all too soon at the door of room 202 once again. This time, she opened the groaning door with purpose and strode in without looking in Courtney's direction. Bracing herself, she handed the late slip to Ms. Krick and sat in an empty desk near the windows.

Wordlessly, Ms. Krick placed the slip on the teacher's desk and continued talking, without looking at Ava.

To Ava's relief, the topic they were discussing was creative writing, which she knew she was good at. Her tenth grade teacher had entered one of Ava's stories in a statewide contest the previous year and she'd won third place. As class was ending, Ms. Krick told them their first assignment would be due Monday morning. Ava doodled in the corners of her class schedule, thinking of possible topics for her one-page assignment. The school bell startled her out of her daydream. Ava looked up to see the dark-haired basketball player she'd watched that morning. He was just standing there, beside her desk, smiling. She hadn't noticed that he'd been in the room.

"Can I help you find your next class?" he asked. His grin seemed friendly enough. "I'd hate for you to be late again."

"Sure," Ava replied.

She did need help finding her next classroom, though she wasn't really in the mood to chat.

"I'm Ethan," he told her, extending his hand in greeting.

"Ava," she replied, shaking his hand.

His handshake was firm and warm.

"Yes, you are," he said, nodding his head.

Ava looked at him. How was it that everyone seemed to know who she was already?

"Here, take this," said Ethan, handing her an empty notebook. "I don't think your class schedule has room for any more notes."

"Thanks," she replied.

Taking the notebook, she realized he must have been watching her doodle on her schedule during class.

He grabbed the schedule she held in her hand and studied it for a moment.

"Hey!" exclaimed Ava.

"You have calculus next," he said. "I'll take you there. It's just downstairs, come on."

Ava was surprised when Ethan boldly grabbed her hand and dragged her into the crowded hall without giving her time to object. He smoothly guided her through the mass of students toward the stairs, still holding her hand in his firm grip.

"So, why does Ms. Krick have it in for you?" Ethan asked over his shoulder.

"I have no idea," said Ava, feeling awkward that he still held her hand. "I was hoping you might know the answer to that."

"Nope," he said, descending the stairs two at a time, pulling her along behind him.

Ava struggled to keep up as he led her through the river of students. If she let go of his hand, they'd be separated for sure.

"My dad roomed with your dad here you know," said Ethan, once they'd reached the bottom of the staircase.

He met her confused look with a shrug.

"You're an alumni kid," he said simply. "You don't get to make your own first impression."

Ethan looked down, as if he'd just noticed that he'd been holding her hand. He quickly released his grip, grinning at her sheepishly.

"But how did you know who I was?" asked Ava, discreetly wiping her sweaty palm on her kilt.

"Our dads were friends for years," he said, "but they haven't spoken since your mom…"

His voice trailed off and he looked directly at Ava.

"Anyway, my dad is on the admissions committee," he continued. "He told me you were coming."

So Ethan was an alumni kid, too.

"You would have made your own impression anyway," Ethan said, laughing. "After all, you practically streaked across campus this morning. Everyone's talking about it. Anyway, here's your calculus class."

They stood in front of an open classroom door.

"I didn't, I mean..." Ava trailed off.

She found herself at a loss for words. Who was talking about her? Streaking? Wasn't that when frat boys ran naked across the football field as a dare? Is that what he'd thought she'd been doing in her swimsuit - getting attention? Ava felt slightly nauseated.

"C'mon." He swept his arms and gave a small bow toward the classroom.

Ava stood in the hall, her arms crossed on her chest.

"Your calculus class awaits," he said grandly, inviting her to enter the room as if it were his castle.

Ava took a deep breath and shuffled past him, careful to keep her distance as she passed. Ethan followed closely behind her.

A man was writing notes on the board. "Mr. Chase?" said Ethan easily. "This is Ava Marshall. She's in your class."

Ava looked up at Mr. Chase and breathed a sigh of relief when she saw his round spectacles and his chin-length blond hair. This teacher was far too young to have taught her parents.

"Welcome Ava. Grab a seat," Mr. Chase said. He gestured to the front row and pushed his hair out of his eyes.

As she sat, Ethan brushed past her, dramatically taking a seat in the back row. Ava couldn't help but laugh at his dazzling smile. He hadn't let on that he was in this class.

CHAPTER FIVE

Destiny

"Ava!"

The previous spring, Ava's dad had called up the stairs of their home in San Francisco.

Ava hurried down to welcome him, though she paused on the bottom step. Her dad's face positively glowed. The absence of his usual gloom put her on guard.

"What?" he asked, with a laugh. "Can't a guy be excited to see his daughter at the end of the day? Are you hungry? I brought take-out for dinner."

Ava looked at the paper bag in his hands. She didn't recognize the restaurant logo on its side.

"It's Malaysian food. Have you ever tried it?" Dad asked, walking toward their kitchen, with Ava trailing behind. "I haven't, but a colleague of mine said it's like a mixture of Indian and Thai. I know you like both of those, so hopefully this will be good. Sorry I'm late, but the restaurant was clear across town."

He unpacked the food on the kitchen counter. Ava just stared at him. Her dad was often late.

"Voilà," he said to her. "Bon appétit!"

Dad opened each plastic container, arranging them in a line on the kitchen counter, and pulled over two stools for them to sit on.

"Of course, they don't speak French where we'll be going," he continued. "So, we'll have to brush up on the local language."

"Going?" Ava asked, watching her dad dish her out a plate of steaming noodles. "Where are we going?"

"Malaysia," Dad declared, beaming.

"When?" she asked, taking the plate from him and digging in. They hadn't taken a real vacation together since her mom died.

"Soon," he replied with a wide grin.

Something about his answer gave Ava pause.

"Dad, you *are* talking about a vacation, aren't you?"

"Nope." Dad still smiled, though Ava noticed a twitch at the corner of his mouth. His mouth had always twitched like that when he was nervous. "Isn't the food delicious?"

"Yeah, it's great," replied Ava warily, putting down her fork. "But I'm waiting for you to explain what you're so giddy about."

"I've been asked to open a new division in Kuala Lumpur," He explained. "You and I are going over there for the year while it gets started."

Ava stared at him in disbelief.

"You should see the great apartment they've got for us," he added quickly. "The ex-pat school you'll go to is terrific. Of course, they'd rather I took on the position permanently, but I told them you'd have to be back on American soil for your senior year. I know that's important for your college applications. I can always head back once you start college if they still need me over there."

Ava's hands trembled in her lap. The day before, she'd received her acceptance letter from St. Augustus in the mail. She hadn't found the right moment to bring it up again with her dad. Ava had lost count of the number of times he'd said no to her attending the school where he and Ava's mom had met.

"Ava, what do you think?" he asked, leaning across the table toward her.

"Can't someone else go?" blurted Ava. She felt like a five year old child trying to convince her parents to stay home from work to play all day.

Dad frowned.

"I thought you'd be excited," he replied.

Ava took a deep breath. She'd practiced her plea many times. This might be her only chance to convince her dad to let her go to New England.

"Dad..." she began, cautiously, "I think you should go to Malaysia. But you and Mom always told me I could go to St. Augustus for high school. I *want* to go."

Ava tried to catch her dad's eye, but he stared blankly at the food on his plate.

"I, um, I've been accepted," Ava admitted, wincing as she anticipated his reaction.

Her confession was met with a stony silence. This wasn't going at all as she'd planned. He still held his fork in his hand, paused in mid-air.

"Dad, talk to me!" Ava exclaimed. "I don't want to go to Malaysia. I want to go to an American high school. I want to be near Gran and be on the swim team, like mom was! Please tell me why you're so set against it? I thought you liked it there?"

"No."

Her dad's answer was barely audible. He set his fork aside without looking at her.

Ava took another deep breath.

"It's what Mom would want for me, Dad," she said quietly. "You know that."

She'd hoped she wouldn't have to stoop so low in her effort to persuade him. She felt herself hold her breath. In the pause that followed, Ava knew she'd won.

Ava picked at the Cheerios in her bowl. It had been a restless night.

"Dad," she said, "Aunt Mia says she'll fly with me to Boston in September and drive me to Evergreen. She wants to stay a little longer and spend a few days with Gran."

Dad didn't look up from the paper he was reading.

"I'm going to live in the dorm," Ava continued, "but I'll be near Gran if I need anything. You and I will see each other at Christmas, right here in San Francisco. You'll be here at Christmas, right?"

"I've already got your ticket to Malaysia," he reminded her, looking at her over the newspaper with a frown. "Everything's been planned."

"Dad," Ava pleaded, "didn't you and Mom love St. Augustus?"

"Some things don't need to be talked about, Ava." He set the paper aside.

"Fine," Ava answered, matter-of-factly. "We don't need to talk about it then, if that's what you want, but please just sign the forms."

Hardly breathing, she pushed the forms across the kitchen table toward him carefully and handed him a ball point pen. Ava watched her dad as he read the top page. He wasn't really going to make her move to Malaysia, was he?

"Your acceptance letter is signed by Jim Wallis," he remarked, touching the page where it had been signed. "I wonder why he's still involved in St. Augustus. He's a big-shot politician now. He was a good guy when we went to school together, he actually tutored me in calculus our senior year. Without him, I'd never have gone to college."

He flipped through the stack of papers and then gently set them aside without picking up the pen.

"Dad, *please.*"

Ava held her breath as her dad slowly picked up the pen and flipped to the page Ava had marked with an 'x.' He carefully signed his name on the line, then put the papers down and left the room.

CHAPTER SIX

New

By the time the morning of her first day of St. Augustus classes was over, Ava's stomach growled. It wasn't like her to skip breakfast. Come to think of it, she'd barely eaten since arriving on campus. No wonder she was feeling so crummy. After a few wrong turns in the long stone halls of the main building, she managed to find the cafeteria. A long line of students snaked out into the hallway. She stretched her neck to see the front of the line. She didn't even care at this point what lunch was, she just hoped the line moved fast.

"Ava!"

Squinting to see into the cafeteria, Ava saw Jules waving frantically. Ava looked around at the students standing near her, but only for a moment. Excusing herself as politely as she could, she wove her way through the line and joined Jules near the front, careful not to meet anyone's eye as she passed. Line-jumpers were the worst.

"Hi," Jules said. "Did your day get any better?"

"I guess so," replied Ava, looking around for the food. "But I can hardly think I'm so hungry."

Jules reached over and grabbed hold of Ava's blouse, tugging it in one motion out of the waistband and smoothing its rumples down over Ava's kilt.

Ava's mouth hung open.

"Sorry," Jules apologized, still patting the wrinkled bottom of Ava's blouse. "I've been meaning to fix that since we parted this morning. Nobody wears it like that. Also, Ava, roll up the waistband to shorten your skirt. It's way too long."

"Uh, thanks," Ava replied, looking down at her dress-code-compliant, knee-length kilt.

Feeling dizzy, Ava looked around the cafeteria at the other girls and realized for the first time that their skirts all looked significantly shorter than her own. She frowned. The brochure on uniforms had clearly stated that the kilts should be worn just above the knee.

They'd reached the front of the line and Jules had wandered off to the salad bar. Ava made a quick assessment of her choices then headed straight for the pasta counter. Taking a large plate, she heaped her plate with spaghetti, meatballs, and cheese. Jules came up beside her as Ava shook red chili flakes on top of her creation. Ava looked up at her new roommate.

Jules balanced a plate full of greens on her tray. She raised an eyebrow at Ava's plate.

"What?" asked Ava. "I swam this morning. I need my carbs."

Ava followed Jules to a table at the far end of the cafeteria, where a few boys sat. Football jackets hung on the backs of their chairs.

"This is my guy, Jake," Jules told her as she set her tray down and took the seat next to one of the boys.

Ava had to stifle a laugh. *Of course* he was Jules' boyfriend. He was the shiniest boy at the table – a regular Ken doll. Still, Jules had been really nice so far. Maybe there was something to him.

"Hi, Ava," Jake said, with a welcoming wave.

"Hi," replied Ava, smiling back.

Everyone here was so friendly, she thought to herself. Well, almost everyone.

"Chloe, Amy, meet Ava," Jules said as a pair of girls sat down at their table "Chloe and Amy are on the cheer squad with me."

"Hi," said Chloe and Amy in unison.

The two girls smiled at Ava, all teeth and dimples. Their long ponytails matched Jules' as if they'd been cloned.

"So, Ava." Jake leaned forward with a gleam in his eye. "I hear you streaked the campus this morning!"

Ava looked up at him, eyes wide. Jules planted her elbow firmly in Jake's ribs before he could say anything else. Ethan had been right, thought Ava. Word did travel quickly around here.

"Oww!" Jake said, laughing and rubbing the spot where Jules' elbow had grazed him.

"I wasn't streaking, I was..." Ava mumbled, looking down at her food. Maybe she'd given him too much credit. "Can we talk about something else?"

Jake sat back in his chair, clearly disappointed.

"Did you get your keys back yet, Ava?" Jules asked, changing the subject.

"Not yet," replied Ava, with a sigh. "I'm meeting Giles at the locker room after school."

"Who has your keys?" asked Jake, jamming three fries into his mouth as he talked.

Ava cringed as she watched him talk with his mouth full. She'd been shoveling spaghetti into her own mouth as just as quickly and probably looked no better. She swallowed her food before answering him and made a conscious effort to twirl fewer strands on her fork for her next bite.

"They're in my locker at the pool," Ava explained.

"Yeah, I heard you couldn't get into your locker after swim practice," Amy piped up. "What happened?"

"Well, I'm not really sure," Ava replied, choosing her words carefully. "But I think Courtney Wallis switched my lock."

The girls exchanged knowing looks.

"What?" Ava asked.

"Well," Amy said, "I wouldn't put it past her. My roommate last year, Rhoda, was on the swim team, and she was pretty good, but Courtney made her life miserable. Rhoda didn't even come back to school this year."

"Didn't she want to go to school at home so she'd be closer to her boyfriend?" asked Jake.

"Well, all I know is that Courtney was very careful," Amy said with a shrug. "It was always Rhoda's word against hers."

Ava followed Amy's gaze and spotted Courtney sitting at a table across the cafeteria. Courtney was surrounded by her small court of girls, just as Ava had seen her the day before in Courtney's room.

"Well, if you ask me," Chloe added, leaning in, "Courtney drove Rhoda out of St. Augustus because she wanted the lucky room. Looks like she got what she wanted."

"That and she knocked out some competition on the swim team," Amy nodded in agreement. "I was annoyed that she got our room, even though I don't believe in that silly superstition. I've been sleeping better in our new room, though. I used to have the craziest dreams."

"Hey," said Chloe, laughing, "you should be glad that Rhoda left. You get to have me for a roommate now!"

"Well," Amy replied, laughing, "I actually liked Rhoda, though she was a little strange."

"Yeah," Chloe told Ava, making a face. "Rhoda had a pet shark in their room."

"A shark?" asked Ava, mopping up the last of her spaghetti sauce with the back of her fork. It wasn't as good as the sauce she and her dad made, but it had really hit the spot.

"Yeah," Amy nodded. "It was just a little one. I don't even think he was really a shark. He was more like a little cranky fish, really. It wasn't so bad, except that he never stopped swimming, even at night. Around and around and around he went, swishing his tail in the water. Maybe that's why I had so many dreams."

"Just remember," Jules reminded Ava, pushing the last of her salad away from herself, "I meant it when I said to stay on Courtney's good side. She could really make things tricky for you if she wanted to. Her family is a big supporter of the school and Courtney gets away with a lot."

"Yeah," agreed Amy, looking thoughtful. "Somehow she always made it seem like Rhoda was the one who was bothering her, when we all knew it was the other way around. I think Headmistress Valentine is scared to call Courtney a liar. But she must know what she's like."

"I've barely even met Courtney," said Ava, with an involuntary shudder.

"Keep it that way, if you can," Chloe advised, taking a sip of her soda.

Jules stood and picked up her tray. "Do you want me to show you where your next class is?"

"Sure," Ava told her, clearing her place at the table. "I have chemistry in the main building with Mr. Roberts."

"No way!" Jules nearly squealed. "Me too!"

"Great!" Ava said. She grabbed her pen and the notebook Ethan had given her.

Ava looked around the table, but the pen and notebook were all she'd brought. It felt strange not to have her phone. It wouldn't be long now before she could get into her locker and this day would be over. Jules chattered on as they left the cafeteria, though Ava wasn't paying much attention. Could Courtney really dislike Ava already? It hardly seemed fair.

Suddenly, Ava felt a thud and the notebook and pen she'd been holding clattered to the floor.

"Hey, watch it!" Ava exclaimed crossly, looking around to see who had bumped into her.

"Ava," Ethan replied, laughing as he stooped to gather the notebook and pen from the floor, "*you* crashed into *me!*"

"Sorry," replied Ava, sheepishly taking back the notebook and pen he'd lent her earlier.

"Did you find your other classes this morning okay?" Ethan asked. He looked genuinely interested.

"Yeah, thanks," she replied, studying the floor.

"Great, well, see you," he said, giving her a wave as he turned to leave.

She watched him as he sauntered away into the cafeteria.

"Ethan Roth?" Jules asked Ava, giggling. "He's quite the catch, if anyone could catch him. He usually keeps to himself, though I know a few girls who've tried to get his attention. He seems to have noticed *you*, though."

"Our dads were friends," Ava said with a shrug. "I've been running into him all day. Not always so literally, though."

"Well, that's a good place to start on your first day. He's *cute*."

"I have a boyfriend back home," Ava answered quickly.

"Well, you don't need to tell Ethan Roth that," Jules said, smiling smugly.

She took Ava's arm and led her toward their chemistry class.

CHAPTER SEVEN

Best Laid Plans

Ava tucked her legs under her, trying to get comfortable against the cement wall outside the girls' locker rooms. She didn't have her phone to tell her the time, but she didn't need it to know Giles was late. She leaned back and closed her eyes. Ava could think of fifty other things she'd rather be doing besides sitting in the hallway of the sports complex.

She wanted nothing more than to talk to Lucas after her eventful day. He'd probably laugh, but he'd be on her side - the side of her that really hated Courtney right now. Ava hugged her knees to her chest, willing Lucas' arms to be around her.

The sound of heavy footsteps jolted Ava out of her state. She scrambled to her feet.

"Hi there," Giles greeted her, bolt cutters in hand. "Sorry, took me a while to find these. They don't get a lot of use."

Ava led him through the deserted locker room.

"So, you forgot your combination?" Giles asked, positioning the bolt cutters.

"Something like that," Ava mumbled.

"Come now," Giles said to her, pausing a moment. "There's no need to be embarrassed."

Ava jumped a little as Giles snapped through the clasp of the combination lock with one clean break. The bolt cutters cracked against the reluctant metal in a sickening snap. He yanked it off and held it out to Ava.

"I, uh," Ava said, staring down at the broken lock in his outstretched hand.

"Oh, of course," said Giles, retracting his hand and tossing the lock into a nearby trash can. "It's not the lock you want."

"Thanks," Ava said to him gratefully.

She moved toward her locker and tugged on the handle. Just as the metal door clanged open, a small plastic container fell out and tumbled onto the floor, its lid coming off in the process. A cascade of tiny pink pills rained down, falling on Giles' work boots.

Ava stood and stared. *Was this her locker?* Her backpack and clothes were there. Ava looked down at the ground where many of the little pills still rolled away, scattering to the far corners of the locker room floor.

Giles bent down and picked up the plastic pill bottle from the floor, bringing it close to his face to read the small print on the label.

"Caffeine pills?" he announced, his eyes wide. "Oh, I don't think you're supposed to take these. St. Augustus has very strict rules for its athletes."

"But I..." Ava started, looking around at the pills and back at the locker.

She didn't even drink coffee.

"Don't bother explaining to me," Giles said to her, his friendly tone gone. "Headmistress Valentine will need to see these, and she can decide what to do about it."

Giles squatted down on the ground and scooped up the scattered pills, popping them back into the bottle. Ava crouched beside him and gathered a few that had rolled under the bank of lockers, sheepishly handing them to Giles, who added them to the container and snapped the lid shut.

"Those aren't mine," Ava told him, reeling as she tidied the floor.

"It's been a while since we had a drug problem with one of our athletes," Giles said, shaking his head and putting the little bottle into his pants pocket.

"What?" Ava said, straightening up from her hunched position on the floor. "A drug problem? No, you don't understand, those aren't mine. My locker..."

She trailed off, as Giles held up a hand for her to stop.

"Save it for the headmistress," Giles said.

He turned and walked away.

Ava left the sports complex feeling like her tires were flat. She had her backpack slung over her shoulder and held her mobile phone in her hand. She checked her phone and saw there had been three text messages from Lucas today. As she read them, she could tell he was getting progressively more worried that she hadn't responded.

All she could think about as she entered the school foyer was that Courtney had to somehow be responsible. For all of it. But why? Thinking for a moment, she dialed her Aunt Mia's mobile number. Mia would know what she should do.

"C'mon, Mia, pick up," Ava whispered into the handset as she cut through the foyer.

The large room was much quieter than when Ava had been there in only her swimsuit that morning. Had it only been that morning?

"Hi Mia, just me, Ava," Ava said when voicemail picked up. "Look, I really need to talk to you about something going on here at school. Could you call me back please?"

She hung up the phone and immediately dialled again, heading back out to the lawn.

"Lucas!" she breathed into the phone as she sank down on a bench far enough away from the main doors to give her a little privacy. "You'll never believe the day I've had."

It was so good to hear his voice. Ava smiled smugly to herself as the two of them came up with all kinds of plans to get Courtney back. She knew she wouldn't actually do any of the outrageous things they'd come up with, but Lucas' willingness to laugh with her gave her much needed relief.

"What I don't get, Ava," Lucas said when he'd stopped laughing, "is why you're letting her get to you. Who cares what she thinks?"

Ava shrugged helplessly, which of course he couldn't see. She knew he was right. But Courtney did get to her, whether Ava wanted her to or not.

"Just ignore her," was Lucas' advice. "She can't prove anything. And besides, you're gonna kick her ass in the pool and she'll have to spend all her free time trying to catch you."

"There you are!" Jules called, just as Ava hung up with Lucas. "I'd almost given up looking for you. Everyone is already in the cafeteria. Let's go."

Ava spotted Jules, who looked terrific in a pair of fitted jeans and a sparkly gold top.

"Are you going somewhere special?' Ava asked.

"Me?" replied Jules. "No, why?"

"Never mind," Ava said, with a laugh.

"So," said Jules, steering Ava toward the cafeteria, "on Saturday, a few of us are going into Evergreen shopping. You should come."

"Oh," said Ava, surprised to feel disappointment. "The swimming time trials are on Saturday. Can we go Sunday instead?"

"Oh, too bad," said Jules. "Most of the stores in Evergreen are closed Sundays, but I'm happy to lend you some clothes until next weekend."

"Sure," Ava mumbled, realizing as she looked down that she was still in uniform.

During dinner, Ava found herself staring over at Courtney's table across the cafeteria. How had she managed to switch Ava's lock? Courtney's friends didn't seem to be having a good time. They all looked very serious in their dark skinny jeans and pastel sweaters. In contrast, Jules and her friends hardly stopped laughing at each other's jokes during the whole meal.

"Sorry to leave so quickly, Ava," said Jules, getting up from the table. "But the girls and I have cheer practice."

"Oh, no problem," said Ava, watching them go. "See you later."

Ava walked back to the dorm alone, using the time to think. Once inside her room, she emptied her backpack on the bed and spread the contents around. Ava picked up her notebook and shook its pages. She then went through all the pockets in her backpack. Nothing else seemed out of place.

She reached for the towel she'd used as a toga that morning, which hung on the back of the door. Tossing it onto the bed, she looked at it, appraising for a long moment. Then she reached down and scooped it up with one hand dramatically. Is that really what had happened? Had Courtney managed to swap locks with Ava under her towel? Was that even possible? She'd been there at the right moment. Courtney was probably laughing about it with the other girls in room sixty-five right now.

Ava squeezed her eyes shut, imagining what she'd say to the headmistress. Caffeine pills weren't actually illegal, were they? A quick search on Google gave back info on illegal coffee trade, but nothing about taking caffeine pills in high school.

She already had an English assignment due on Monday. Maybe once Ms. Krick saw that Ava could write, she'd stop singling her out. She grabbed a pen and a notebook from her backpack and opened the notebook to the first page. She stared at the blank white sheet in front of her.

One page was all she had to write. Easy.

St. Augustus, she wrote, then crossed it out, thinking it was too obvious a choice. Besides, she wasn't sure she could paint this place in a positive light right now. She wondered what Ms. Krick would think about a paper that described a political, mean-spirited St. Augustus. Not a good idea. Tapping her teeth with her pen, she wrote a list of topics:

Swimming
Lucas' music
Mom

Staring at the last entry, she smiled a little to herself. Based on Ms. Krick's comments this morning, she hadn't been crazy about Ava's mom, Mariam. Tearing the page from the notebook, she crumpled it up and tossed it into the trash can under her desk.

Sitting back against the pillows on her bed, she wondered what else she should be doing. Ava started as a knock sounded at the door.

"Hello, Ava." It was Bessie, the dorm supervisor. "Are you settling in okay?"

"Um, yes," replied Ava.

"I have a note for you from the headmistress."

Ava drew a sharp breath in.

"Well, perhaps you know what this is about then," said Bessie, looking at Ava with a curious expression on her face. "It only says you are to come to her office after school tomorrow."

Ava nodded her head; sure her face had turned a sickly green.

"If you'd like," Bessie said, looking keen, "I can come with you to the meeting."

"No!" Ava blurted out quickly. "I mean, there's no reason for that, thank you, Bessie."

"Ava," said Bessie, her tone wary, "are you in some kind of trouble already?"

"Uh, no," replied Ava, trying to smile. "At least, I don't think so."

"Well, if you're sure," said Bessie, looking disappointed as she handed Ava the note. "Make sure you mind the curfew."

"Good night." Ava said as she closed the door.

She'd barely heard the latch click when the door opened again and Jules bounded in.

"What was Bessie doing here?" said Jules. "Are you breaking rules already, Ava?"

"She just wanted to remind me what time curfew is tonight," lied Ava, quickly closing her palm over the note.

Jules pulled out a pair of purple silk pajamas from her chest of drawers and started getting ready for bed. Pulling on her pajamas, she filled Ava in on the cheer squad practice she'd just come from, and which freshman girls she thought would make the team.

Ava lifted her pillow to retrieve the grubby shorts and T-shirt that she'd slept in the night before, while she listened to Jules. Replacing her pillow on the bed, she discreetly slipped the note from Bessie underneath.

Jules' chatter was pleasantly distracting as Ava tried to forget the anger she'd felt toward Courtney that afternoon. She straightened her phone beside her on the bed stand. Mia still hadn't returned her call. It would have to wait until the morning as it was almost lights out and she had a feeling that also meant silence. She nearly giggled out loud as she thought how hard it must be for Jules to be silent.

"So," Jules whispered as she snapped out the lights, "you have about three minutes before lights out to tell me about this boy from back home that makes you pretend not to notice Ethan Roth."

Ava couldn't help but smile.

"He's my best friend," said Ava, hugging herself into the darkness of her new room.

CHAPTER EIGHT

Headmistress Valentine

"I can't believe your dad finally agreed to let you go to Massachusetts!" Lucas had said last spring. "I guess that's good news."

He picked up his guitar from the corner of his bedroom and sat down next to her on his bed.

"At least I'm not going to Malaysia for a whole year," Ava answered, laughing.

She flipped through a Rolling Stone magazine he'd left on his bedside table, drumming her fingers on its pages in time to his beat.

"I like it," she said. "What's it called?"

Lucas put his guitar down and ruffled her hair.

"It's called *Ava Come Back*!" he shouted.

"What? " Ava squealed.

"The track," he answered. "I call it *Ava Come Back.*"

"Well, I don't like the title," she said, "but I like the tune; it's catchy."

"I'm happy you're not going halfway around the world anymore," Lucas confessed, suddenly serious. "A three-hour time difference is going to be hard enough."

He pulled Ava gently toward him where he sat on the bed. Ava let him put his arms around her, leaning against his chest.

"I can't remember not knowing you," he whispered.

"You'll still know me, dummy," Ava scolded, playfully.

"Yeah," he replied, "but it'll be different."

"Hey, don't get all pouty on me," said Ava. "Just think of all the free time you'll have after school to practice your music without me around to distract you."

Lucas shook his head.

"Nah, I'll be too busy texting you all day to play any music."

"I think I know you better than that," she said, laughing.

Lucas picked up his guitar and played *Ava Come Back* again. Ava watched him carefully. The song was perfect to announce the threshold of their new adventure. He'd always been able to express himself best through music.

A few hours earlier, when Dad had signed the admission papers, Ava had felt she could fly. Now comfortable in Lucas' room, where they'd spent countless Saturday afternoons just like this one, she wondered what the next year would bring.

"I've changed my mind about liking the song," she told him, interrupting the melody. "It sounds too sad."

He stopped strumming and reached for her hand. His fingers found hers and interlaced.

"It is," he replied.

Her second morning at St. Augustus, Ava woke after a pleasant dream. She'd been gathering flowers with her mom, something they'd done every spring. Before. They'd deliver them in bunches to local businesses, to brighten up their stores. Ava could still remember the expressions on the shopkeepers' faces. Some had even thought that Ava and her mom wanted money for the bouquets. She'd thought a lot about those moments over the years -- why her mom had insisted on giving the flowers away.

Being with her mother on those days had made Ava proud and happy.

Ava smiled and stretched her arms above her head, kicking the covers off. She took in her surroundings and felt her stomach tighten. Her meeting with the headmistress wasn't until after school today. She wished she could go now, to set the record straight. What was she going to tell her? Maybe the headmistress would think a few caffeine pills were no big deal. Ava would just have to wait and see.

She dressed quickly, glancing over at Jules, who had begun to stir. The thought of taking anything to make her swim faster, even something as mild as caffeine, made Ava's stomach feel queasy.

Ava quietly grabbed her cosmetic bag and made her way through the hall toward the restroom. Her day always looked much better after a shower - surely even a shower in one of the small dorm stalls would help.

That second day of classes was much less eventful than her first. The halls and classrooms were even starting to feel a little familiar. Thankfully, Courtney hadn't been in any more of her classes. By the time chemistry, her last class, came along that afternoon, Ava realized that she hadn't heard back from her Aunt Mia. What was she going to say to the headmistress?

After she'd dropped Ava off at St. Augustus on the first day, Mia had gone to spend a few days at Gran's house just on the other side of the woods. Ava felt sure that Mia would help her decide whether to point the finger at Courtney, or play dumb. They both had their drawbacks, but she was having trouble seeing the bright side of either plan. Ava thought briefly of calling her dad, but she didn't want to worry him on his first week in Malaysia. No, she'd have to face the meeting with the headmistress alone.

"Just tell them what happened and it will be fine," Ava told herself, muttering aloud in the hallway as she made her way to the headmistress' office after school.

Miss Samantha's smile waited for her when she arrived, giving Ava reason to hope. Perhaps she wasn't in trouble, after all. Most kids she knew drank cola and coffee. What was the big deal?

"Hi, Ava," Miss Samantha greeted her. "Headmistress Valentine is just finishing another meeting that came up. Have a seat and she'll be right with you."

"Thanks," Ava said, feeling lighter.

She sat down on a bench by the door and picked up a school pamphlet from a table to flip through while she waited. She'd expected so much out of this school. After a few minutes, the door to the headmistress' office opened, and Ava heard voices.

A girl's voice floated out. "Thank you for your understanding, Headmistress Valentine."

Ava knew that voice. She looked up in time to see Courtney exit the headmistress' office and saunter over to Miss Samantha's desk.

"Thank you for squeezing me in to see the headmistress, Miss Samantha," Courtney said, flashing the secretary a sweet smile. "I really appreciate your help."

Ava stood up from the bench, her mouth hanging open. *What was Courtney doing here?*

"Why, hello, Ava," said Courtney, with exaggerated politeness. "It's nice to see you here."

Ava could only stare in bewilderment as Courtney left the office by the main door.

"The headmistress will see you now, Ava," Miss Samantha told her, still smiling.

Ava nodded in silence and entered the headmistress' office.

"Ava Marshall," said Headmistress Valentine, without looking up from her writing as she sat behind her large wooden desk. "Have a seat."

Ava looked around the dark office for somewhere to sit, and settled for a hard wooden chair. She felt her stomach drop as she saw the bottle of pills that had been in her locker right in the center of the desk.

"Well, Ava," the headmistress looked up at her, smiling drily. "I must say, in all my years at St. Augustus, this has to be a record for how quickly a new student has found themselves in my office."

"Headmistress Valentine," said Ava meekly, her heart pounding. "I can explain."

"Yes, please do." The headmistress looked at her evenly, folding her hands in front of her on her desk. "Also, I have just been informed that you have tried to convince your teammates that they should be taking stimulants as well, so I wait for your explanation."

"Miss Valentine?" Ava stammered. "Other teammates?"

"You may call me 'Headmistress Valentine,'"

"Sorry... Headmistress Valentine," Ava repeated, bowing her head. Her pulse raced. "The pills aren't mine. Courtney..."

"Yes, Courtney." Headmistress Valentine nodded her head. "I have just spoken to Courtney about her involvement in this, and she knows that she should have come to me sooner."

Ava listened keenly.

"She told me that she refused the pills outright," Headmistress Valentine recounted, "but she wanted to make sure the younger girls on the team don't feel pressured to improve their performance with such chemicals."

"I have never taken anything to help me perform," Ava blurted. She got to her feet and placed her hands firmly on the desk in front of her. "I train hard to swim as well as I do. Those pills were put in my locker. Courtney put them there!"

"Ava, you're only going to get yourself in more trouble by lying," the headmistress told her, clucking her tongue in a condescending way. "Now, St. Augustus doesn't actually have a formal policy regarding its athletes and caffeine, though it seems we need one. I'll be discussing this with your coach before we decide how to proceed. In the meantime, you're not to attend classes. In fact, why don't you take the weekend and think long and hard about whether St. Augustus is the right place for you. I know having a family legacy to uphold can be a lot of pressure."

Ava could hardly believe what she was hearing.

"We'll meet back here Monday morning at eight o'clock," the headmistress continued. "We can decide then what is to be done."

"But Headmistress Valentine," Ava said, trying to keep her voice from shaking, as she sank back down into the hard wooden chair, "you don't understand."

"No, Ava Marshall," Headmistress Valentine said, holding up her hand. "*You* don't seem to understand. St. Augustus has very little patience for cheaters, or for liars. We will discuss this again on Monday. Good day."

Ava stood, steadying herself on the back of the wooden chair she'd sat in. She'd never been called a cheater or a liar before. She knew she was neither of these things. She understood that she'd been dismissed, but what was she to do now?

CHAPTER NINE

Fountain Encounter

Ava couldn't get off the campus fast enough. She stopped at the dorm just long enough to stuff a few things into her overnight bag before heading to Gran's. She couldn't bear the thought of Jules or anyone else seeing her ashen face. Besides, if she left before it got dark she could take the shortcut through the woods.

Minutes later, she'd already crossed the campus lawn, passed the West Building and reached the edge of the woods. Ava found the poorly marked trail that she knew led to her Gran's house. She frowned darkly as she tripped over tree roots that had grown into the path. She'd taken this way many years ago with her mom, but she didn't remember it being this rough.

Ava could have kicked herself for not speaking up and naming Courtney earlier. The right thing to do would have been to tell Coach Laurel what was going on as soon as she'd been late for swim practice. Or she could have let a teacher know that her lock had been switched before the pills were found. As mad as she was at the headmistress, Ava knew she looked guilty.

Her fists flexed at her sides as she walked. Surely, she'd be given a chance on Monday to prove she was telling the truth. She'd been told Courtney had pulled tricks like this last year on another girl. What was her name, Rhonda? Something like that. Couldn't the headmistress see the pattern? Jules had said that

Courtney got away with a lot because of Senator Wallis' involvement with the school. But would Courtney really let Ava get suspended - or even sent home?

How on earth was Ava supposed to convince everyone of Courtney's meddling if the headmistress didn't let her tell her side of the story? Mia would help, Ava felt sure as she walked as quickly as the uneven path would allow. An overgrown tree branch she'd pushed away suddenly snapped back and slapped her on the cheek.

"Oww!" yelled Ava.

Grabbing the offending branch, she tore it from its tree and hurled it into the path in front of her. The branch cut through the trees and landed in what looked like a field ahead.

"Great," muttered Ava to herself, squinting through the trees at the field. "It figures, now I'm lost."

She stepped off the path into the long reedy grass. The last light of the day streamed into the clearing, spreading its glow to the edges that were lined with trees.

"Ohhh."

Ava heard her own voice echo into the open space.

At the center of the field stood a large stone fountain, its spout spraying water that sparkled in the afternoon sun. Ava walked toward it suspiciously. What was a fountain doing in the middle of the woods? *This must be somebody's yard*, she thought. She looked around her, and saw she was surrounded by trees on all sides. If it was somebody's yard, it hadn't been mowed all season. Make that several seasons.

Ava stepped toward the rushing water. The fountain looked out of place, somehow. Its white stone was grayed with age, long cracks zigzagging across its surface, which was partially covered by long vines that had grown up from the ground. Ava tilted her head to the side. This fountain looked much older than even the buildings on campus.

Ava leaned over the fountain's basin, fine mist tickling her face from its spray. She could see past its water to the bottom, where a handful of coins lay. The clear water looked pure enough to drink. Someone must look after this fountain, despite its crumbling stone, Ava thought. Did it belong to St. Augustus?

Ava perched herself on the edge of the fountain's basin and let one hand dip into the water. It wasn't surprising that she'd taken a wrong turn. The path was in pretty bad shape. She closed her eyes and tried to recall the times she'd been in these woods with her mother. It had been so long ago. Which way had they walked?

Looking around the clearing, it still seemed familiar somehow, though she felt certain she'd never seen this fountain before. What was it about this moment that reminded her so much of her mom? Stretching her hands into the waterfall cascading from the top she reached through to the space on the other side.

This week had been so busy she hadn't had time to think much about her mom, who she usually missed each day that went by. Ava closed her eyes to let her memories in, mixing with the soothing sounds of the water rushing into the basin.

Almost on impulse, she wiped her wet hands on her sweater and reached into her pocket, drawing out a coin.

She remembered her mother holding Ava's own small hand.

"Fountains hold a special kind of magic, Ava," her mother had told her with a sparkle in her eye. "They present themselves to us when we are most in need. Never let an opportunity go by to wish for what is in your heart."

Her mom's pockets had always held pennies for just such occasions and the two had whispered to each other the wishes they'd made. Ava looked at the coins in this fountain and felt certain her mother had been to this fountain before, so close to where she'd lived. Her mom had always made a point of wishing on every fountain she saw and had taught Ava to do the same. Had this fountain meant something to her mom?

"I wish St. Augustus had never heard of Courtney or her family!" Ava shouted at the fountain, her voice echoing back through the trees.

She drew her arm back and hurled her coin into the basin. The result of her throw was less than spectacular as the quarter floated gracefully to the bottom. Ava watched it land as she felt the first teardrop on her own cheek. Giving a voice to her frustration felt good. She could fight back against Courtney. She'd have to.

"Mom," whispered Ava into the air as she sank to her knees beside the fountain and finally let herself cry. "You're supposed to be here for me."

Heavy sobs rocked through her as she sat with her head in her hands on the hard ground beside the fountain. Dampness from the soft ground seeped through her kilt. She felt the hurt from the last few days roll down her cheeks with her tears. She couldn't explain why she felt the need to be at St. Augustus, why she felt she belonged here. If she had to fight to stay, she knew that she would.

She rested her head on the fountain's stone and stared through her tears at the carvings on its side. A strange assortment of Cupids, trees, and flowers decorated the fountain. A Cupid's arrow was filled with dark green moss. A delicately carved tree's pointy branches bent gently as if blown by the wind.

After a time, Ava found she had no tears left and sat listening to the gurgle of the fountain. Looking up, she realized that the sky was growing dark. Shivering from the dampness of the tears on her cheeks mixed with the spray from the fountain, she wondered how long it had been since she'd left the campus. Was she lost? It was almost completely dark outside.

Stiffly, she pulled herself from the ground and brushed off her kilt. Bending over the fountain's basin, she splashed its water on her face in an attempt to wash away any tear stains. The water felt surprisingly warm. Dabbing her eyes with a corner of her sweater, she looked around, resting her gaze on a clump of evergreens at the edge of the woods. Ava tilted her head to one side, staring at the trees. They looked incredibly familiar. Spinning herself around slowly, she let memories flood back to her of playing fairies with her mom under the evergreens. *This was the clearing that her mother used to take her to when they'd come to visit Gran.*

"Every night for a week before graduation your dad had snuck out to meet me out here after lights out," her mother had confided, sitting in their secret place under the trees. "We looked at the stars and talked for hours."

Her laugh rang in Ava's ears as if it were here in the clearing now.

"Don't tell your Gran," her mother had said. "She would have a fit if she ever knew that I snuck out of the house."

Ava gave her head a quick shake. How could she have forgotten that there was a fountain in this place where they'd played? She studied the stone fountain closely. It had definitely been here a long time.

It was now almost dark. Gran and Mia would be getting worried about her. *What if they decided to call the school?* She shuddered at the thought of them talking to the headmistress before she'd had the chance to explain. She'd ask Mia about the fountain tonight, right after they figured out what to do about Courtney. She walked over to the clump of evergreens and found the gap in the trees, just to the right, where the path continued.

The overgrown path was barely there, but Ava felt certain that it was the same path she remembered. After taking one last look back at the fountain in the gathering darkness, Ava broke into a run toward Gran's, trying to avoid the uneven parts of the ground as she ran.

CHAPTER TEN

You Can Always Go Home

"Ava, is that you?" called Mia, from the front of the house. "Honey, are you all right? We were starting to get worried!"

Mia rushed into Gran's kitchen and took Ava into her arms. The swinging door that led to the front of the house banged shut behind her.

"You're wet!" Mia exclaimed, drawing back in alarm. "Is it raining?"

Ava shrugged as she felt Mia studying her.

"Do you have dry clothes in that backpack of yours?" Mia asked, ushering Ava to the back stairs. "Go change. You can tell me how you got so wet over dinner. It's all ready."

"Okay," Ava answered finally, dragging her backpack toward the back stairs.

"Did you use the forest shortcut?" Mia called after her.

Ava stopped at the bottom of the stairwell and looked back at her aunt, noting a warning in her voice.

"Yes," replied Ava.

"I meant to call you. Gran said it's not used much anymore," Mia said to her. "St. Augustus students are apparently banned from the woods."

"Why?" asked Ava.

"It's safer that way, Ava," Mia answered. "You should probably use the main road when you come to visit."

"Oh, okay," said Ava.

She hadn't given a thought to her safety, even when she thought she might be lost in the woods, though of course that made sense.

"Your mom used to tell me stories about the woods," said Mia with a laugh, as she prodded Ava gently toward the stairs. "It all seems silly now, but she made me terrified of going in there. I don't think I walked to school that way once the whole time I went to St. Augustus."

"Really?" asked Ava, smiling at the thought of her Aunt Mia being scared of anything.

"Go! Get changed!" said Mia.

Ava scooted up the steps and ducked into her mother's childhood room. She'd stayed here plenty of times when she and her mom had visited Gran, though it had been a while.

Hurriedly, she wiggled out of her wet uniform and pulled on the jeans and long-sleeved shirt she'd brought. Checking the result in the white-framed mirror hanging on the bedroom wall, she smoothed back a few stray hairs before heading downstairs to dinner.

"I am really glad to be here, Gran," said Ava, as she arrived in the formal dining room and leaned over Gran's wheelchair to give her a kiss on the cheek.

"Yes, it's about time you came for a visit," replied Gran, though not unkindly.

Ava took her seat at the place that had been set for her, placing her linen napkin in her lap. She eyed the blue-and-white china plate before her and remembered how upset Gran had been when a five-year-old Ava had broken one by dropping it onto the hardwood floor. It had smashed into about ten pieces, like uneven slices of pie. She'd been served on Gran's everyday plates when she'd come to visit after that.

The last time she'd seen Gran had been at her own mother's funeral. That had been the one and only time Gran had come to California, though Ava and her mother had visited Evergreen every year.

Her mother's memorial service had been at Trinity church, at the end of the street from their house. Ava remembered her father arguing that Mariam wouldn't have wanted a religious service, but in the end, Mia's practical sense prevailed, since the church was the largest venue in their neighborhood. The service had been standing room only.

Ava had opted to sit in the balcony instead of joining her dad in the front row pew that day. Every adult around, it seemed, told her that it was okay if she wanted to cry. She'd wondered if perhaps they'd all feel better if she did. Lucas had sat with her in the back row of the balcony and held her hand without saying anything at all. That had been the first time they'd held hands.

As the minister had talked on and on, and she'd watched from above, Ava had been comforted to see Gran's wheelchair parked in the aisle beside the pew where her dad sat with Aunt Mia and Uncle Chuck. Ava had looked forward then to her next visit to Gran's. If she'd known that she wouldn't see Gran for so many years, she might have come down from the balcony.

Ava pushed her beef around with her fork, watching the gravy pool at the edges of her plate. She didn't want to burden Gran with her problems already in the first week of school. She needed to talk to Mia alone.

"So, did you know that Ava is an amazing swimmer, Ma?" Mia asked Gran. "You'll have to make it over to the school to cheer her on."

"Oh. No," Gran chuckled. "That sounds like too much excitement for an old lady like me. I don't leave the house much anymore unless I need to."

"Oh, Ma," said Mia, sounding exasperated. "The doctors all say you're doing better than fine. You could do with a little excitement in your life."

Ava looked at Gran, who wore an apricot-colored crepe dress accented by a string of pearls around her neck. Gran's hair was neatly curled into a slate-gray halo which framed her face. She presided over the dining room from the place of honor, her black-and-silver wheelchair tucked up underneath the table so that, from where Ava sat, it was out of sight. Ava sat next to Mia and across from Gran. The small trio barely registered at one end of the large table. The place at the other end of the table usually reserved for the host remained vacant. Ava had never known her grandfather—he'd died when Mom and Mia had been in grade school.

"Gran," said Ava, hoping to change the subject, "I was planning to spend this weekend here, if that's okay with you?"

Gran's housekeeper appeared from the kitchen to clear their plates. Ava couldn't remember her name; there had been several women who'd served as caregivers and housekeepers for Gran over the years, all occupying the bedroom just off the pantry. Gran wasn't mobile enough to live by herself.

"Of course, dear," said Gran, beaming. "You can stay here as often as you wish. In fact, I hope you do. It'll be nice to have some young energy around here. You can stay in your mother's room, right Theresa?"

"Yes, of course," The lady said, smiling.

Theresa. The housekeeper's name was Theresa.

"I thought you were going to go back to campus tonight, Ava," said Mia, helping herself to some more potatoes from the serving dish on the table.

"I changed my mind," said Ava, flashing Mia a look.

Aunt Mia narrowed her eyes but didn't say anything.

"You'll have to excuse me," said Gran when the meal was done, "I'm feeling tired. Good night everyone. I'll see you tomorrow."

"Good night Gran," Ava said, standing up from the table and moving to Gran's side.

Ava gave her a hug, bending low over the wheelchair. Gran's lavender perfume reminded Ava of her mother's favorite soap. Ava closed her eyes and inhaled deeply.

"We'll talk more tomorrow?" asked Ava, pulling away from Gran's embrace.

"I'd like that," said Gran, giving Ava a tired smile.

Mia and Ava cleared the table together and went to the kitchen as Theresa helped Gran over to the stairs. Ava winced at the laborious sounds coming from the stairwell as Theresa helped Gran climb.

"Mom always made us wash the dishes, even though we always had housekeepers after she got sick." Mia said, smiling.

"Sure," replied Ava, stacking the plates beside the sink. She was grateful for the distraction. The familiar chore reminded her of being with her dad.

"How were your first few days of school?" asked Aunt Mia as she ran water in the sink and handed Ava a dishtowel. "Were they everything that you expected?"

"It's been, um...interesting," Ava began, bracing herself as she remembered what she'd wanted to tell Mia. "Actually, not everyone at St. Augustus seems happy to have me here."

"Oh, honey – they'll come around once they get to know you, and..."

Mia paused as she looked at Ava's face.

"It's that bad, huh?"

"Yeah," replied Ava, sighing as she slowly swirled the dishcloth around inside the pot that Mia handed her. "I think I've set a record for the worst first week ever."

"Why, what happened?" asked Mia, still washing dishes.

"Well, first I was late for swim practice," said Ava, her words tumbling out. "Then my locker wouldn't open and I had to walk across campus in my purple bathing suit, having everyone stare at me like I was crazy. Giles, the maintenance guy, had to cut my lock off the locker. I was even late for a class and Ms. Krick sent me to the office. The whole week I felt like I've been drowning."

"Ah, Ms. Krick," replied Mia with a cluck of her tongue. "Is she really still teaching?"

Ava nodded miserably, gearing up to tell Mia about her suspension.

"I'm sure it wasn't as bad as you feel," said Mia with a broad smile, as she handed Ava a dripping wet platter. "I think it's normal to feel out of sorts your first week at a new school. I'm sure once you make some friends you'll feel more at home."

"Well, my roommate Jules did turn out to be great," replied Ava. "She showed me around and introduced me to some of her friends. But I met this girl, Courtney, and I could swear that she's behind everything bad that's happening to me."

"Why would someone want to make things difficult for you?" Mia asked her, looking perplexed.

"I guess she doesn't want me to make the swim team," Ava said simply, opening and closing cupboard doors, trying to find a home for the pot she'd just dried. "It was Courtney who gave me the wrong time for swimming practice. Then suddenly I couldn't get into my locker to get my clothes after. She has this stupid grin – it makes me so mad I could spit."

Ava opened a cupboard near the oven that had a bunch of pots inside. She found a gap and put the pot she'd been holding inside.

"And then when I opened my locker..." continued Ava, working her way up to the part she was dreading.

Mia held up her hand to pause Ava mid-sentence as she dried off her hands and patted down her blazer pocket looking for her vibrating mobile phone. Ava froze. The call could be from the headmistress. Mia scowled as she studied the number on her caller ID.

"Sorry, honey," said Mia. "It's still early on the West Coast. I need to take this call from my office. I've been waiting for some information on a case I'm working on."

Ava relaxed. It wasn't the school calling. Mia gave Ava's hand a warm squeeze before ducking into the back stairwell to take the call.

Ava took over the washing that Mia hadn't finished just as Theresa entered the kitchen and started putting away the dishes Ava had left on the counter.

"Theresa, what do you know about the fountain in the West Woods? I don't remember it being there when I was here as a kid."

"Fountain?" asked Theresa. "What kind of fountain?"

"I dunno," said Ava with a shrug. "A stone fountain. I saw it on my way over here."

"Oh," replied Theresa, crinkles appearing at her temples. "I wouldn't go into those woods. Not that I believe the stories that they're haunted by old Mr. Young. Me, I never go out there, but I don't know anything about a fountain."

"Do you mean Isaac Young?" asked Ava. "The founder of St. Augustus?"

"Yes, that's him," Theresa nodded. "I've been living with your gran a while now and I hear things in town. The kids from the school aren't allowed in those woods. People say there's been funny business in there, though nobody ever says exactly what. I don't know that there's any real danger, but you'd best use the road, especially after dark."

"Yes, Mia mentioned that," Ava said thoughtfully, "but who owns those woods?"

"The school I suppose," Theresa answered, wiping a dishrag across the spotless countertop.

Why would the school have built a fountain in the middle of the woods?

"I'll finish up these dishes, dear," Theresa told her with a smile. "Your mother's old room is all made up for you. Feel free to go up and get settled."

"Thanks," replied Ava, drying her hands on her jeans.

As Ava climbed the back stairwell, she had to sidestep Mia to pass. Mia had parked herself on a step halfway up, still deep in conversation on her phone. Mia smiled at Ava apologetically, but made no indication that her call would be over anytime soon.

Ava retreated to her mother's childhood room and took a good look around. It was easily twice the size of her bedroom in San Francisco. Its high ceilings and large windows gave it an open feeling. Not much had changed since she'd visited as a child. Her mother's antique desk still sat unused in a corner. The broad window seat was still covered in lacy cushions and her mother's brass-framed bed was covered with the same bright patchwork quilt it always had been. Ava remembered her mother being proud of the bookcases that lined the walls of the room.

"Pick a book, Ava," her mother used to say when it came time for Ava's bedtime stories. "There isn't a bad one on these shelves. They're all my favorites."

Her mom had even talked about having the whole lot of books shipped out to their house in San Francisco, but she'd died before she'd gotten around to it. Ava looked at the books now and was glad that they were still here. She'd have lots of time to read every one in the next two years. That is, if she got to stay for two years.

Ava picked up her damp uniform from where she'd left it on the floor earlier and hung it over the desk chair to dry. After she'd pulled on the shorts and T-shirt she'd brought to wear to bed she padded out into the hallway, listening at the top of the back stairs. Murmurs from below confirmed that Mia was still on the phone, talking in a serious, low voice.

Returning to the bedroom, Ava lay down on the bed, folding

her arms behind her head with a sigh. After this call, Mia would be in work mode and even more wound up when she found out Ava had essentially been suspended from school. She closed her eyes and took a deep breath, reminding herself that she'd done nothing wrong.

She reached for her phone and dialed Lucas' number. She really needed to talk to someone before the thoughts swirling around scrambled her brain.

"Ava!" Lucas exclaimed, his breathless voice answering on the fifth ring. "I'd almost given up on you."

"Very funny," replied Ava drily. "It's kind of been a busy week."

"It's been busy here too," Lucas told her. "We're auditioning a new drummer for the band."

"What happened to Brock?" asked Ava.

"Oh, his mom said he has to focus more on his studies this year," replied Lucas. "So he can't practice with us. Anyway, I think we found someone and he's really good. This could really be the boost we need to get noticed."

Lucas rambled on about the new drummer, while Ava stared up at cracks crisscrossing the ceiling. She waited for him to finish recounting his week. He seemed really excited.

"That's great, Lucas," said Ava. "It sounds like everything there's going well."

"Yep," Lucas replied. "So, will you get to swim every day? Is it awesome?"

"Well," Ava replied slowly, "there's only been the one swim practice so far, but the time trials for the team are tomorrow."

As soon as she said it out loud, Ava sat up in bed. She'd nearly forgotten about the time trials. The headmistress had forbidden her from attending classes, though she didn't have any before their meeting on Monday. Was she supposed to attend swim practice?

"That's great, Ava," said Lucas. "I'm sure you'll swim circles around them."

"Yeah, right," said Ava, clearing her throat. "That's enough about me. Tell me more about the band. Have you guys booked any gigs yet?"

Listening to Lucas talk about his band was a welcome distraction. Ava knew the last thing she wanted was for him to hop on a plane to come and 'rescue' her, and that's exactly what he would try to do if she told him about being suspended.

"Lucas," interrupted Ava shyly, "I really do want to hear all about the band, but I need to talk to Mia before she goes to bed. I'm staying at Gran's tonight."

"Oh," said Lucas, not hiding his disappointment. "I want to hear more about your week."

"I know," said Ava, feeling a twinge of guilt, "but I'll call you tomorrow and fill you in. It's just that I need to catch up with Mia."

"I guess," replied Lucas. "I know Mia can be tricky to pin down. Well, 'night, Ava."

"'Night, Lucas," replied Ava, fighting back tears. "I miss you."

"I miss you too, Ava."

She stared at the phone for a long moment after she'd hung up. Getting up off her bed, she opened the door just enough to poke her head out into the hall. Mia's faint voice floated up the stairs toward her. She was definitely still on the phone.

Ava leaned back against the doorframe. Leaving Lucas and San Francisco with tearful goodbyes seemed so long ago, although it had only been a few days. She closed her eyes and imagined Lucas' arms around her now, longing to feel safe. Why hadn't she told him what her week had really been like?

Closing the door, she returned to the bed and sank down on it with a sigh, folding back the quilt and stretching her body out under the covers. The cold sheets slowly warmed to her limbs. She yawned as she listened for Mia's footfalls on the stairs.

Ava awoke to silence and complete darkness. Mia must've turned off Ava's light on her way to bed. Ava gave her pillow an angry punch. She'd need to get up early to catch Mia before Gran was up and about.

She knew morning had arrived when she heard someone shuffling in the hallway outside her mother's room, but Ava couldn't seem to wake up from her dream. Trying to sit up before she was fully awake, she became entangled in the sheets. Ava groaned. She wasn't what you'd call a morning person. Bright sunlight streamed warmly onto the bed through lacy curtains. She rolled over toward the bedside table and checked the time on her phone. It was already 9:45. So much for getting up early.

Shaking herself free of the weight of the covers, she stepped down onto the hard floor, one hand resting on the bedspread to steady herself. Walking toward the door, she bent down to pick up a piece of paper lying on the floor. Ava's heart sank as she read the note written in her aunt's flowing hand.

Ava,
Sorry our chat last night was cut short! I had to take an
early flight home this morning. The case I'm working on
unfortunately can't wait until Monday. I'm sure this week
will be better for you. Keep your chin up, and call me if you
need anything.
Lots of love,
Mia.

How was she going to face Headmistress Valentine alone? She tried dialing Mia's number, but it went straight to voicemail. Crumpling Mia's note into a ball, she hurled it toward the windows. Ava sighed deeply. Trying the number again, she decided to leave a message.

"Aunt Mia, I hope all's well with your case," said Ava. "Can you give me a call when you land? I'd like to finish our conversation."

Ava hung up the phone, wondering if she should have left Mia more information. No, she thought, she really didn't want to worry Mia if she had work to do today.

Ava had made up her mind during the night to attend the time trials, which meant she didn't have much time to get ready. She'd done nothing wrong, she reminded herself, again. It was probably best to act like everything was fine. Hurriedly, she decided the shorts and T-shirt she'd slept in would have to do for the day, or at least until she got to the pool. Wriggling into her bra and panties, she pulled the T-shirt and shorts back on. She would have to grab her swim gear from the dorm room on her way.

Theresa was in the kitchen when Ava came down the stairs. The smell of fresh baking made Ava's mouth water.

"Good morning," Theresa said. "What can I fix you for breakfast?"

"Oh, I..." Ava stammered. "I'm actually heading out to swim practice. Sorry, I forgot to mention it last night. What time did Mia leave this morning?"

"Oh, she was out before dawn," replied Theresa. "I made muffins. Why don't you take one and eat it on your way?"

"Sure," said Ava with a grin, taking a warm blueberry muffin with each hand from the basket that Theresa offered. "Tell Gran I'll be back at dinnertime."

"She's in the parlor having a cup of tea if you'd like to tell her yourself," answered Theresa.

Ava nodded and set her muffins down on the kitchen table

before heading to the front room of the house. She hadn't spent much time in the parlor, with its prim and proper couches. Breakable knick-knacks decorated the small side tables. Ava steered clear, not wanting to knock them down.

Gran lay on one of the couches, her legs covered with a rose-embroidered afghan. Her wheelchair was parked next to the couch, looking out of place and modern in this formal room. A cup of tea sat steaming on an end table within Gran's reach.

"Oh, hello Ava," Gran greeted her warmly. "I was wondering how long you'd sleep. Me, I get up once the morning light hits my window, but I remember when the girls were young."

"I just came in to say hello, Gran," Ava told her, moving toward her and giving her a hug. "I have swim practice this morning. It's the time trials I need to complete to make the team. I'm just on my way out."

"From the way Mia spoke of your swimming," Gran said, "you hardly need to worry about making the team. You remind me so much of your mother at your age."

"Really?" replied Ava, feeling pleased.

"Be a dear and bring me the package on the seat of my chair?" asked Gran, motioning toward her wheelchair.

Ava took the heavy manila envelope that sat on the seat and handed it to Gran. She ran her hands tenderly across the surface of the envelope before handing it back to Ava.

"These were your mother's diaries when she attended St. Augustus," said Gran to her. "I know she would want you to have them. Perhaps you won't feel alone while you are here."

"Oh Gran, thank you," Ava breathed, taking the envelope from Gran's outstretched hands.

"You're welcome, dear," Gran answered. "Make sure you get some of Theresa's muffins on the way out, they really are quite good."

"Thanks Gran, I will," said Ava, gently sliding the envelope into her backpack. "I'll be back tonight for supper and I plan to stay until Monday, so we'll have time to visit."

"I'd like that," said Gran with a smile.

Ava gave Gran a quick hug and left hurriedly for the kitchen.

"Theresa," asked Ava tentatively, as she entered the kitchen, "is Gran doing okay?"

"Oh, yes," replied Theresa with a half-smile as she handed Ava the muffins she'd left on the table. "As good as she's ever been, but she doesn't have much energy. She keeps them guessing at the hospital, that's for sure."

"Thanks, that's good to hear," said Ava, waving goodbye with her hands full of muffins and leaving by the screen door.

CHAPTER ELEVEN

Eerie

"There you are!" exclaimed Jules brightly, pulling Ava into their room. "Where have you been? Did you stay at your grandma's last night? I was worried, but Bessie was frantic - you should have seen her waving her little arms in the air!"

"Hmm?" asked Ava absently, bending to grab her swim gear from where she'd stashed it under her bed. "Bessie was looking for me last night?"

"Well, I told her that you'd gone to your gran's for dinner," said Jules with a shrug. "That seemed to make her relax a little. I figured you'd spent the night. Is that where you were? Bessie said she called your aunt a few times, but it went straight to voicemail. You need to talk to Bessie right away."

Ava looked up at Jules long enough to absorb what she was saying. The puzzled look on Jules' face told Ava that her disgrace over the alleged "drugs" hadn't reached the campus gossip mill yet. Ava's hand under the bed rested on something cold and hard. Pulling it out, Ava looked blankly at the combination lock in her hand. Instinctively, she spun her old combination around its dials and it opened. Ava scowled at it. How on earth had her lock gotten under her bed? Was there no limit to what Courtney was capable of?

"Ava?" Jules prodded. "You really need to go see Bessie. You could get in a lot of trouble for missing curfew last night."

"Okay, um, I'll talk to her," promised Ava.

She stood and tossed the lock into her backpack.

"I've got to get to swim trials now though, so it'll have to be after that," Ava continued, hurriedly. "I'll be staying at Gran's until Monday morning, actually, so I'll let Bessie know."

Ava couldn't help but notice Jules' look of disappointment.

"I'll explain everything later," Ava told her. "Sorry, I gotta go!"

She grabbed her backpack on her way out of the room before jogging down the hallway and out onto the lawn.

As she neared the pool, Ava slowed to a walk. She had plenty of time to get to practice, although she certainly didn't want to be late again. She kept rehearsing what she was going to say to Coach Laurel. Of course, she'd know about Ava's suspension by now.

Ava reassured herself that the headmistress had only said she was to stay out of *classes* and swimming was not technically a *class*, though her stomach felt unsettled. If she didn't swim today, she might not qualify for the team. Tentatively, she pulled open one of the metal doors to the sports complex and stepped inside, making a beeline for the locker room.

"Hi, Ava," a girl greeted her with a wave as Ava stepped inside the change room. "I'm Margaret."

"Hi," replied Ava.

She recognized her as one of the girls in Courtney's room the day that Jules had shown Ava around.

"I saw you swim on Thursday morning," said Margaret. "You're lucky: you'll have no problem making the team."

"Thanks," replied Ava, warily. She unpacked her backpack on a bench next to Margaret. "I'm sure you'll do well too."

"Maybe," said Margaret with a shrug. "It's my third year on the team, though I barely made it the other years. I struggle with my freestyle times."

"Oh," replied Ava, not sure what else to say.

"Maybe a few extra practice laps will help," said Margaret, with an unconvincing laugh.

Margaret pulled on her swim cap with a snap and headed toward the pool with a wave.

"See you out there," said Margaret.

Ava stared after Margaret for a moment as she slowly pulled on her own swim cap, tucking her stray hairs underneath its rim. She hadn't expected a friend of Courtney's to be so nice. She slung her full backpack over her shoulder. She was going to bring all her things out onto the pool deck so that Courtney couldn't mess with her today. Somehow she'd have to manage to keep an eye on her stuff, even while she was swimming. That could be tricky.

"Ava!" Called Coach Laurel, waving her over to a table where some teachers sat with clipboards in front of them.

She beckoned Ava over and clapped her on the shoulder when she reached the table. Ava blinked in surprise at the warm welcome. Maybe the headmistress hadn't meant she'd have to miss the time trials, after all.

"All of these teachers have volunteered to help me time today," said Coach Laurel. "Team, this the one I've been telling you about. Ava's going to win us some championships this year."

Ava recognized Mr. Chase, her calculus teacher.

"Hi, Ava," said Mr. Chase with a wink, handing her a square of cloth with a safety pin at the top. "Here's your number, you can pin it to your swim cap, though the way Coach Laurel is talking, we'll know the swimmer out front is you."

"Thanks," said Ava, smiling weakly as looked at the cloth number. Coach Laurel had talked about her swimming. Not about her suspension. That was good.

After standing in front of the table a moment longer than she felt comfortable, she moved to the starting blocks and pinned the number to her cap. Her body felt numb. *She was going to be allowed to record her times.* There was no need for her rehearsed defense. Still, she'd probably feel better if she had the chance to explain. She'd talk to the coach after the trials.

"Ava?"

Ava turned to see a woman coming toward her, holding a clipboard and a stopwatch.

"I'm Miss French," said the lady. "I teach senior chemistry. I'll be timing you today, whenever you're ready. You'll be asked to swim 100 meters and then 400 meters of each stroke. We can start with whichever one you'd like."

Ava blinked at Miss French then looked over to find Coach Laurel, who was now at the other end of the pool deck. She'd never been to a time trial like this. This morning was not going as she'd expected. She still hadn't seen Courtney among the swimmers and thought bitterly that Courtney was probably guaranteed her spot on the team and didn't have to try out.

"Ava," said Miss French kindly, "do you need a few minutes in the pool, or are you ready?"

"No, I think I'm ready," said Ava, taking a deep breath. "I'll start with breast stroke, 100 meters."

"Whenever you're ready," Miss French said to her with a smile.

"You've got this," whispered Ava under her breath to herself. She pushed all thoughts of the tough conversation she was going to have later out of her mind.

Splashing into the pool, she let her training take over. One by one, she performed the strokes and the distances, resting only moments in between. She didn't need to ask Miss French for her times to know that she was swimming well. By the time she was on her last set of laps, a small crowd of girls had gathered to cheer her on. She'd saved her strongest stroke for last.

"You're almost there, Ava!"

Ava blocked out the cheers from the pool deck as best she

could and kept up her front crawl, feeling every muscle in her body fire as she made the turn into her last length. As she reached her arm out for the finish, she heard applause erupt from the pool deck. Breathing heavily from her exertion, she blinked up at the gathering, clinging to the end of the lane. It'd been a while since she'd swum that hard.

"Great job, Ava!" declared Coach Laurel, beaming as Ava climbed out of the pool. "That's got to be the fastest time trial I've ever seen. I look forward to having you as part of this team."

Coach Laurel waved away the girls who had gathered to cheer Ava on.

"Okay, show's over. Those of you who still haven't finished your laps," Coach Laurel continued, "please make sure you have times recorded for each stroke with your time-keeper."

The crowd dispersed and Coach Laurel turned to time a girl in another lane. Ava went over to grab her towel from her backpack sitting on the pool deck. Her breathing had returned to normal, though she enjoyed the feeling of her arms and legs tingle from the exertion. Looking around, she noticed that there were still many girls who hadn't finished their trials.

"That's all we needed, Ava," Coach Laurel called from the starting blocks. "You can go. See you Tuesday morning."

Ava waved to the coach and went to take a shower, replaying her last few laps in her mind. She wondered if any of her times had been a personal best. She'd have to ask the coach for her times at the next practice.

Once dressed, she tied her hair into a damp ponytail. To think she'd almost stayed home from the trials. Did Coach Laurel already know about the pills? Not likely. Even if it wasn't officially against school rules, she would have said something if she'd known. Ava chewed her lip as she slipped on her shoes. She'd been dismissed. Should she go back and wait for the chance to talk to the coach? Would that make her look guilty? After a long moment of hesitation, Ava pushed open the locker room door and took a step out into the hallway, toward avoidance. Not watching where she was walking, Ava ran smack into Ethan.

"Well, hello again," said Ethan with a laugh, wiping his sweaty brow with his towel. "Don't you ever look where you're going?"

Ethan's shirt was off – tucked into his basketball shorts at the back. Ava noticed his smooth, sculpted chest before looking down at the ground.

"I, uh…" said Ava, feeling her cheeks grow hot "I'm just heading from swimming, I was going to get some lunch."

"Great," replied Ethan, punching her lightly on the shoulder. "I'm buying. I've gotta hit the showers, but I'll meet you in the foyer."

"Very funny," Ava said, laughing. "You'll buy me a free meal in the cafeteria?"

"Nah," said Ethan, smiling. "We can go into town; it's not far. Besides, the cafeteria only serves sandwiches for lunch on the weekends. Nobody eats on campus on Saturday."

"I'll keep my clothes on to walk across campus this time, okay?" replied Ava.

"What?" Ethan asked, looking at her quizzically, before ducking into the boys' change room.

Ava strolled lightheartedly across the lawn toward the dorm, breathing in the smell of the freshly mown grass. Ethan seemed to have forgotten about her embarrassing swimsuit stroll. Maybe the rest of the campus would forget, too. When she reached Bessie's door, she knocked, but nobody appeared to be home. A pen and a clipboard marked MESSAGES hung beside the door. Ava scrawled her plans for the weekend on the sheet of paper for Bessie and included her mobile number, in case Bessie needed to reach her.

Turning to go, she checked her phone for messages, though there were none. She really felt more like calling Lucas right now than going into town with Ethan. He was an alumni kid, though. Maybe he'd shed some light on what Courtney was up to.

Entering the foyer, she spotted Ethan easily, sitting on a bench. They were the only ones there. Seeing her cross the floor toward him, he got to his feet and waved. She waved back. Ava knew students were allowed off campus on weekends until lights out. Noticing that the lounge in the balcony was quiet as well, she wondered where all the students had gone. Jules and her friends had surely left for their shopping trip already.

"Let's go," said Ethan, gesturing toward the door.

"Lead the way," answered Ava, following him out toward the lawn.

"Have you been to Luigi's yet?" he asked as they crossed the lawn toward the road.

Ava shook her head.

"Well, you're in for a treat, then," he told her. "Their pizza is awesome; much better than the cafeteria's. The place is packed on the weekends."

"Mmm," Ava replied, her mind elsewhere.

"You're awfully quiet, Ava," said Ethan.

"This place is tiring me out," Ava answered walking with her hands in the pockets of her hoodie.

"Oh?" asked Ethan.

"Yeah," said Ava as they turned onto the sidewalk and walked in the opposite direction from Gran's. "What can you tell me about Courtney Wallis?"

Might as well skip straight to the punch, she thought to herself. Ethan seemed like he could handle it.

"Courtney? I'm not sure I know a Courtney," he replied. "Is she a student here?"

"Really?" asked Ava, recoiling. "You don't know Courtney? Bright red hair, swim team, she's in our English class..."

"Sorry," replied Ethan, continuing along on the sidewalk. "I guess I'm not very observant."

"Well, she's not a very nice person," grumbled Ava, kicking a stone off of the sidewalk in front of her. "I was kinda hoping you could help me figure out why she's trying to ruin my life."

"You're right," said Ethan, grinning as he mocked her a little. "She doesn't sound nice at all."

Ava made a face.

"She's trying to ruin your life?" he asked, more seriously, as they walked together.

"Well, it seems like it," said Ava, biting her lip and lowering her voice. "She made me late for swim practice, locked my clothes in my locker, then made it look like I'm taking caffeine pills to boost my swim times and even claims I offered them to her. Now I'm basically suspended from school."

"You're suspended from school?" exclaimed Ethan, giving a low whistle. "A girl in our class did all of that?"

"I think so," Ava replied.

"Why?" asked Ethan, looking perplexed.

"I don't really know," replied Ava, her voice trembling slightly. "I guess she doesn't want me to make the swim team. She's made a few comments about my parents, so I'm thinking she holds a deeper grudge. Her dad's on the admissions committee with your dad."

The sidewalk had led them to a small strip of shops just a few minutes' walk from the school, only a block from downtown Evergreen. Ava recognized the grocery store and pharmacy down the street that she'd been to with her mother. Evergreen didn't seem to have changed much over the years, she thought as she looked around. Funny, her mother had said it looked much the same as when she was a kid as well.

"We're here," Ethan told her, holding the door to Luigi's open for her. "Ladies first."

Ava looked at the neon sign and wondered if her parents had

ever come here for lunch. It had surely been here for years. As they entered, a middle-aged waitress greeted them and led them to a booth. Ethan waved to some classmates at another table as they passed. Ava thought a boy sitting at that table looked familiar. He might have been from one of her classes.

"I'll have a Coke, please," said Ethan.

"I'm fine with just water, thank you," Ava said.

She shifted in her seat. Sitting across from Ethan in the booth, this felt suspiciously like a date. Perhaps she shouldn't have been so quick to accept his invitation. Ava glanced around the restaurant, but nobody seemed to be looking their way. Best to keep the lunch short.

"So," said Ethan with a grin once the waitress had left, "tell me - do you actually take caffeine pills? I've just ordered a Coke, so I guess I'm not opposed to caffeine, though I don't think it would help my performance much."

"Of course not!" replied Ava, laughing despite herself.

"Then this will all blow over," said Ethan. "If you're half as good a swimmer as this Courtney person is worried about, let her do the worrying, not you."

"Thanks," replied Ava, managing a thin smile just as the waitress came to deliver their drinks.

"We'll have a large pepperoni with the works," Ethan said to the waitress, looking at Ava. "That okay with you?"

"Sounds good," replied Ava, closing her menu.

"So, what did Courtney say about your parents?" Ethan asked as the waitress walked away.

"Um," Ava replied, trying to remember what exactly Courtney had said. "She said something about my family connections when she told me about the first practice, and then the coach said something about me bragging that I would get on the team because my mom had been a great swimmer."

Ava felt her throat tighten.

"Did you know that my dad was madly in love with her?" asked Ethan.

"With Courtney?" she asked incredulously.

"No, silly," he said with a chuckle. "He was in love with your mom. She and my dad were an item for most of high school. But sometime during senior year, she dumped him and starting dating your dad out of the blue."

"What?" asked Ava, feeling stunned. She knew very little about her parents' years at St. Augustus.

"From what I understand, my dad stepped aside," Ethan continued, sitting back in his seat, "but I know he's always thought of your mother as the 'one who got away'."

"Oh," replied Ava, not quite sure what to say. "How did your parents meet?"

"They were set up on a blind date by my mom's sister," Ethan replied. "They married and had me within the year, divorced the year after that."

"Sorry I asked," replied Ava, grimacing.

"It's okay," replied Ethan. "My mom remarried a few years later. When I got old enough, I asked if I could live with my dad. My mom's new husband had three daughters that lived with us every other week. I guess I kind of liked it being just me and my dad."

The waitress arrived at their table, carrying their pizza on a tray. Ava's mouth watered at the sight of the cheese oozing off the sides. She was surprised to find this didn't feel like a date, after all. It felt like she'd known Ethan for years.

"Anyway, since you haven't heard the story before," said Ethan, grabbing a slice after the waitress set it down, "your mom was supposed to go to prom with my dad, but showed up with Steve, ignoring my dad all night. I happen to have heard the story lots of times from my dad."

"Really?" mused Ava, swallowing a mouthful of pizza and taking a sip of her water. "That doesn't sound like my mom, at least not when I knew her."

"Apparently your parents were inseparable after that," Ethan continued, reaching for another slice. "My dad tells it like he just gave up. He and Steve had been friends for a very long time and it was so close to graduation. They stayed friends, even after. Though I imagine it was never the same."

Ava chewed her pizza thoughtfully. She'd heard about prom from her Mom before, though this story was very different. She'd never even heard of Ethan's dad.

"Our dads played basketball together," said Ethan. "They'd roomed together since freshman year. In their senior year they lived in the "lucky" room."

"Room 65?" she asked.

"That's the one," Ethan confirmed, grinning. "See? You really are an alumni kid - legends of the school and all."

Ava looked at Ethan now, feeling very uneasy that he knew so much about her family, more than she did, in fact. Her dad had always been so closed-lipped about the past.

"Does your dad believe the room is lucky?" Ava asked, taking the last slice of pizza, though she was full already and knew it would probably sit in her stomach like a lump all afternoon.

"He always jokes that it was lucky for your dad, stealing his girl," replied Ethan, laughing.

Ava didn't respond, leaving an awkward silence hanging between them. This was the first lull in their conversation all afternoon. It seemed to Ava like it stretched forever. She put down the second half of the pizza slice she'd taken. There was no way she could finish.

"We could just stay sitting here and order dinner, it's almost five o'clock," Ethan said finally, looking at his watch.

"I've got to be getting back to my gran's," said Ava, shifting in her seat. Looking around the restaurant, she noticed that they were the only customers left from the crowd that had been there at lunch. "I'm staying there for the weekend."

"Why? You just got here."

"I thought I'd lay low until my meeting with the headmistress on Monday," Ava said.

"Well," said Ethan, his eyes playful, "get this all cleared up with Valentine in time for English class on Monday, I wouldn't want you to hand in your assignment late."

"The only good thing about meeting the headmistress on Monday morning is that I'll probably get to *miss* English class!" groaned Ava.

"Writer's block?" teased Ethan.

"Nah," Ava replied. "I've got all day tomorrow to do the assignment. There's not much to do at Gran's."

"Can I copy yours?" Ethan asked her, with mock-seriousness. "It'd free up my day tomorrow to work on my free throws."

"You think Ms. Krick is that batty she wouldn't notice us handing in the same paper?" Ava asked, laughing. It felt good to laugh.

Ethan shrugged, tossing cash on the table and getting up.

"Oh, please," Ava said, reaching into her pocket. "Let me pay."

"Don't be silly," Ethan replied, laughing. "You can buy next time."

"Okay," replied Ava, sliding out of the booth and feeling pleased that there would be a next time.

"Your grandmother lives nearby?" Ethan asked as they walked back toward the campus. "That must be nice to have family around."

"Yeah, her house is just on the other side of the woods," replied Ava.

"She lives near the West Woods?" he asked, sounding interested. "If you aren't expelled for your drug habit, you definitely will be if you go in there."

"Hey!" said Ava, hitting him playfully, but hard, on the shoulder.

"Ouch," he complained, laughing.

"I actually did walk through the woods last night," said Ava as the campus came into sight up ahead. "I had no idea we weren't allowed, I'd gone that way loads of times with my mom. Did you know there's a fountain in the middle of the woods?"

"Well," he suggested, with a sparkle in his eye, "maybe we'll have to break the rules and go see it sometime."

Ava smiled. He really was easy to talk to. Her issues with Courtney didn't seem so bad now that she'd said them out loud. No way would she actually be suspended for something she hadn't done.

"I'll want a full account of your showdown with Valentine on Monday," Ethan told her, as they stopped in front of St. Augustus. "So make sure you take notes."

"Sure," said Ava, rolling her eyes as she waved goodbye and continued on the sidewalk toward Gran's.

As she walked away, she felt her cheeks hurt from all the smiling she'd done that afternoon.

CHAPTER TWELVE

Gone

The Fountain
By Ava Marshall

A gasp fills the clearing, and at once I realize the gasp is mine. The fountain is so unexpected, standing out here in a clearing in the woods. Its round, smooth stone walls tower over their own shadow in the undergrowth. I wonder why or how it is here.

Picking my way through the vines and leaves toward it, I reach out to touch the stone. Marble, even on a hot day, should feel cool to the skin, but this marble is warm. I lay my cheek against its rim to take the chill from my bones and rest for a moment, the sound of its splashing water a welcome melody. My cheek and face become wet with its warm spray, sweet water dripping into my mouth.

Stepping back, I blot my face dry with my sweater. Intricate carvings dance along the side of the basin, animals and angels smiling back at me. My fingers bump along the ridges in the stone. Time hasn't been kind to the carvings, so smooth now they would be invisible but for the damp green moss that has grown in its shapes.

The constant crash of the water blocks out my thoughts, which is a welcome interlude from reality and the harshness of life. Water shimmers in the sunlight, diamond flashes reflecting across its

The Fountain

surface. I squint against the glare. Coins litter the bottom of the basin, wishes of those who had come before. I feel my shoulders relax, and settle in to visit for a while.

Ava reread her assignment, smiling smugly to herself as she sat at her mother's old desk. It'd had taken her all evening, but it was ready. Reading through her paper, Ava could almost feel herself standing back in the clearing. She'd found the fountain at the exact moment that she'd needed it. Ms. Krick would surely have to admit that her paper was good.

Looking around her mother's room, Ava felt glad that she'd left campus for the weekend. Aunt Mia had texted late Sunday afternoon to say she was swamped and she'd call Ava on Monday. In the morning, Ava would face the headmistress alone, though this time she was determined to tell her side of the story.

Crossing the room, Ava tucked her English assignment inside her backpack and climbed into her mother's childhood bed. Carefully, she set the alarm on her phone to be up in plenty of time to drop her assignment off at Ms. Krick's classroom before visiting the headmistress.

Ava snapped off the lights and settled in for sleep, though her mind didn't shut off. So many times in her life she'd wondered how things would be different if her mother hadn't gotten into the car that day. Ava longed now to cry on her mother's shoulder and be told that everything was going to be okay.

The next morning, Ava smiled to herself as she entered the headmistress' office, realizing that she hummed Lucas' song, *Ava Come Back.* Her mood had greatly improved following her relaxing Sunday at Gran's. Sunlight shone through the windows of the office, brightening the ornate woodwork to a warm glow. Surely the headmistress would be more in the mood to listen to the truth today.

Miss Samantha sat at her desk, clicking away at her keyboard with her long, manicured nails.

"May I help you?" Miss Samantha asked brightly, looking up.

"Good morning, Miss Samantha," said Ava, smiling. "I have an appointment to see Headmistress Valentine."

"Oh?" Miss Samantha replied, frowning over her glasses at a large appointment book in front of her. "What's your name, dear?"

"Ava Marshall," replied Ava, looking at Miss Samantha curiously. It seemed strange that she didn't recognize Ava. That might be good news.

"Oh, Ava," said Miss Samantha smiling warmly, "so nice to meet you. I've spoken to your aunt a few times on the phone. Are you settling in to St. Augustus all right?"

"I, uh," Ava stammered, feeling overwhelmed with a sense of déjà vu. "Headmistress Valentine asked me to come see her this morning before class."

"Are you sure?" Miss Samantha asked, frowning as she rechecked her date book. "Well she isn't here right now, but I'll ask her about it. I can send for you in class if she says she needs to see you."

"So, I should go to class?" Ava said, shifting uncomfortably.

"I don't see why not," replied Miss Samantha.

She scribbled something in the margin of her book then looked up, as if something had just occurred to her. Ava braced herself for Miss Samantha to comment on what was found in her locker.

"Perhaps the headmistress asked you to come because there was confusion about your being at your grandmother's for the weekend." Miss Samantha suggested. "Bessie let us know on Saturday that it'd been all cleared up, so there's no problem now."

Ava glanced over at the headmistress' closed door behind Miss Samantha's desk. She'd come to the office that morning prepared to leaving nothing unsaid. She wanted to get this over with, but now she was being offered the chance to delay the inevitable. Could she really just go to class? If the headmistress still wanted to see her, surely she'd come and find Ava.

"Really, there's no problem, Ava," said Miss Samantha, interrupting her thoughts. "I'll tell her that I sent you to class. You needn't worry. You'll be late though if you don't hurry. And because of your family's history with the school and your lovely Gran, we understand that you'll want to be off campus from time to time. But you need to make sure the proper paperwork and approvals are in place. Can't have you wandering off."

"Uh, thanks," Ava stammered, wondering if she should trust Miss Samantha to tell the headmistress she'd been here. Her memory didn't seem great.

Turning her back on Miss Samantha and the headmistress' office, she realized that she'd been looking forward to clearing the air. Ava thought it strange that the headmistress hadn't talked to the coach or to Miss Samantha about the pills. She could only hope that meant that the headmistress had realized how absurd her accusation had been. Still, the headmistress had been clear about the time. What had changed?

Ava scanned the campus uneasily as she crossed the lawn toward the West Building, as if the headmistress would appear at any moment.

Ms. Krick's classroom was noisy as she entered. Ava's classmates leaned against their desks in groups, talking about their weekends. Ava noticed students dropping their papers off on a stack that sat on Ms. Krick's desk. Her assignment should already be in that pile somewhere. The bell rang just as Ava took her seat and she was grateful that she wouldn't be expected to chat.

"Open your textbooks to page thirteen," Ms. Krick said to the class sharply. "Read chapters two and three during this period while I grade your assignments. If you don't finish those chapters during class you can read them for homework."

Ms. Krick took a seat at her desk, in front of the stack of

student papers. Sounds of low groans and books shuffling filled the classroom as the students settled in uncomfortably for a whole period of silent reading. Ava looked again at the papers sitting on the teacher's desk. Had Ms. Krick read her assignment when she'd found it slipped under the door? Or had she simply put it in the stack?

Ava opened her book along with the other kids, though she kept one eye on the classroom door, expecting the headmistress any moment. Ava couldn't concentrate on the words on the pages and watched Ms. Krick reading behind the teacher's desk instead.

Suddenly, Ms. Krick snapped her head up, catching Ava's eye with a fierce expression on her face. Caught staring at her teacher, Ava buried her nose in her book and didn't look up again until the bell rang.

Ava stood up with the other students at the sound of the bell, opening her backpack to put away her English book.

"Hi."

She looked up to see Ethan standing beside her desk. She'd momentarily forgotten that he was in this class.

"So, which one is Courtney?" Ethan asked in a low voice as they walked toward the door.

Ava looked around the room quickly at the students filing out of Ms. Krick's classroom.

"I don't see her," Ava replied, shaking her head. "I don't think she was in class today."

"Ms. Marshall," Ms. Krick called loudly from her seat at her desk, "would you stay behind for a moment, please?"

"Uh, sure," Ava answered.

Something about Ms. Krick's tone made Ava uneasy. Had the headmistress summoned her? No, Ava thought to herself, if Ms. Krick knew that Ava had been suspended, surely she'd have said something at the beginning of class. Perhaps she only wanted to commend her on her essay.

"I'll catch you after calculus," Ethan told her.

His eyebrows gave Ava a quizzical look.

Ava just shrugged as Ethan backed his way out of the room and shut the door, leaving Ava alone with Ms. Krick.

After the door clicked shut, Ms. Krick crossed the floor toward Ava, waving a sheet of paper in the air.

"What's the meaning of this?" Ms. Krick hissed.

Ava took a step back to avoid the paper hitting her in the face.

"Do you think you're really clever?" demanded Ms. Krick.

Ava blinked at her with complete surprise. What was she talking about?

"Did you do it to mock me?" Ms. Krick continued in a harsh whisper. "Or did you simply copy your mother's assignment and think I wouldn't notice? That's called plagiarism, Ms. Marshall."

"I'm sorry, Ms. Krick," Ava said, her heart racing. "I'm not sure what you're suggesting. I simply wrote the assignment about the fountain in the woods near my Gran's. I know now that students aren't allowed..."

"Liar!" Ms. Krick interrupted in a low voice, her dark eyes seeming to look right through Ava. "There is no such fountain. Who put you up to this, your father? What did he tell you?"

"I, uh..." Ava stammered, feeling her hands shake.

Her father hadn't told her anything. What was she talking about?

"Well, you get an F on this paper," Ms. Krick said coldly, sitting back behind her desk with a thud. "I'm watching you, Ava Marshall."

Ava gaped at Ms. Krick, who sat behind her desk, studying some papers. Ava watched Ms. Krick for a moment, realizing that she'd been dismissed. She clasped her hands in front of her as she left the room, trying to stop them from shaking.

"There you are!" Ethan exclaimed, pushing himself off the wall in the hallway outside the classroom door. "What did Krick want?

She didn't sound happy."

"She..." Ava said, her voice breaking as she spoke. "She accused me of plagiarizing my assignment. She says I copied it from one my mother wrote."

Her backpack slipped off her shoulder and she held it protectively in front of her body.

"Oh," said Ethan, taking her backpack from her to carry it for her as they walked.

Ava let him take her bag, still feeling shaky.

"Did you?" Ethan asked her simply.

"Of course not!" exclaimed Ava, her face hot with temper. "I have no idea what she's talking about. She says my mother wrote a paper on the same fountain. My mother went to school here over twenty years ago! Why Ms. Krick would remember a paper that she wrote, or care that we had the same subject, I have no idea."

"That is strange," said Ethan, as they slowly made their way down the staircase toward calculus class. "Man, Ava, you're having a tough week."

Ava looked at the clock on the wall when they'd reached the bottom of the stairs. The hall was nearly empty now; the bell was about to ring.

"How did your meeting with Valentine go this morning?" Ethan asked, handing back her bag. "You came to class, so I take it you're no longer suspended, does that mean you're off the hook?"

Ava shrugged.

"Did you tell her what Courtney did?" asked Ethan. "Is that why she wasn't in English class?"

"No," replied Ava. "It was weird, actually. The headmistress wasn't even there when I showed up this morning and Miss Samantha told me to just go to class. I'll have to meet with her at some time today, but I'm dreading it."

They stood just outside the door to Mr. Chase's classroom.

"Maybe you could ask Ms. Krick to put in a good word for you." Ethan teased.

The clang of the late bell covered the sound of his chuckle.

"Very funny," replied Ava, as she yanked open the door to the classroom. "I can't wait for this day to be over."

They walked quickly into the room and took their seats. Ava glanced nervously over at Mr. Chase, knowing that she and Ethan had entered after the bell, but he just smiled and went to the board to show them the equations they were going to discuss. Ava felt herself relax as she slumped into her front-row seat.

Ava had biology class next, in which they talked about recessive genes. Sometime during biology, Ava stopped watching the door for the headmistress.

Walking toward the cafeteria for lunch, her jitters were back. Ava had reached a crossroads in the corridor of the main building. If she turned left, she would find herself at the headmistress' office. Turning right, she'd be in the cafeteria. The suspense was killing her.

"Ava!"

Jules came rushing up behind her, locking arms with Ava.

"You look lost," Jules told her, leading her down the hallway to the right. "The cafeteria is this way."

"Thanks," Ava mumbled, following Jules into the cafeteria.

There wasn't much of a line.

"How was your weekend at your grandma's?" Jules asked, stepping up to get some food.

"Good, actually," replied Ava, scanning the crowd. "Have you seen Courtney?"

"Who?" Jules asked her as she put a can of diet soda on her lunch tray.

Ava narrowed her eyes at Jules, but said nothing. Instead, she quickly grabbed a sandwich from the closest display and followed Jules toward her usual table.

"So, who's everyone going with to the homecoming dance?" Jules asked the others with a giggle, after they'd sat down. "Wouldn't it be fun if we all had dates and went together?"

Ava wasn't listening. She'd seen a flash of red hair across the cafeteria and squinted. It was only a tall red-headed boy walking across the far end of the room.

"Ava?" asked Jules. "Are you listening? Do you think Ethan will ask you to the dance?"

"What?" asked Ava, tuning back into their conversation. "No. No, of course not. I don't even think I'll go."

"Oh," Jules said, frowning.

"Actually," said Ava, standing up from the table, "I just remembered I have to get something from our room before class. I'll see you girls later."

Ava walked in a daze toward the dorm. When she'd arrived in her hallway, she paused at the door of room 65. She stared at the numbers on the door. Made of black wrought iron, they curved in the same loopy style as the numbers on her own door. Ava raised her hand and knocked. She felt her heart race as she waited, but there was no answer. Ava turned to go.

The door to room 65 opened with a creak and Ava spun around, expecting to see Courtney. Instead, she found herself staring at a brown-haired girl.

"Hi," said the girl, looking surprised to see Ava standing there. "You're Ava, right?"

"Yes," replied Ava, warily.

This girl must be one of Courtney's friends.

"I'm Rhoda. I don't think we've actually met yet, but I'm on the swim team," said the girl. "Sorry it took me so long to answer the door, I spilled soup on my kilt at lunch. I just came back to the dorm to change."

"I... uh," said Ava as she glanced at the number on the door again to be sure. "Sorry, I must've gotten confused, I was looking for someone else."

"No problem," replied Rhoda as she came out into the hall. "Your swim trial was awesome, by the way. We're lucky to have you on the team. "

Ava felt herself at a loss for words.

"Well," said Rhoda, shutting the door to room 65, "see you later!"

Rhoda walked away, leaving Ava in stunned silence. *What was going on?*

CHAPTER THIRTEEN

Changed

Ava firmly closed her dorm room door behind her once she'd stepped inside, and took a few deep breaths. Courtney was probably just sick, or had gone home for a few days. Yes, that had to be it, though hadn't Jules said that Courtney didn't have a roommate? Who was Rhoda and why did her name sound so familiar? She'd met so many kids since she'd arrived it was hard to keep everyone straight.

Ava took out her mobile phone and stared at it for a moment before scrolling through its address book, searching for the number her dad had given her to contact him in Malaysia. She hadn't spoken to him since she'd arrived at St. Augustus and she suddenly felt homesick. Finding her dad's entry, she brought it up on the screen. Ava frowned. The only number listed was his mobile number in California. Where was the number he'd given to her to reach him in Malaysia? Ava distinctly remembered putting his number into her phone before he'd gone. Suddenly noticing the time, she laughed. She would have been calling her dad in Malaysia in the middle of the night. She called Mia's number instead.

"Hello, Mia Taylor speaking," Mia answered on the first ring.

"Hi, Mia," said Ava. "Is this a bad time?"

"Ava!" Mia replied. "How's school? I'm never too busy for my favorite niece."

"Okay," replied Ava, laughing. "Though I'm your only niece, Mia. Listen, I seem to have lost my dad's new number. Do you have it?"

"New number?" replied Mia. "I don't think he has a new number. He's probably at the house."

"At the house? Why isn't he in Malaysia?"

"What's that, Ava?" Mia asked. "I didn't quite catch that. Sorry, I'm still working on the notes for that case I had to come home for. Just wait a second and I'll close the file while we talk. Okay, there. What I was saying was that I think he's at home. It's raining pretty hard here and his crew is paving this week, but they aren't working today because of the rain."

Ava felt cold all over. Her dad was an engineer, but he worked in an office. She'd never known him to do anything with paving before. And why was he even in San Francisco?

"So," Ava asked carefully, "is he at my house or your house?"

"Very funny, Ava," replied Mia with a chuckle. "You know that Uncle Chuck and I consider it your house too. How else would I get the chance to watch you grow up from the day you were born?"

Ava drew in a sharp breath of air. Shivers ran through her to her fingertips.

"Honey, are you all right?" asked Aunt Mia.

"Um, I'm not sure," replied Ava. "Everything is a little, uh, strange today."

"It's strange to have you so far away from home, honey," replied Mia. "You really should give your dad a call. I'm sure it would be good for both of you. He's having a hard time with you so far away, you know."

"Thanks, Mia, I will. Bye." said Ava, hanging up quickly.

Why wasn't her dad in Malaysia? He lived with Mia and Chuck? Why did Mia think that Ava had lived there too? The prickly feeling she'd had all day suddenly came into focus. Ava felt all the blood drain from her face. She thought of her coin floating slowly in the water of the fountain. The answer had been there all along. But she couldn't turn away from it now.

I wish that St. Augustus had never heard of Courtney or her family.

What had she done?

Panicked, she pulled up the contacts on her phone again and then breathed a huge sigh of relief. Lucas' number was still there, along with his text messages from the last few days. She closed the contacts and Lucas' his smiling face next to hers on the screen. That picture had been taken of them together the day she'd left California.

She put her phone down on her bed and stared at the beige wall of her room, trying to recall everything she knew about Courtney and her family. Dad had said Jim Wallis had tutored him. Without Jim Wallis, he'd told her he never would have passed high school. Ava felt a wave of nausea wash over her and clutched at her stomach, though she didn't seem in immediate danger of losing her supper. Is that what had happened? Because of her, had her father never become an engineer?

The warning bell for afternoon classes rang through the dorm hallway, snapping Ava back to the present. Ava looked at her phone and then at the door to the hallway. She'd never skipped a class in her life. If she called Dad now she could find out for sure, though what would she say? She needed to think.

Slowly, Ava raised herself off of her bed and focused simply on putting one foot in front of the other on her way to her next class, her mind racing.

Ava barely paid attention to anything her teachers said that afternoon. Luckily, they didn't seem to notice how distant she felt.

She kept coming back to her mother's conviction that wishing wells contained real power.

"When you have a wish in your heart," her mother had told her, "you just need to trust in yourself and it will happen."

When her long afternoon of classes finally ended, Ava found herself walking aimlessly down the hallways of the main building. Ava had never believed in that kind of magic, yet she felt certain now that her mother had. She thought she understood why.

Clutching her backpack to her chest, her mind replayed the night in the clearing. She could see herself sitting beside the fountain as if it had happened moments ago. *Could Courtney really be gone?* Ava sifted through the events of the last few days, trying to make some sense of them. *Where did she go?* Suddenly, she realized that she'd taken a wrong turn in the main building and walked down an unfamiliar hallway. Ava looked around at the stone walls of the school, finding herself in front of the library. Ava entered.

"Excuse me," Ava said to the librarian behind the large desk in the entryway.

Ava's own voice sounded too loud in the quiet library.

"I'm... uh, doing a project on the town of Evergreen," Ava continued in a lower voice, almost a whisper. "I'm looking for information on Evergreen history and legends, that sort of thing."

"Well," the librarian started slowly, looking up from the book she'd been reading, "there are a few local history books here that I can show you. But legends? What exactly do you mean by that?"

"Legends," repeated Ava. "Specifically about St. Augustus."

The librarian looked at Ava curiously.

"I guess I'm looking for anything about St. Augustus' founder," Ava continued, "or something about the St. Augustus buildings and the campus."

Ava looked evenly at the librarian. Jules had said that alumni kids talked about these things. Surely they'd be written down somewhere.

"Well, I've certainly heard stories about Isaac Young," said the librarian, sounding brighter. "Though I don't know that any of them are written down. However..."

She motioned for Ava to follow her across the small library.

"We do have some books that were from the founder's estate, including some of his journals," explained the librarian. "I don't think you'll find any legends here, but you might get a sense of who he was. There are also some books in this section about the history of the town, so maybe you'll find something interesting in there to put in your report."

"Great," said Ava, already scanning the titles on the shelf.

"You might want to ask Matilda Krick as well," the librarian suggested. "Ms. Krick's been teaching here an awfully long time and is known as a bit of an expert on St. Augustus history."

"Uh, thanks," stammered Ava.

"Good luck," said the librarian, smiling at Ava and walking away.

Ava found herself alone in the aisle. It was a dead end in one corner of the library. She ran her fingers along the spines of the books on the cluttered shelf. There were so many titles. How would she know where to start?

Most of the books reminded her of the boring texts lining her father's study back home. Books that were in the house that Ava had grown up in, not far from Mia and Chuck's - but not Mia and Chuck's. *Did someone else live in that house now?* Ava gave her head a shake and pulled a book off the shelf entitled *"A History of Evergreen"*. On a whim, she flipped to the back. Pulling the card gently out of the pocket glued to the inside back cover of the book, Ava studied the handwriting closely. The book had been checked out three times according to the card, and always to the same person.

Matilda Krick.

Ava's scalp prickled. Ms. Krick had read this book - more than once. She might be on to something. She picked the next book off the shelf – really more of a thick pamphlet than a book - this one called *"Evergreen's Bicentennial Celebration"*. Again, only Ms. Krick's name was printed neatly on the card at the back.

Ava scanned the shelf, searching for the journals the librarian had mentioned. She spotted a set of about a dozen leather bound binders at the end of the shelf, next to the wall. She reached over and pulled the first one out. Its brown leather cover was cracked with age. She felt the grooves under her fingertips. Holding her breath, she opened the journal and quickly flipped to the back cover.

This time, the list of names that had checked out the book almost filled the entire card.

Lucy Sawyer
Timothy Agneau
Robert Moss
Mariam Taylor
Matilda Krick
Steven Marshall
Matilda Krick
Rebecca Frost
David Earl
Matilda Krick

Ava gasped. Her mother and father had both read this book. Ava gently ran her index finger over her mother's name. It had been written in Mariam's own teenage handwriting. Her father's name had certainly also been written by him, she recognized his boxy letters.

Ava gave a furtive look around the library, though the librarian was nowhere to be seen. Snapping the book shut, she tucked it under her arm and walked toward the librarian's desk. She'd have plenty of time to read it back at the dorm.

"Ava!" A loud voice called to her from the foyer of the otherwise quiet library. Ava looked up to see Ethan crossing the library toward her, wearing a broad smile.

"Fancy meeting you here," he said, winking at her. "Don't tell anyone I know how to read, it'll ruin my image."

Ava managed a thin smile.

"What's that book you have there?" he asked, gesturing to the journal tucked under Ava's arm. "It looks old."

"It is," replied Ava. "It's something my parents checked out when they went to school here. I thought I'd give it a read."

"May I?" asked Ethan as he reached over and took the book from her.

Ava prickled, but didn't stop him from taking the book.

"Isaac Young," Ethan said, reading the cover. "The founder of St. Augustus? Why were they interested in him?"

Ethan had already started flipping through the pages, having taken a seat in a comfortable armchair in the center of the library. Ava sat down on the edge of the chair beside him, fiddling with her hair. How could she politely tell him she'd just like to be alone?

"So, what happened in the end with the headmistress?" Ethan asked, while turning the delicate pages of Isaac Young's journal. "Did you tell her what Courtney's been up to? By the way, I still have no idea who Courtney is. Did you find out if she came to school today?"

"Um," started Ava. How was she going to explain?

Ethan looked up from the book.

"Do you remember the fountain I told you about in the woods?" Ava began, in a rush of words. "It's what I wrote about for my assignment, the one Ms. Krick said I copied from my mother. Ms. Krick flunked me on it, by the way."

"Go on."

"Well," Ava continued, words tumbling out, "I couldn't understand why Ms. Krick was so mad. Also, I didn't copy the paper from my mother. But I think the fountain may have belonged to Isaac Young, so I thought his journals might help me understand the connection."

"Okay," said Ethan slowly.

"Look at the card in the back," said Ava, reaching over and flipping the pages of the book, pointing to the card at the back. "Both of my parents' names are there as well as Ms. Krick's. I don't know what it means yet. I'm hoping this journal will help me figure that out."

"The first I'd ever heard of the fountain was when you told me about it this weekend," said Ethan, studying the names on the card. "Actually, I've never had a reason to go into the West Woods."

"Of course not," said Ava, practically. "The woods are off-limits to students."

"That doesn't usually stop me," said Ethan, grinning. "I have heard that Isaac Young was a strange dude, though. Why would he put a fountain in the middle of the woods?"

"Ethan," Ava said quietly, looking around the library, "do you believe in wishes?"

"I don't know," Ethan answered with a shrug. "I make 'em like anybody else, but I don't ever expect them to come true."

"And what would you think if they did?" Ava asked, her voice barely a whisper.

"Well," replied Ethan slowly, no longer smiling, "that would be a good thing, wouldn't it?"

Ava looked at him with a pained expression on her face.

"You wished on that fountain you found?" Ethan asked her loudly, looking straight into her eyes. "For what?"

"I, uh," Ava struggled to speak her confession, her eyes filling with tears. "I wished for Courtney to go away."

Ethan's laugh made her jump out of the seat she'd been perched on.

"And you're worried because she wasn't at school today?" Ethan asked her, smiling and shaking his head. "Like, somehow you made that happen?"

Ava stood in front of him with her arms folded across her chest. It all seemed rather ridiculous now that she'd said it out loud.

"Man, Ava, you are full of surprises," said Ethan, relaxing back into his armchair. "Don't worry. I'm sure there's a much more logical reason for her missing class today."

"But lots of things are different," Ava blurted out impatiently. "Nobody seems to even know who Courtney is. And someone named Rhoda lives in Courtney's room, and my dad..."

"Whoa," said Ethan, reaching boldly forward and wiping away a tear from her cheek. "Ava, there are lots of people at school that I don't know. I'm sure there's an explanation for all of these things. How about I help you find it?"

He stood up beside her, still holding the journal.

"Let's start with this book," he continued. "You definitely need to pull up your grade in English. If you get an F, you'll be off the swim team. Learning about something that Krick is interested in seems like a good way to get on her good side. C'mon, let's go sign it out."

Ethan draped his arm playfully around Ava's shoulders, leading her toward the librarian's desk. Of course, he was right, she thought to herself, feeling grateful for his level-headedness. There had to be a more rational explanation for everything that had happened.

CHAPTER FOURTEEN

Shared Secret

Crack.

Ava opened her eyes that night in the dark dorm room and wiped away the sleep. What had woken her? She blinked, adjusting to the dark. Jules seemed undisturbed under her bedcovers. Gentle snores interrupted the otherwise quiet room. Ava exhaled loudly, immediately wishing she'd done so more quietly.

Wiggling her limbs, she felt circulation returning. She must have imagined the sound. Nightmares were no stranger to Ava. She sank deeper beneath her cocoon of a quilt and let herself drift back to sleep.

Crack.

Ava nearly jumped out of bed. Her heart raced. It was the same sound that had woken her before. This was not a dream. She held her breath.

Crack.

The noise seemed to be coming from outside the window. Releasing her breath, Ava slowly eased herself off of the bed and edged her way toward the outside wall of her room. Gently, she lifted an edge of the curtain.

Crack.

Ava dropped the curtain quickly. Something was striking her

window. She looked over at Jules, who was still sleeping soundly. Should she wake her up?

Crack.

Extending her shaking hand, she tore the curtain back as if she were pulling off a Band-Aid. Looking out into the night, Ava scanned the shadows below her window. She gasped as she saw someone standing at the edge of a clump of trees a few feet from the wall. She stood frozen as she watched him raise an arm to throw something, then seeing her, the figure started to wave its arm up at her. Ava squinted her eyes out into the night and breathed a sigh of relief. It was Ethan.

Her heart still racing, she glanced over again at Jules' sleeping figure before pushing the window open a crack. She winced as the window groaned.

"What are you doing here?" she hissed at him.

His Cheshire-Cat grin hung in the shadows, glowing faintly white in the darkness.

"I found something you need to see," Ethan called up to the window in a hoarse whisper, moving toward the wall. "I'm coming up."

He'd already started to climb up the wall. The window frame creaked loudly as Ava shoved the pane upward. Cold air rushed into the room as Ethan scrambled through the window and landed on the floor with a thud.

"Well?" Ava asked, in a pointed whisper. "What's so important it couldn't wait?"

She stood facing him, her arms crossed on her chest over the thin shorts and T-shirt she wore. Ethan looked over at Jules, who'd rolled over sleepily, apparently unaware of Ethan's intrusion.

"Voilà," Ethan replied, pulling a sheet of white paper from under his coat with a flourish. "Behold - your mother's essay."

"Really?" Ava asked with a gasp, forgetting her annoyance.

She reached toward him eagerly to grab the crisp paper. Scooping up her phone from her bedside table, she turned it on for the light and settled down on her bed to read.

"*The Fountain,*" she read in a whisper.

The title on her mother's essay was the same as hers.

Ethan sat down beside her and flopped back to lie down, propping Ava's pillow behind his head. Ava shoved his sneakered feet off her quilt without looking up from the page. Ethan sat up with a sheepish grin.

"How did you get this?" she asked.

"After lights out," he whispered, "I went to Ms. Krick's classroom."

"What?" said Ava, appalled. "You broke in?"

"Yeah, I guess so," Ethan said. "After I saw you in the library this afternoon I went by her classroom. She was talking to one of the other teachers in the hallway. I told her I'd forgotten something and went inside. I opened one of the windows at the back of the room just a crack so I could come back."

"But Ms. Krick's classroom is on the second floor," said Ava, staring at Ethan.

He shrugged. "I climbed the big tree outside her window." he replied. "Anyhow, your essay and your mother's essay were in a folder just sitting on top of Krick's desk. I probably could have found them this afternoon if I'd been looking. Don't worry, I scanned them into my phone and printed it in my room. This is just a copy."

Ava looked at him curiously. Had he slept at all yet tonight? "I've broken into the library a few times when I couldn't sleep," he offered, as if he could read her mind. "But Ms. Krick's classroom was a first. Actually it was pretty easy, I'd do it again – can you imagine the look on her face if there was a frog in her desk?"

Ava's stomach felt tight as she looked at his grin. If Ethan were caught, she could get in even more trouble. Wasn't he worried about being seen?

"Anyway, I can see why Ms. Krick thought you'd copied it," he continued. "It's uncanny, really. Are you sure you never saw it before?"

"Whose side are you on, anyway?" Ava asked him in a low voice. She scowled as she read through the rest of the page.

Her mother's paper had certainly been written about the same fountain. Some of the phrases they'd used were almost word for word the same. Ava shifted uncomfortably on her bed. Her mother had taught her to wish on fountains, but Ava had never seen this paper before - or the fountain, for that matter. She ran her hand lightly over the script on the page. It was unmistakably her mother's writing, though the letters were more perfectly formed than the hurried hand Ava remembered. The printer ink sat smooth and dark on the white page, a false replica of the ballpoint pen her mother had probably used.

"Ava, there's more," Ethan continued quietly. "I also went and visited the headmistress' office."

"What?" Ava whispered, her eyes wide. "Tonight?"

This guy was too much. She looked over again at Jules, who didn't seem to be waking up.

"It's pretty easy to move around the main building after hours actually," Ethan said with a small laugh. "Our house mother sleeps like the dead, though the lock on the office door was tricky, it's pretty old. Then, after a few tries, I guessed that Miss Samantha's computer password is *St. Augustus*. Not a very secure password, actually."

Ava could only stare at Ethan, who seemed at ease with coming and going anywhere he pleased and obviously made a habit of roaming restricted areas of the campus at night. She wished he would get to the point, as her feeling of dread mounted.

"Anyway, Ava," Ethan continued in a serious tone, "there's

nobody named Courtney in our year. Actually, there isn't a Courtney in the whole school. Do you think maybe she has a different name?"

"What do you mean?" asked Ava, feeling suddenly cold.

"I did a pretty thorough check, actually," Ethan told her, a grim expression on his face. "I even looked up the swim team roster from last year in the yearbook. Nobody named Courtney."

"But that's impossible," breathed Ava.

"I don't know why, Ava," said Ethan, looking at her evenly, "but somehow I think you're telling the truth about this wish nonsense. I just don't know what to make of it all."

"Ethan," said Ava, grabbing his arm. "I have to undo my wish as soon as possible. We could go to the woods now, out the window?"

"No, not now," said Ethan, looking down at his watch. "It's almost morning. I have to get back to my room before our house mother gets up. She's usually up pretty early. We could go tomorrow night, though. I'll come and get you around midnight and you can show me your fountain."

Ava nodded silently, feeling light-headed.

"Good night, Ava," said Ethan, giving her hand a quick squeeze as he got up to leave. "Try to get some sleep."

"Good night," Ava replied, finding her voice. "And... thank you, Ethan."

"My pleasure," he said as he climbed out of the window.

He dropped from the open window to the lawn, waving to Ava before he jogged away across the dark campus. She felt the lingering sensation on her hand where he'd squeezed moments ago. A gesture of comfort, nothing more, she assured herself. He'd gone to a lot of effort tonight to help her, Ava realized as she watched him disappear behind the building on his way to the boys' dorm. Selfishly, she willed him to get back safely before his absence was noticed. If he were caught tonight, she wasn't worried that he'd implicate her, only that there would be no way they'd get to the fountain tomorrow.

She looked down at her phone. It was nearly 5 a.m. She had to be up for swim practice shortly. Ava's hand shook as she tucked her mother's essay under her pillow. Her stomach churned as she settled back into bed. A fitful sleep would be better than none at all, she thought. Lying on her side, she stared straight ahead and was spooked to see Jules sitting up, facing her in the other bed, a broad grin on her face.

"So, you and Ethan are *just* friends?" said Jules with a chuckle. "What were you two talking about? I could hardly make out a word. Your voices were all just a mumble. It was all I could do to pretend I was still asleep."

"He's, uh..." said Ava, not in the mood for a girl chat. "He's helping me with something, that's all."

"O-kay," replied Jules, slowly. "Still, one week at school and you are sneaking Ethan Roth into our room? I think I'm going to like being your roommate, Ava."

"Good night, Jules," said Ava. She rolled away to face the opposite wall. "I have swim practice in two hours," Ava mumbled. "I need to go back to sleep."

"Hey," said Jules, with mock annoyance. "I'm not the one entertaining a boy in our room at this hour!"

Ava was tired, but she couldn't help but giggle with Jules. She had a point.

CHAPTER FIFTEEN

Wait

Ava stood on the campus lawn early the next morning, staring across to where the woods stood thick and dark. She shivered, feeling very far from home. The woods weren't far. If she ran, she could make it to the clearing, throw a coin into the fountain to undo her wish and make it back in time for swim practice.

Ava looked at the woods, then back in the direction of the sports complex. Either choice made her skin prickle. What would happen if she actually managed to undo her wish? She could find herself expelled from school, or worse. If she went to the woods now, would Courtney be at the swim practice when she returned? What if it didn't work? She stood on the grass for another moment before taking a few tentative steps across the open lawn toward the woods.

"Ava!"

Ava stopped walking, her heart pounding. The voice had come from behind. She turned around to see who had called her.

Mr. Chase stood on the lawn a few feet away, looking at Ava intently.

"Where are you going, Ava?" he asked.

"I, uh... swim practice" she managed, meeting his gaze.

"You're going the wrong way," he said, frowning slightly.

"Oh, uh..." Ava replied, turning away from the woods, though keenly aware of their presence. "Right."

"Your grandmother lives that way, doesn't she?" he asked. He'd walked over to where Ava stood.

"Yes," she mumbled, "I played in there as a kid."

Why was she talking about the woods? She should leave. Now.

"Well, I'm sure Ms. Krick would love to talk to you about that," Mr. Chase answered, smiling.

Ava's pulse quickened. Ms. Krick? She was not going to discuss the woods with Ms. Krick.

"She's spends a lot of time there, herself," he continued, with a chuckle. "The staff tease her that she's looking for the fountain of youth – you ever seen it in there?"

"What?" Ava said, balking.

"Oh, of course there's no such thing," Mr. Chase replied, with a laugh. "But she's obsessed with the history of this school. We just wonder what it's all about, is all."

Youth? Is that what Ms. Krick wanted? Ava wasn't sure.

"Don't you have to get to practice?" Mr. Chase asked.

"Uh, yes," Ava answered, turning on her heel.

"But seriously, Ava," Mr. Chase called after her, as she walked away. "Stay out of the woods. It's forbidden."

"No problem," Ava answered over her shoulder.

Ava's feet felt heavy with every step. If only she'd acted faster, she could be in the woods right now putting a new coin in the fountain. Of course, Mr. Chase might have seen her, but maybe he wouldn't have turned her in.

The unease in her gut mounted with every day that passed. Would everything she'd done since Friday be erased? She debated turning around. The thought of attending practice when she knew Courtney wasn't coming – might never come again – may not even exist - made her stomach ache. She could tell Coach Laurel she was sick. She gave her head a quick shake. No, swimming was a better distraction than sitting in her dorm room, going over and over events in her mind.

Ava counted silently on her fingers as she walked. She'd made her wish on Friday, which was now four days ago. Who knew what kind of trouble Courtney would have cooked up for Ava if she'd been here that whole time? Ava shuddered as she thought of the mess she could find herself in once Courtney came back. Would she really be expelled? One thing was for sure, Ava wasn't going to be making any excuses for Courtney this time. She'd make sure that the headmistress and everyone else saw Courtney for who she really was. Feeling her arm shake a little, she opened the heavy door to the sports complex with a tug and entered.

Down the hall, a group of noisy girls gathered outside the locker room. Ava approached cautiously. She recognized a few of them from the swim trials.

"Ava!" Margaret squealed, breaking away from the group and rushing toward Ava. "I made the team!"

She gave Ava a big hug and Ava returned the embrace half-heartedly. She'd momentarily forgotten that the team list was going to be posted today.

"Of course, you made the team too," Margaret continued. "But I've been so worried. I know I didn't swim my best on Saturday. I'm sure I was the last one to make the cut."

Margaret gleefully spun around in a circle in the middle of the hallway. Ava looked away, dizzy from watching Margaret. *Would Margaret be on the team if Courtney had been here?* Margaret stopped spinning and hooked her arm through Ava's, leading her toward the other girls.

"Great job, Ava!" Rhoda said, speaking over Ava's shoulder.

Ava counted fifteen names on the list, with Ava's name the first one listed and Margaret's appearing at the bottom of the page. Beside each name was the girl's best time for each stroke and distance. The girls in the group buzzed with excitement, laughing together and sizing up their competition. Beside them, a blonde girl sat sobbing on the floor.

"Um, hadn't we better get to practice?" Ava asked nobody in particular.

"Yes, let's go girls!"

Ava didn't recognize the girl that spoke. The throng of girls squeezed through the locker room doors. Ava followed them in and hurried to get ready. Snapping on her swim cap, Ava stepped out onto the pool deck, carrying her backpack. Courtney or no Courtney, she wasn't taking any chances.

The new swim team milled about in their suits excitedly, waiting for Coach Laurel to speak.

"Ava!" the coach called to her. "Would you come up here please?"

Ava bristled, wondering what she'd done now. She set her backpack down near a wall and stepped forward.

"Team," Coach Laurel announced loudly once Ava had arrived, "meet Ava Marshall, this year's team captain!"

An excited cheer erupted from the girls. Ava's stomach lurched. The echo in the vast room amplified the sound of the voices around her.

"That is," added Coach Laurel, watching Ava, "if you accept this responsibility, Ava? It's really quite an honor."

Ava's mind raced, unsure how to react. Tomorrow, Courtney would be the rightful team captain, Ava told herself. She nodded her head slowly in agreement.

"Good!" said Coach Laurel, smiling broadly. "All right, everybody in the pool. We have our first meet right here, just a few weeks after homecoming. I still need to figure out our line-up for the freestyle relay, so swim your best! I want ten laps to start. Go!"

Ava moved toward the pool with the rest of the girls, but Coach Laurel caught her arm gently.

"I'm sorry, Ava," the coach addressed her quietly. "Maybe I

should have asked you about being captain in private. I just thought it would be a nice surprise."

"I...I'm certainly surprised," said Ava. "But it's fine."

"Good," said Coach Laurel. "Come by tomorrow after school and we'll talk more."

"Sure," replied Ava.

She edged her way toward the pool. The meeting tomorrow would never happen. Courtney would be back tonight, after Ava and Ethan's visit to the fountain.

Walking to class after swim practice, Ava thought of pinching herself to make sure the last few days hadn't just been a dream. People didn't really do that, did they? The thing was, Ava was surprised to find it was mostly a good dream. The woods seemed further away than they had this morning.

In a daze, she nearly walked under a ladder propped up against the wall of the West Building, where her first class was that morning. She looked up to see Giles perched midway up the tall ladder, hanging a silver banner advertising the homecoming dance. He briefly looked down at Ava then continued his task without saying hello. His expression was blank. Ava felt chilled. Of course. She would never have met Giles if Courtney hadn't messed with her locker. Giles didn't know her anymore - or *yet*? This was all very confusing.

Ava gave the ladder a wide berth as she walked up to the door, not wanting to tempt fate. She noticed the homecoming banner had been professionally printed. The posters for dances at her school in San Francisco had always been hand drawn with markers or paint. Ava and Lucas hadn't gone to the dances back home. Instead they went to lots of movies at the second-run theatre downtown, or spent low-key time together hanging out at home. Homecoming seemed like a really big deal here. Jules kept telling her that she should go. Ava bit her lip. The homecoming dance was the last thing she needed to think about. A nagging voice told her she should really call Lucas. She had no idea what to say.

Ava sighed as she reached the door to calculus. Every class today brought her closer to tonight, when she could end this mixed up reality. She pulled open the door. She was glad English class wasn't on today's schedule. No Ms. Krick.

"Ava Marshall?" a voice called to her from behind her in the hall.

Ava turned and felt her stomach churn as she saw Headmistress Valentine walking toward her. She steeled herself for the onslaught.

"Ava?" said the headmistress, standing beside Ava's classroom door. "I'm Headmistress Valentine."

"Uh..." Ava stammered, her skin prickling. "It's nice to meet you."

Of course, there had been no meeting about the caffeine pills. There was no Courtney.

"I just wanted to welcome you to St. Augustus," the headmistress continued. "I took a guess that it was you just now. I met your Aunt Mia and you look so much like her."

Ava looked curiously at the headmistress, who was smiling.

"I spoke with Coach Laurel this morning," the headmistress continued. "She tells me you've agreed to be team captain. Did you know you'll be the first junior team captain the Owls have ever had? The position is always reserved for a senior. You must have really impressed her."

"Oh," said Ava, at a loss for words.

"Well, don't let me keep you from class," said the headmistress with a laugh as she urged Ava into Mr. Chase's classroom.

Ava walked slowly into the classroom and took her seat, feeling uneasy. St. Augustus was an entirely different school today.

Ethan entered the room smiling, just as the bell rang. He brushed past Ava, casually dropping a folded note on her desk as he passed to take his seat. Ethan's dark hair was neatly combed, though his St. Augustus tie was askew. Ava marvelled that he was on time for class at all, given he'd been up half the night sneaking around. She felt a pang of guilt that she'd asked him to stay out again tonight. She hoped he could run on little sleep.

Ethan's note felt heavy in her hands under the desk as Mr. Chase excitedly talked about the role of the x and y axis. *What was so important that Ethan couldn't wait to tell her until after class?* What if he wasn't going to go with her to the fountain, after all? She waited for an opening, and when Mr. Chase turned to draw a large graph on the blackboard, Ava lowered her eyes to read the note.

It read:

Congrats on team captain!
-E.

That was all he had to say? Ava scowled as she quickly tucked the note into her calculus book. Word really did travel fast around here.

"Are you okay, Ava?" Mr. Chase asked, eyeing her.

"Yes, fine," replied Ava, looking up at the chalkboard.

"All right," he said, "then perhaps you could tell me what the x intercept is on this graph?"

Ava answered easily, glad that she'd read the chapter in the textbook already.

Ava made it through the rest of the morning by taking meticulous notes in her classes to keep awake. She welcomed the chance to focus on something other than Courtney's absence.

"I can't believe you get to be a team captain, Ava," Chloe said at the lunch table. "Man, I wish I was an alumni kid. That'll look great on your college applications."

"Chloe!" Amy scolded. "Ava was asked to be team captain because she's a good swimmer, not because her parents went here, right Ava?"

"Well, my mom did swim for the Owls," Ava replied, as she unwrapped her roast beef sandwich. "But my family isn't involved with St. Augustus, really. I don't think they have much pull."

"Is this seat taken?" Ethan asked, pulling out the empty chair beside Ava and sitting down.

Jules' smug smile made heat rise into Ava's cheeks. Ava felt sure that Ethan had never eaten with Jules and her friends before. She watched him warily as he joined in the conversation with Jake and his buddies easily, debating the football team's chances at the homecoming game. Their group was one of the last to leave the cafeteria.

As they walked out of the cafeteria, Ethan sidled up beside Ava.

"So, things seem to be going pretty well for you today," he said to her, in a low voice. "Are you absolutely sure you want to go tonight?"

"Yes, of course," Ava hissed.

"Whoa, whoa," said Ethan, laughing. "It was just a thought. I've got basketball after school, but I'll see you around midnight?"

"Thanks," Ava replied quietly, silently calculating the long hours until they could go to the fountain.

CHAPTER SIXTEEN

Irreversible

Ava lay in her bed listening to the patter of rain on her window that night after lights out. Eventually, it slowed to drizzle then finally stopped. She lifted the curtain to look onto the dark lawn again. There was no movement aside from some water that still dripped down the window pane. It was after one in the morning, and Ethan hadn't come.

It wasn't in her nature to assume the worst. Had he fallen asleep, or been caught? Ava didn't think she could take another restless day waiting to visit the fountain, second-guessing whether or not to undo her wish. She'd have to go tonight.

Shoving the window upward quickly, she winced when it squeaked. Darting a look at Jules, who appeared to be sleeping peacefully, she turned back to the open window. Ava stared at it helplessly. If she closed the window behind her, she wouldn't be able to get back in when she returned. She shut her eyes to think. The rain had stopped and it was now still outside, though the air was thick with dampness. Jules might not wake up, but if she did, Ava thought it unlikely she'd report Ava missing.

Ava swallowed hard as she looked out the window at the eight-foot drop to the ground. Ethan had made this look easy. With a deep breath, Ava swung her legs over the windowsill and eased herself outside. Pressing her body against the wall, she let herself down carefully, struggling to get a grip with her hands on the damp stone. Reaching down with one foot, her sneaker made contact with a rock but slipped, sending her crashing the final few feet to the ground.

Ava's heart raced as she scrambled up off the wet grass and flattened her back against the wall. Had Jules heard? Ava's shoulders slumped as she looked at the woods. The fastest way to get there would be to walk straight across the open lawn. Moonlight cast an eerie glow across the grass.

After a few minutes of keeping still, Ava stepped away from the wall and looked up at her window, half expecting to see Jules' face peering out. How on earth was she going to climb back up there when she returned?

Ava turned to stare at the woods. Feeling exposed, she hurried over to the stand of trees where she'd seen Ethan the night before. She surveyed her options. If she crept along the wall, she'd get a little closer to the woods, which would be more discreet, or she could just make a run for it from where she stood.

She scanned the campus again and froze, catching movement at the far end of the dorm wall. Ava ducked behind a narrow tree and held her breath. Peeking out, she saw a dark shadow move quickly along the wall toward her.

"It's about time you showed up," Ava called quietly, breathing a sigh of relief. "Where have you been?"

Ethan jumped at the sound of her voice.

"Impatient, are you?" he teased, joining her where she stood in the trees. "What, were you going to go by yourself?"

"Yes, of course I was," replied Ava.

"Don't be mad," he said. "I got stuck outside the staff quarters. I almost got caught, actually. I had to wait until Ms. Krick went to bed."

"Ms. Krick?" Ava nearly squealed. "She *lives* here?"

"Yeah," replied Ethan. "Krick, Giles, Valentine, and a handful of others have apartments in the big house on the other side of the boys' dorm. It used to be servants' quarters when this place was built. The rest of the teachers and staff live in town."

"Anyhow," he continued, "I stuck close to the house on my way over here to stay out of the rain and got caught when Ms. Krick came out onto the covered porch with Giles. I had to lie low in the bushes until they were finished their conversation. It was a while before I was sure they'd gone to bed."

"Ms. Krick and Giles?" asked Ava in disbelief.

"Nah," replied Ethan, laughing. "There's nothing romantic there, I don't think. They've both just been at St. Augustus for a long time. I guess that's why she confided in him. About you."

"Me?" asked Ava, his tone giving her a chill.

"Well, about the fountain, anyway" Ethan told her. "Ava, she mentioned your essay, saying, 'It's starting again, and with her daughter.'"

"What?" Ava's arms and legs felt numb.

"She told Giles that she'd all but given up," Ethan continued. "She said that at first she'd thought you were pulling a prank. Then when she confronted you about it, she was sure you didn't know about the connection to your parents. Ava, she called finding the fountain 'her life's passion'. But, the funny thing is, she doesn't seem to know where it is."

"That seems strange," said Ava, her voice trembling. "It's not hard to find, it's right on the path. Do you think we should still go tonight?"

"I think so," replied Ethan. "If you're still up for it, that is. I waited till Krick turned her lights out, so she must've gone to bed. But Ava, you've stumbled onto something big here."

"Let's go," she said. It didn't matter to her what the fountain meant to Ms. Krick. It just mattered that she got there. Tonight.

Ava quickly started across the lawn, not wanting to waste

another moment. Without having to turn around, she felt Ethan's presence as he followed close behind her.

"The path is over there," Ava said in a low voice as they neared the edge of the campus, pointing up the hill beside the West Building to a gap in the trees.

The air felt cool after the rain and she imagined the breeze blowing into her open dorm room window. She hoped Jules was a deeper sleeper than she'd been the night before. She glanced over at the thin hoodie Ethan wore and felt shivers herself. He'd been outside since before midnight. It had still been raining then, his clothes must be damp. She snuggled deep into her own dry sweater and walked quickly, leaving him to follow behind again.

Once they'd reached the trees, Ava relaxed a little. The earlier cloudburst had knocked leaves off the trees, coating their path with a shiny green carpet that sparkled in the moonlight. Ava reached forward to steady herself against a tree. Its trunk was bloated with rain. She'd left her phone back on her bedside table and was relieved when Ethan pulled an actual flashlight out of his pocket and snapped it on, lighting their way.

Ethan seemed so at ease being out here. If Ava hadn't slept the night before, she knew she wouldn't look so put together.

Ava was startled by a hoot of an owl erupting from the treetops. Losing her footing, she stumbled close to the ground, her heart pounding. The owl's lonely call echoed overhead through the trees. Ava shivered as she imagined the owl's call daring Ms. Krick to find her and Ethan out in the middle of the night.

Walking side by side now, Ava looked gratefully to Ethan, glad she wasn't out here alone. Still, she imagined a paper-thin wall hovering between them as they moved together through the trees. Part of her wanted to reach over for his hand to steady her as they walked, but she didn't.

Would Lucas have come with her tonight? She thought she

knew the answer. She hadn't had a real conversation with Lucas since she'd made her wish. How was she going to explain all of this?

"You and your silly wishing wells," Lucas might've said, mussing her hair.

If she could click her heels three times and be home in San Francisco, would she go? The owl's cries had faded and the silence was comforting as they picked their way along the path. The musty smell of wet leaves filled the air, the ground squishing beneath their feet.

"Ethan!" Ava screamed.

Suddenly dancing as if she were on fire, Ava grabbed at her back. Something cold and slimy slowly crept down the middle of her spine. Ava screamed again. Ethan quickly clamped a hand over her mouth, muffling her scream. Without hesitation, Ava shoved him hard with both hands, knocking him to the ground. Winded from her blow, he sat on the ground at the edge of the path, clutching his rib cage. Ava tore off her sweater and threw it in his direction, frantically shaking her T-shirt away from her body.

"Ava, talk to me! What is it?"

Ethan shone his flashlight toward her, staying on the ground where he sat against the trees. Ava stood in the middle of the path, staring at something she held in her hand. Hurling it with a loud yell out into the woods, she sank down into the wet leaves beside him with a loud sigh.

"What was that?" Ethan whispered urgently.

"Leaves," replied Ava, grimacing.

"What?"

"Leaves," Ava repeated, impatiently. "Wet, muddy, gross leaves on a branch dropped down inside my shirt. I thought it was...I thought something was grabbing me and I..."

Ethan laughed loudly, rolling over onto his side in the

undergrowth.

"The girl who isn't afraid of expulsion is afraid of leaves?"

Ava pouted. She wasn't in any mood to be made fun of.

"I'm *terrified* of expulsion," she corrected him in a fierce whisper, "but this isn't negotiable. Go back if you're scared. I never asked you to come."

Ethan's grin faded and they sat in silence.

"So, when we get to the fountain," he asked, "you'll just throw a coin in and we head back? Is that the plan?"

"Beats me," Ava replied, throwing her hands up in the air.

"Have you thought about what you'll say?" Ethan probed.

Ava was surprised to realize she could talk to Ethan.

"I was thinking I would just wish to undo my wish," Ava told him. "Does that make sense?"

"I assumed you'd have to make a counter-wish," Ethan replied. "Something like, *I wish for Courtney to be back at St. Augustus...*"

"Yeah, I thought so too, at first," said Ava, really wanting his opinion and trying not to sound condescending. "But I don't think that'll work. I need Courtney's dad to have been here too, to help my dad pass high school. I don't think I explained that part to you. Things with my dad seem to have, uh, changed. I couldn't begin to name it all with one toss of a coin."

She realized that she'd been rambling, though Ethan looked at her with a steady gaze.

"Obviously I've done some thinking on the subject," said Ava, giving him a weak smile.

"Obviously," Ethan agreed. "Though I still think you should be very specific."

"I dunno," replied Ava. "I guess it wouldn't hurt."

"Tell me again why you can't just leave things the way they are?" Ethan asked.

"My dad..." Ava started, staring off into the night. "No way, I'm not that selfish."

"Suit yourself," Ethan said with a shrug. "But if it were me, I wouldn't be in a hurry to reinstate my own suspension and face Valentine."

Ava bristled at his frankness. Did he even believe her, Ava wondered. She thought he wanted to. That was something, at least. Would he remember, after the wish?

Ethan got to his feet and pulled her up onto the path in one fluid motion. Ava groaned a little as she realized how wet the seat of her pants had gotten sitting in the leaves. She self-consciously brushed some of the mud off the seat of her pants, plucked her wet jeans away from her skin and pulled her sweater down over her bottom.

They started out again on the path, Ethan walking behind her, shining his flashlight. Soon they'd be in the clearing. Ava felt like she walked in a daze. Was this all really happening? A shudder of doubt rocked through her. Had Ethan come just to laugh at her? That didn't seem like something he'd do, did it? It was hard to believe she'd only known him a few days. She took shorter steps until Ethan walked beside her on the path. She had one hand in her jean pocket, fingering the coin she'd brought, feeling its weight. Her other hand swung close to Ethan's as they walked.

I wish to undo the wish I made here on September 14th that made Courtney disappear.

That sounded right. Would it work?

"We're almost there," said Ava, breaking their silence.

When they'd reached the edge of the clearing, Ava stopped with her arm outstretched to keep Ethan from going any further.

The view across the clearing was unobstructed. Its field was bathed in moonlight. Long, reedy grasses swished back and forth in the wind. Ethan swept his flashlight across the expanse, but there was nothing else. There was no fountain.

Ava's hand opened and she dropped the coin she'd held in her grasp into the long grass. She struggled to breathe. Aware that

The Fountain

Ethan watched her, she looked his way helplessly. As their gazes locked, Ava's heart quickened. How could she ask him to believe her when she hardly believed what was happening herself?

Ava felt herself fall, and then Ethan's warm arms were around her, holding her up. Resting her head against his chest, she couldn't help but notice his heart beat nearly as fast as her own.

CHAPTER SEVENTEEN

Research

Ava's head pounded as she walked toward English class the next morning. *How could the fountain be gone?* The question made her temples throb. She hadn't slept much the night before. Walking back together toward her dorm in silence, Ethan had led her by the hand. Instead of making her feel uneasy as it had the day they'd met, she'd found it a comfort.

"It's going to be okay," Ethan had said to her. "We'll figure this out."

Ava nodded her head slowly, not meeting his gaze. She wouldn't have blamed him if he thought her whole story was made up. Standing by the dorm wall, he'd embraced her in a reassuring way. She thought she'd felt his lips brush her hair just before he'd let her go, though she couldn't be sure.

Ethan had hoisted her up the wall to her open window and she'd climbed easily over the sill. Lowering herself down onto the floor of her dorm room, she'd kept her eyes on Jules. Miraculously, it appeared that Jules hadn't missed her. Ava had stared at Jules for a long moment, in case she was pretending again, but she hadn't moved. Ava had shut the window gingerly, looking down at the ground for Ethan, though he was no longer there. She hoped he'd get some sleep.

Now, the morning after, her stomach was in knots at the

thought of seeing Ethan, though she wanted to show him what she'd found. Would he laugh now? She hadn't been able to show him the fountain.

Finding herself unable to sleep, she'd dressed quietly just before seven in the morning. She headed for the library, arriving just as the librarian unlocked the door. After saying good morning, she'd headed over to Isaac's journals and grabbed the next volume she saw. Examining it, she'd found that it was mostly filled with clippings from local papers about the construction of the school, punctuated by the occasional handwritten note. She chose three more journals to check out and brought them up to the front desk. The librarian barely looked up from her coffee as she stamped the cards at the back and typed something into her computer.

After grabbing a quick breakfast in the cafeteria, Ava headed to class, finding that she was the first one to arrive. She took her front row seat and pulled out her English book, taking care not to disturb the journals that filled her backpack. She zipped it up quickly, her pulse quickening. It certainly wouldn't do for Ms. Krick to see the journals in her bag.

Ava looked up to the classroom door to see Ethan ushering Ms. Krick inside, the two of them deep in conversation. She could hear Ethan ask their teacher about the assigned readings and Ms. Krick's pleasant response. Ava stifled a laugh as Ethan flashed a grin at her from behind Ms. Krick's back.

"Good morning, Ava," Ethan said to her, leaning on her desk. "Sleep well?"

"I uh..." Ava replied.

She kept her voice low - aware that Ms. Krick watched them. Ethan didn't wait for her to answer, instead leaving to take his seat at the back of the classroom. Ava looked back to where Courtney had sat last week, seeing an unfamiliar boy sitting at what had been Courtney's desk. Ava now dreaded English class, though it had been one of her favorite subjects back home. Ms. Krick's voice droned on about sentence structure while Ava watched the clock. When the bell finally rang, Ethan caught up with her and suggested that they meet for lunch later at the student lounge.

"Uh, sure," Ava replied.

Looking around the crowded hallway, she knew that she couldn't tell him about the journals now.

"Bye!" Ethan said with a smile and a quick wave as they parted.

Ava looked back over her shoulder. He didn't seem different. He hadn't laughed.

When the lunch bell finally rang, Ava made a beeline for the lobby and climbed the staircase to the lounge. Ethan was already there, though the rest of the room was deserted. She walked over to where he sat, in a circle of casual chairs stationed around a low table, like in a coffee house. As she approached she saw that he had three more of Isaac Young's journals spread out on the table.

"How did you beat me here?" Ava asked him, looking down at the books. She'd come straight from her class, which had been in the main building.

"I might've cut class." Ethan told her, with a grin.

Ava frowned.

"Don't worry," Ethan laughed, "it was only health class I told the teacher I had something to do for basketball. Here, I brought you something from the cafeteria."

He tossed her a sandwich wrapped in plastic wrap.

"Thanks," said Ava, glancing over to the student lounge concession which appeared to be closed.

"This concession is only open after school. I grabbed these in the cafeteria," Ethan explained, taking a bite of his own sandwich. "This place is usually pretty quiet the first half hour of lunch, but starts to fill once people have eaten. Anyway, I went to the library and took out some more of the journals so that we could take a look, but Ava, three more were missing from the shelf. I'm thinking maybe Krick went and checked them out again."

Ava reached down wordlessly and pulled the three journals she had out of her backpack that sat on the floor, placing them on the table beside his. Ethan's tense expression dissolved into relief.

"I couldn't sleep," Ava said, by way of explanation.

She unwrapped her sandwich. It was roast beef, the same kind she'd chosen for herself when they'd eaten together the day before in the cafeteria. He'd been paying attention.

"That's good," said Ethan.

Ava looked at him quizzically.

"I mean it's good that you have the journals, not that you couldn't sleep," he added quickly, correcting himself. "I thought maybe Krick was onto us."

"Looks like we had the same idea," said Ava. "I haven't read them all yet, but I found this written at the back of the first book. Take a look."

Ava flipped to a page she'd marked in the back of the journal she held and handed the book to Ethan, who read aloud from the handwritten page.

Rushing water. Crashing. Eroding evidence of things that were real, since the beginning of time.

A never ending cycle of water, trapped in cold stone to be beheld but once.

Hidden away the fountain waits for each, minutes and hours to be lost gazing in its streams.

Students who dream, and wish for something else.
–I.Y.

Ava sat on the edge of her seat, watching his reaction, hoping he wouldn't laugh. He looked up at her, a puzzled expression on his face.

"There are other handwritten notes, but I haven't read them all yet," Ava explained, hurriedly. She hoped he would draw the same conclusion that she had. "He must be talking about the fountain, right?"

"Looks like it," replied Ethan. "What does he mean, *to be beheld but once*?"

"That's the part I thought was interesting too," said Ava.

She lowered her voice. A few students had entered the lounge since they'd arrived and were seated nearby.

"It seems crazy that I could be the only one who's ever seen the fountain. Is that possible?" Ava asked.

"No, you're not the only one," replied Ethan, shaking his head. "Your mother's essay describes the same place. She must've seen it too, at some point. Maybe it means each person can only see it once? It says *the fountain waits for each*, after all."

"That makes sense," replied Ava, feeling a little foolish that she'd thought she'd been the only one. Of course her mother had seen it. "I hadn't thought of that."

"What's this at the bottom of the page?" Ethan asked, running his index finger over a small ink drawing.

Ava reached over for the book to take a closer look. The page with the passage was numbered in the bottom right corner, with a drawing of an owl, his wings spread, intertwined the numbers. The drawing was done in black ink, and smudged a little so that the owl's face was slightly obscured.

Ethan began flipping absently through the other volumes that they had on the table, checking the back pages.

"Interesting," he said.

"What?" asked Ava.

"That same drawing is in the corner on the last page of each volume," he said, still flipping through the books. "But even more interesting is that each volume has 65 pages."

"Well, all the books are alike," said Ava. "They probably came with the same number of pages."

"Maybe," Ethan replied, studying one of the drawings. "Though the drawings are deliberate. They're all identical, except for the one that got smudged, though I doubt that was intentional. I think the number 65 might be significant."

"65?" Ava gasped. "Like the lucky room?"

"Maybe," said Ethan, with a shrug. "Who lives in the lucky room this year?"

"Well," replied Ava, "Courtney was in the room last week by herself, but Rhoda seems to live there now. I was sure I remembered her name, I think she's the one that didn't return to school this year because of the things Courtney did to her."

She watched Ethan as she shared this information, knowing it was a lot to take in.

"Sounds complicated," offered Ethan.

"I don't know if Rhoda has a roommate," Ava told him. "Though I think Amy or Chloe said they roomed with her last year, I can't remember which."

"Can you get in there to take a look?" Ethan asked, separating the books into two stacks and handing one stack to her. "Maybe there's something to the legend of the lucky room after all? There could be a clue in there to the fountain. Who knows if it would still be there, though, after all this time?"

Ava was surprised to notice that the lounge had filled up around them. The clock on the wall announced their lunch hour was almost over. She tucked the stack of books Ethan had given her into her backpack and zipped it tightly closed. If the fountain only appeared once, how was she ever going to set things right?

"I'll go this weekend," said Ethan, standing up from the table.

"What?" asked Ava, distracted. "Where are you going?"

"To the fountain," continued Ethan. "I'll go to the fountain this weekend."

Ava looked at him blankly.

"The way I see it," Ethan explained, "if it appears for each person once, then I get a wish. I'll undo your wish. If that's what you want."

Ava's pulse quickened. Would that work?

"I'll probably have to wait a few days until the heat is off," continued Ethan. "But we're allowed off campus on weekends. I think I can find the clearing from the other side of the woods. You say the path leads to your grandmother's yard? There'll be less chance that Krick or someone else will see me if I get to the fountain from there."

Ava looked at him with disbelief. Ethan would be able to wish for anything he wanted.

"Besides," he continued, with a laugh, "I could use some sleep. This sneaking around at night is starting to take its toll."

"I'll go with you," said Ava, decisively.

"I don't think you can," Ethan told her, shaking his head. "We were both there last night, remember? And there was no fountain. No, I think I have to go alone. If it's going to show up at all, it'll be if I visit by myself."

He offered Ava his hand to help her up. Ava's mind raced. Would she really have to wait until the weekend? It was only Wednesday.

"In the meantime," said Ethan as they walked out together from the lounge, "we can read the rest of the journals in case there's anything else helpful."

He looked at Ava, who hadn't said much.

"It's going to be okay," Ethan assured her, stopping to face her as they descended the long staircase into the main foyer. "I'll undo your wish and everything will go back to... well, you know."

He looked straight into her eyes.

"That is," he continued, "if that's really what you want?"

"Yes," Ava told him, without hesitation.

"Even if it means you are expelled?" Ethan asked, in a serious tone.

"Even then," Ava replied, in an even tone.

"Then it's settled," said Ethan. "See you later?"

"Sure," Ava replied.

Ethan turned to go to his next class while Ava lingered for a moment in the busy foyer. Would the fountain really appear for Ethan?

"There you are!"

Ava turned to see Jules standing right beside her.

"Come on," said Jules. "We can walk together to gym class."

Ava nodded and the two of them started off in the direction of the sports complex.

"Can you help us make decorations for the homecoming dance after school today?" Jules asked as they crossed the lawn. "We could use the help."

"I uh..." stammered Ava, as they entered the complex.

She wasn't really paying attention to what Jules had been talking about. She looked up to see Coach Laurel coming toward her down the hall.

"Ava," Coach Laurel called out to her, "I'll see you for our meeting today after school?"

Ava gave a start. She'd forgotten all about the team captain meeting. But Courtney wasn't back yet. The job still belonged to Ava. Ava nodded her agreement to Coach Laurel and gave her a wave as they passed each other in the hall.

"Sorry, Jules," Ava said. "I almost forgot, I have a meeting after school."

"That's okay," Jules answered brightly, as they entered the girls' locker room. "There'll be more work to do for the dance again tomorrow."

Ava groaned inwardly. She had a feeling that Jules wasn't going to give up easily.

"So," said Jules, with one eyebrow raised. "Did you have lunch with Ethan again today? We missed you in the cafeteria."

Jules pulled off her uniform quickly then reached into her backpack for her gym strip. Ava noticed that Jules' bra and panties matched perfectly, once again. Today they were sky blue with lace trim around the edges.

"Yes," replied Ava simply, turning away from Jules to get changed.

It was probably easier to let Jules think what she wanted, rather than try to explain.

"How's friend-boy in San Francisco, then?" Jules probed, pulling her gym shirt over her head.

Ava winced. She hadn't thought about Lucas all morning. She didn't think she'll be able to avoid his calls until everything was set right again on Saturday. She'd have to speak to him tonight.

"Hmm, I see," said Jules, watching Ava. "Well, he's a long ways away. What he doesn't know won't kill him. Besides, Ethan Roth's pretty cute."

Ava's stomach felt tight as she pulled her own T-shirt over her head. Let Jules think what she wanted. She couldn't exactly explain what she and Ethan were working on. The wish had changed things. What if things were different now between her and Lucas? If she'd grown up living in Mia's house, it was still close by, but not right next door to him. In this post-Wallis world, was her relationship with Lucas the same? She'd been trying not to make any major decisions or interact too much this week, in case it messed things up for when it went back to normal. What was she going to talk about with Lucas?

CHAPTER EIGHTEEN

Reality

Reaching her empty dorm room later that afternoon, Ava closed the door and eagerly pulled one of Isaac Young's journals out of her bag. During her meeting with Coach Laurel, her mind had been far away, the journals weighing heavy in her pack. Ava knew that she'd never have been chosen as team captain if Courtney had been here. Courtney had better be back to plan the swim meet. Event planning wasn't exactly Ava's forte.

Settling in on her bed, she carefully opened the next journal. Its pages were yellowed and felt brittle in her hands. Cracks had appeared on the edges of the paper. Stencilled neatly on the front page was the date January, 1932. The diary was really old.

Ava flipped to the last page and ran her fingers over the small drawing intertwining the number 65. Pasted on the page was a sketch of St. Augustus, signed illegibly on the bottom. Ava squinted at the signature. It started with a long straight stroke, almost certainly an "I". Had it been signed by Isaac Young himself? The sketch was detailed, considering its size, with the main building looking more like a castle than a school, just as it did today.

Ava turned back to the beginning of the volume and Isaac's loopy scrawl filled the page with an introductory letter. Flipping through the first volume, she saw that documents and contracts pertaining to the building of the school were intermixed with Isaac Young's notes. Ava skipped over the documents and started reading the handwriting slanted across the pages. She was amazed to see the school's construction plans unfold as she read.

The second and third volumes held more of Isaac Young's thoughts as the building materialized. He certainly was passionate about the place. Just as she neared the end of the third volume, her phone rang. She checked the call display. It was Lucas. Suddenly, she felt like she really needed to hear his voice. She wanted his advice.

"Hello?" Ava answered her phone on the third ring.

"Ava!" exclaimed Lucas. "Are you dodging my calls?"

"No," replied Ava, laughing nervously. "I've just been busy, that's all. You're speaking to the new team captain of the St. Augustus swim team, you know."

Ava slapped herself on the forehead as her news slipped out before she had the chance to think. She hadn't meant to share anything with Lucas that was remotely related to Courtney. After Saturday, she wouldn't be the team captain.

"Really?" asked Lucas, with hesitation in his voice. "That's great - that is, if it's something you want. You've never said anything about wanting to be a team captain. It doesn't really sound like your style."

"It's okay," replied Ava, wanting desperately to change the subject. "I only agreed to do it for a short time. Someone else is, uh, supposed to be the captain, but she's away. It's keeping me pretty busy, that's all. Our first meet is in a few weeks, after homecoming."

Ava wasn't used to lying – especially to Lucas. A small sensation of panic rose into her chest.

"Homecoming?" Lucas asked, laughing a little. "I thought they only did that in the movies."

Homecoming was a safer topic, Ava thought to herself. Her

wish hadn't changed anything about that, had it?

"No, it's a pretty big deal here," Ava replied, feeling a little embarrassed at the excitement in her tone, even if it was feigned. "There's a football game, events for alumni, and there's a dance."

This was Lucas on the phone. She could tell him anything, right?

"Of course," Ava continued, filling the silence, "I don't plan to go to the dance."

"When is homecoming?" asked Lucas.

"Oh, it's not for a few weeks," replied Ava. "Hopefully everything will be back to, uh, normal by then."

This was a good time to tell Lucas what was really going on, if she was going to. Would he remember after the wish was undone? Ava's stomach felt queasy. She'd just remembered that Courtney's dad had been slated to give a speech at homecoming - so much for homecoming being a safe topic.

"Oh?" said Lucas. "Ava, is everything okay? You don't seem yourself."

"Me?" replied Ava quickly. "I'm fine."

"It's just that," Lucas continued, "maybe being team captain is too much on top of the new school and all. I'm sure they'd understand if you didn't want to do it."

"No," Ava answered, perhaps a little too quickly. "I mean...well things here have been a little strange."

"You haven't met someone new, have you?" Lucas joked.

"No, of course not!" Ava exclaimed. "Nothing like that. It's just that the school, it has some strange history. And I have a teacher that taught my parents and didn't really like my mom, and now she doesn't like me. It's all been very confusing."

"Oh," Lucas replied.

He didn't sound convinced.

"So," Ava continued, searching for the right words, "I'm trying to find out why she didn't like my mom and I've learned about some of the school legends."

She tensed, expecting him to laugh at any moment, though he didn't. What should she say next? Nothing she'd said so far had been entirely untrue. Ava twirled a lock of her hair around her finger. Just then, Jules entered the dorm room, shutting the door loudly behind her.

"Lucas," Ava said, lowering her voice, "I should go. I haven't had the chance to eat dinner yet."

"Oh," replied Lucas. "You should definitely go eat then, it's late there!"

"Okay," Ava said, hesitating. "I'll call you soon, Lucas."

Truthfully, she couldn't wait to hang up the phone.

"Ava," Lucas said to her seriously, "you shouldn't worry too much about one teacher. You're smart, she'll come around once she realizes that. Please don't wear yourself out trying to please her."

"Okay," said Ava, choking back tears that threatened to fall.

Lucas always knew what to say.

"G'night Ava," said Lucas.

"Good night," Ava whispered into the phone, hanging up.

"Was that Mr. San Francisco?" Jules asked her, kicking off her shoes and flopping down on her bed.

"Yes," replied Ava, bristling as she stuffed her phone into her sweater pocket.

She expected Jules to tease her about Ethan next, but she didn't.

"I wondered where you were when you didn't show up for dinner," added Jules. "Did you say you haven't eaten yet?

"Yeah," replied Ava, "I had to meet with my coach, then I lost track of time."

She hadn't realized it was already eight o'clock.

"Well," said Jules, sitting up and smoothing her black pencil skirt, "the cafeteria closed at seven thirty, but the lounge is still open; you can grab a sandwich or something."

Ava felt her stomach growl. She'd been eating a lot of sandwiches lately, it seemed. Ava noticed Jules, eyeing the journals spread out on Ava's bed. Hurriedly, Ava gathered them up, stuffing them into her backpack.

"What are you reading?" Jules asked, pointing toward Ava's overstuffed pack.

"Oh, nothing important," replied Ava. "Just a little project I'm working on."

"Would that be the project you claim Ethan Roth is helping you with?" Jules asked, looking unimpressed.

"Yeah," Ava answered slowly. "That'd be the one."

"He had books like that in the cafeteria at dinner." Jules added.

"He did?" Ava asked.

She hoped she didn't sound too interested in what Ethan had been up to, though she was inwardly pleased he'd been reading the journals. Maybe he'd found something.

"Yeah," continued Jules. "At first I thought you were with him again when you didn't join us for dinner, but then I saw him. He just sat there through dinner, reading all alone."

"Oh," said Ava, trying to keep her voice even. In truth, she was a little choked up, "well, I'm going to go to the lounge now to get something to eat."

Ethan might still be around. She was bursting to talk to him about the journals. Ava might be able to catch him in the library or the lounge. She jumped to her feet and slung her backpack over her shoulder.

"I could use a latte," said Jules, pouting as she put her shoes back on. "I'll come with you. I feel like I've barely even seen you this week. Besides, I had some thoughts on what I could lend you to wear for the homecoming dance."

"Uh, sounds good," replied Ava, not having the heart to say no.

✧✧✧

"I didn't see you at dinner last night," said Ethan the next morning in the cafeteria.

He put his tray down on the table where she sat eating breakfast by herself. Ava was surprised at his tone. He actually sounded annoyed. She'd looked around the lounge for him when she and Jules had arrived the night before, but she hadn't checked the library or anywhere else, for fear that Jules would invite herself along.

"I caught a late dinner in the lounge with Jules," replied Ava. "I looked for you there."

"Oh," replied Ethan, his voice softening. "I went back to my room after you weren't in the cafeteria. Did you find anything in your journals?"

"No," replied Ava. "I didn't see any references to the fountain either, other than the poem we looked at, but his notes were fascinating all the same. It seems there was some controversy around building the school. The school was built during the Great Depression. It seems not everyone thought New England needed another fancy private school. Isaac Young had to fight pretty hard to get it built."

"Go on," said Ethan, leaning forward in his chair.

"From Isaac Young's notes and the newspaper clippings," Ava continued, "it sounds like the town of Evergreen was supportive of building the school, since it would provide jobs. He also talked about groups that opposed the school, citing his "ill-gotten" money. Do you know what that was about? The journal didn't say."

"I think so," replied Ethan. "There wasn't anything in the journals I read about his money, but it's well known that Isaac Young was a rum runner."

"A rum runner?" Ava asked, scrunching up her nose. "What's

that?"

"It means that he smuggled alcohol illegally during the Prohibition," Ethan explained. "There was a period of time in America when selling alcohol was against the law. We studied the 30's in history class last year. We did a brief section on Isaac Young. Come to think of it, Ms. Krick actually came in to talk to us about him that day."

Ava listened, her mind racing.

"I remember it," said Ethan, looking thoughtful, "because I always thought it strange that nobody seems to know how he amassed such a fortune. Smuggling booze doesn't explain it all. That would never happen today. Everyone knows everyone's business."

"Oh," said Ava, disappointed.

Somehow this information didn't match the image of the selfless man she'd visualized while reading his journals.

"If it was well known that he was a smuggler," asked Ava, "why didn't he go to jail?"

"I don't think that's how it worked back then," replied Ethan. "From what we learned, smuggling alcohol wasn't even frowned upon. In fact, the police were some of their best customers. You didn't study this in history?"

Ava shook her head.

"Did you find out anything more about the fountain in the journals you have?" she asked.

"Nothing about the fountain," replied Ethan. "There were a lot of entries about Isaac Young's mother. It seems like he built the school to fulfill a dream that she'd had. I kind of skimmed the pages about that."

"So it's a dead end," Ava sighed, sitting back in her seat.

"Maybe," Ethan conceded. "But remember, I'm going to the fountain first thing in the morning on Saturday, so the rest of this doesn't matter."

How could he be so callous? Ava felt something inside her break. She couldn't hold it in.

"It does matter," she snapped at him. "Ethan, I've *killed* someone. Maybe more than one someone. Her whole family is missing, Ethan. *Where are they?*"

Ava's chest felt tight. Her breathing was shallow. She'd named what had been eating at her. Courtney and her family were dead. Or missing. Or something worse. It was all she could do to keep her hands on the table in front of her and not hug her ribs. Her hands shook on the table.

"Ava," said Ethan, putting one hand on top of hers and pulling his phone out of his shirt pocket with the other, "How many times have you thrown a coin in a fountain?"

Ava was glad his question was rhetorical. She would have to admit, she'd thrown a coin in every fountain she'd ever come across. Her gaze didn't meet his eyes.

"And those wishes never came true." Ethan continued. "I'm sure she's not dead. You didn't wish her dead. It should be easy enough to find out. What did you say her dad's name was?"

His hand felt warm. Her hand still shook – though maybe a little less.

"Jim," replied Ava, taking in a deep breath. "Jim Wallis."

Ethan typed the name into Google and hit search.

"Voilà," said Ethan, holding out his phone for her to see the search results on the screen. "There's a Jim Wallis who's a Massachusetts senator, is that him?"

"Yes!" Ava exclaimed. She pulled her hand out from under Ethan's and placed it in her lap.

Jim Wallis was still in government, even if he hadn't attended St. Augustus. His job hadn't changed. He wasn't dead. Ava breathed deeply. There were enough moving parts to keep track of without worrying about Jim, too, whom she'd never even met.

"There's no address or number listed," continued Ethan,

scrolling through the results on his screen. "Though, that makes sense if he's a bigwig."

"Any mention of Courtney?" asked Ava, craning her neck to see what he'd found on his phone.

If her dad was fine, maybe Courtney was fine, too.

Ethan typed Courtney Wallis into his phone then hit search. He frowned at the results that were returned.

"What?" Ava asked. She felt the bottom drop out of her stomach as she waited for his answer. It seemed like a very long time.

"There are lots of hits on her name," he replied, with a frown. "It's hard to tell which one is her. It shouldn't be too hard to find information on the daughter of a senator, though. It'll take some time to sift through all this, but right now I've got to get to class."

Ava sat at the table for a long moment after Ethan had gone. Lots of hits on her name were good, right? If Courtney's dad still existed, there was probably still a Courtney - wasn't there? Maybe none of this mattered after all. If Ethan's wish worked on Saturday, things would go back to how they were supposed to be - whatever that looked like.

If.

In the meantime, her concern for Courtney gnawed at her. If Ethan couldn't undo her wish, Ava was responsible for whatever changes had happened in Courtney's life.

Every Christmas, Ava and her dad sat down together to watch the black-and-white version of "It's a Wonderful Life." In it, George Bailey's life had touched so many. The ripple effect of his wishing he'd never been born completely devastated those around him. Ava felt a shiver. What if Courtney's life were changed like that from not coming to St. Augustus? Worse, how would Ava know? The little she'd known of Courtney before she'd disappeared hadn't been much.

Ethan's wish had to work. No matter what the cost.

CHAPTER NINETEEN

Boston

Ava drummed her fingers on the table at Luigi's, where she and Ethan had agreed to meet. She'd been a few minutes early, but by now Ethan was definitely late. Frowning, she realized it was nearly an hour past when she'd expected him.

Had he seen the fountain? Ava felt the waitress eyeing her while taking an order from another table. She probably wanted to give Ava's table to someone else. A line had formed at the front of the restaurant, waiting for tables.

Ava sat on the edge of her seat, keenly watching the door. Ethan should have been at the fountain undoing her wish at the same time as she'd been in swim practice that morning. She'd felt skittish the whole practice, wondering if Courtney would just suddenly appear on the pool deck after Ethan had thrown his coin. The thought had terrified her. How would everyone else in the room react if that happened? Would they notice? Worst of all, would Ava notice? After all, this would be Ethan's wish, not hers. Nobody else seemed to notice when Courtney had disappeared. Only Ava had known what changes her wish had made. But there had been no sign of Courtney. And now there was no sign of Ethan. These details had never featured prominently in the fairy tales she knew about wishes. She rested her head in her hands, closing her eyes. All this thinking was giving her a headache.

"Am I interrupting something?" asked Ethan, who'd arrived unannounced beside the booth.

"Ethan!" cried Ava, opening her eyes. "I was so worried."

She jumped up to embrace him.

"Whoa," Ethan said, laughing as he returned her hug, giving her a quick squeeze. "I took a little detour before I came to meet you. That's all. Nothing to worry about."

"It's just that you were late," said Ava, drawing back from his embrace and returning to her seat. She blushed a deep shade of red.

"I know," Ethan replied.

He slid into the booth on the bench across from her. She knew from his pained expression that he didn't have good news to report.

"I'm sorry, Ava, I couldn't undo your wish."

Ava felt her shoulders slump, although she'd prepared herself for this possibility.

"What happened?" she whispered, looking around the restaurant to make sure nobody was in earshot.

"The fountain just wasn't there," said Ethan.

Ava felt her lower lip begin to tremble. He was going to think she was crazy.

"Hey, I still believe you," Ethan assured her, grabbing her hand on the table and looking straight at her. "Ava, there's obviously something strange going on. We just haven't figured out how this wish thing works yet."

"But Courtney," Ava stammered. "I need to find her. I've done this to her. I need to bring her back to St. Augustus where she belongs. At least I can do that. Ethan, I looked up the Wallis' property tax records yesterday. They live just outside of Boston. I have the address."

"Great," said Ethan. "I had a feeling that you'd say that. I actually got their address too, though I had to do a lot of digging. I eventually found it on an unofficial lobby group site, encouraging supporters to mail Senator Wallis directly at his home. Nice thinking on the tax record. That would've been much simpler. Anyway, my detour on the way here was to get us bus tickets. We're going to Boston the Saturday of homecoming."

"Really?" asked Ava. "You're okay with missing homecoming?"

"Yeah, it's no big deal," Ethan told her. "The bus ride to Boston is only an hour, but we'll still have to get out to the suburbs from there, so we'll need lots of time. Everyone on campus will be busy with homecoming and less likely to ask where we've gone. Besides, curfew on that Saturday gets extended to 1 a.m. for the dance, so we can take the late bus back and still be in our rooms before we're missed. I'm pretty sure we're not supposed to leave Evergreen though, curfew or not."

"So, we're going to just show up at her house?" said Ava, her mind racing at a thousand miles per minute. "How do you know she'll be home? What will we say?"

"I didn't say it was a foolproof plan," replied Ethan, frowning. "You said you wanted to make sure Courtney was okay and we can do that. I checked the Senate schedule too. They aren't in session next week, so her dad will hopefully be home. I'm sure we'll think of something once we get there. Besides, we have time to plan."

"I guess so," said Ava. Her lower lip protruded.

"Great, then it's a date," said Ethan, opening the menu in front of him. "We'll go to Boston on Saturday and find Courtney."

"Yes," said Ava, though she felt unsure. "It's a start, though it won't reverse the wish. We have to keep looking. I haven't gotten anything else from the journals."

"I'll tell you what," said Ethan, winking playfully at her. "If I find a way to fix the wish before homecoming, I'll take you to the dance instead of Boston."

"Ethan, I..." Ava stammered, looking down at the table.

"Oh," interrupted Ethan quickly, "I just thought it might be fun for you, being new to campus and all."

Ava looked at him across the table. He was being sincere.

"It was just a thought," he added.

"I wasn't really planning to go anyway," said Ava quickly. "I'm not much for dances."

"Me either," Ethan replied. "But if I solve the riddle of the fountain before then, I won't let you argue with me about the dance."

Ava avoided his steady gaze by looking down at her menu.

"I don't feel like we're any closer to figuring it out," she said. "I spent some time yesterday afternoon in Rhoda's room. I asked her to help out with the swim meet coming up. It's Amy that's her roommate."

"That's good news," said Ethan, smiling encouragingly. "It'll give you another reason to be in the room. Is Amy the blonde?"

Ava shook her head.

"No, Chloe is blonde," she said.

"Oh," replied Ethan. "I can never keep those two straight. It's a bummer that you have to plan the swim meet, though. I know you expected Courtney to take that over. Is there anything I can do?"

"Get your friends to come cheer us on?" Ava asked, sheepishly. "I think our advertising for the meet is going to be a little weak. I can't rival Jules' glitzy homecoming banners, that's for sure."

"I think I can probably get some guys from the team to come," said Ethan. "Who wouldn't want to watch a bunch of girls in bathing suits?"

"Ethan!" exclaimed Ava, giving him a swift kick under the table.

"Ouch," Ethan complained. "I won't be able to come cheer you on if I can't walk!"

"Sorry," apologized Ava. "I didn't mean to kick you that hard."

Ethan winced dramatically, rubbing his leg.

"I didn't see anything when I was in the lucky room that might be a clue," Ava continued. "Did you know Rhoda has a pet shark, though? Other than that, it looks the same as my room and probably every other room one on that floor."

"She has a shark?" asked Ethan. "Like, a big one?"

"Well, she called it a rainbow shark," Ava said. "It looked more like a fish to me. She said they gave her room 65 because it has a little extra space for the tank. I'd like to get in there alone to take a good look around, although I doubt that an eighty-year-old clue will still be there."

"Beats me," Ethan said, flipping through Luigi's bright-colored menu. "Maybe it's an invisible clue, like the invisible fountain."

Ava gave him a hard look. Could he be serious for even a minute?

"Ava," said Ethan, looking up at her, "I'm not making fun of you. I'm only saying that the fountain seems to be mostly invisible, except under some circumstances. If we figure out the fountain's rules, maybe it'll help us figure out the clue?"

"Maybe," Ava groaned, "but isn't the clue supposed to help us understand the fountain, not the other way around?"

"Very good point," said Ethan. "Though I think that you making friends with Rhoda and Amy is a good start. We just need a plan to get into their room without either of them there."

Ava nodded, deep in thought.

"Are you ready to order?" the waitress asked, startling Ava back to the restaurant.

"Sure," Ethan answered without missing a beat. "let's get some pizza. I'm starving."

Mariam ran through the woods barefoot, with Ava following behind, struggling to keep up. The woods were shrouded in silence.

The Fountain

Even Mariam's footfalls as she ran made no sound at all. Ava looked around her. The colors in the forest had faded. Each tree shone a muted shade of gray.

Ava's mother hurried back and forth between large white stones littering the forest floor. Each time she reached one, she'd turn it over to peer beneath, waving her arms for Ava to come join her.

Though she tried to run lightly like her mother, Ava's legs felt as if they were weighted with lead. Arriving beside stone after stone, Ava's frustration built each time she was unable to share in her mother's obvious delight. There was nothing under the stones that she could see but mud and leaves.

Looking, looking, never finding. Each stone brought new hope and disappointment.

Ava felt her subconscious pull her away from the seemingly endless dream. Opening her eyes, she found herself in her dorm bed, no longer wandering in the forest.

The dream had seemed like it had lasted for hours. Melancholy dreams about her mother had plagued Ava for years, but they'd faded over time. Ava shivered, despite her warm covers. She'd forgotten how real the dreams could feel.

She rolled over and closed her eyes again, yet the frustration she'd felt in the dream lingered. Her mother had known about the fountain.

Leaning over the side of her bed, she pulled out her mother's diaries. She'd almost forgotten about them. In the dark room, she unsealed the manila envelope that Gran had given her. Inside, she found three small diaries, each equipped with a miniature lock. She studied the locks for a moment then grasped the manila envelope, turning it upside down and shaking it. A set of tiny keys jingled as they fell onto her bedspread. Ava groped in the dark to find them in the folds of her covers then tried the keys in the first lock.

The lock on the diary opened easily. Ava smiled. She guessed any of the keys would probably work in any of the locks. Had her teenaged mother really thought that her thoughts were safe in one of these flimsy books?

She held her phone's light near the pages of the diary she'd opened. Jules slept with her back facing Ava. The diary she'd opened had 1988 written and underlined on its first page. Ava drew in a breath. That was the year her parents had graduated, the year when her parents had fallen in love.

Without thinking, Ava looked for entries about her mother's prom. The prom Mariam had planned to attend with David Roth. She found June and started to read.

Dear Diary,

June 3, 1988

David said he loved me today! It was after the swim meet and I'd gotten my medal. He met me at the locker room door and swung me around. He was so happy that I'd won and said, "I love you, Mariam!" Of course I said it right back. I've been dying to. Something about his smile that makes me know we're going to be together forever. Our children will be beautiful...I hope they have his dark eyes. I hope we have a daughter. I like the name Ava.

I'm on cloud nine. I wonder if I look different. I feel like people can tell.

Ava stared at her mother's name written over and over in the margin of the page. Mariam had practiced her signature as *Mariam Roth* and *Mrs. Mariam Roth* in different script. Ava felt dizzy. Her mother had wanted to marry David Roth - Ethan's dad - and have a daughter. She could have been David Roth's daughter. Would that make her Ethan's sister? Or would that mean neither she nor Ethan would exist? Some other girl would be named Ava. Her hand shook as she turned the page to the next entry.

The Fountain

Dear Diary,

June 8, 1988

Mom took Mia and me to Boston this weekend to shop for my prom dress. I drove, which was the longest I've ever been allowed to take the car out. It was hard for Mom to get around the shops in her wheelchair, but she didn't complain. Mom really liked the lavender dress, but I picked one that was electric blue, since it's David's favorite color. I didn't tell Mom and Mia that, though.

I knew Mia was annoyed, because she'll probably have to wear the dress as a hand me down to her prom next year. The lavender one was actually nicer. On the car ride home, Mia barely spoke, which was fine with me. It's my prom and my dress. I spent the drive imagining what David's face will look like when I come down the stairs. He'll know I bought the dress for him.

Dear Diary,

June 10, 1988

I can't believe it's almost prom! I can hardly think of anything else. David says he'll get me a white corsage to go with my blue dress. Mia says I shouldn't have told him what my dress looked like, that it's bad luck, but that's just for wedding dresses. Mia can be so stupid.

Dear Diary,

June 20, 1988

Prom was amazing. Steven was the perfect date, we danced all night. He's really great. Why didn't I notice that before? He told me he's failing calculus, but he's got a plan to pass it. He's been accepted to college in California, and he hinted that I should go with him. I got some brochures about schools there. I hope it's not too late. I've never been so sure of anything in my life. I haven't even told Mia yet. Mom's going to have a fit.

Ava stopped reading, leaving the diary open on her pillow. A line she'd read in her mother's fountain essay ran through her mind.

A wish for a different life.

What had happened in the ten days between the two diary entries she'd just read? Despite being intrigued, Ava felt exhausted. She'd had trouble sleeping since she'd arrived at St. Augustus and it was starting to catch up with her. She yawned and switched off her phone, tucking the journals back under her bed.

Her mother had loved Ethan's dad.

CHAPTER TWENTY

Surprise

Homecoming seemed to take forever to come. The plan to go to Boston seemed more surreal with each day that passed. Was Courtney going to be home? Were they just going to ring the doorbell - and say what, exactly? Ethan had reassured her that they'd figure something out, but Ava wasn't so sure. Courtney was going to think they were nuts. That didn't matter so much if Ava could know that her wish hadn't ruined Courtney's life.

She'd packed and repacked her backpack for Boston at least a dozen times before the day finally arrived. Had she brought everything she needed? She silently inventoried the contents of her backpack as she walked down the dorm hallway the morning of homecoming. She'd brought her phone, wallet, a raincoat and a few protein bars. She'd gotten everything ready the moment Ethan had suggested they go to Boston.

Ava had been waiting on pins and needles, but she felt sure that finding Courtney was okay would somehow lead her to the fountain. She felt like skipping on her way to meet Ethan to catch the bus to Boston.

It seemed she couldn't help being early for most things these days. They didn't have to be at the bus station for another hour. Entering the school foyer, she stopped short. She stared for a moment at the boy sitting alone on the bench by the door.

"Lucas!" she cried, as she rushed toward him. "What are you doing here?"

Lucas grinned broadly and stood up to take her into his arms. All the weeks they'd been apart melted away into his embrace.

"I'm here for homecoming, of course," he replied, with a hint of mockery in his tone.

His bangs were longer than Ava remembered, almost completely covering his eyes. She pushed back his hair to get a good look at her childhood friend and boyfriend.

"And I've been really worried about you," he added more seriously, shaking his head slightly, so that his hair fell back into place.

"When did you get here?" Ava asked, still reeling.

"Late last night," he replied. "Mia arranged for me to stay at your gran's so that I could surprise you this morning. I thought if I got here early, I'd catch you before you went off somewhere, but the school office isn't open yet, so I guess I was a little too keen. Mia said I was supposed to sign in or something. Anyway, I was thinking I'd wait until someone around here woke up and ask them to go find you."

"Well," said Ava, "I'm certainly surprised."

"But you're glad to see me, right?" Lucas asked shyly.

"Of course!" Ava exclaimed.

"Then my mission's accomplished," said Lucas, looking relieved and planting a kiss on her lips.

Ava wrapped her arms around his neck. She'd missed him so much. He pulled away all too soon, taking her hands in his once again.

"So, do you want to tell me what you're doing up so early?" Lucas asked, eyeing her backpack. "You're not exactly a morning person."

"I, uh…" Ava stuttered.

She noticed the back door to the foyer was open and Ethan

entered, approaching them across the stone floor.

"Ethan!" she exclaimed, letting go of Lucas' hands. "This is, uh, my boyfriend Lucas. He came from San Francisco last night to surprise me."

"Oh, hi," Ethan replied, shaking hands smoothly with Lucas. "Ava and I were..."

"Just going for an early breakfast to discuss the upcoming swim meet," Ava interrupted, shooting Ethan a pleading look. "Ethan's helping me plan it."

"Yeah, Ava," said Ethan, looking into her eyes, "about that. I think you'll be on your own. It turns out I'm busy this morning. Basketball practice."

"Uh, okay," replied Ava, looking first at him, then back at Lucas.

"See you later then," Ethan said coolly, turning to go. "Nice to meet you, Lucas."

"*Sorry,*" she mouthed to Ethan.

Lucas waved to Ethan as he left. Ava watched as Ethan left the foyer, resisting the urge to run after him. The trip to Boston evaporated as the door closed behind him.

"So, what's on the agenda for homecoming?" Lucas asked brightly.

"I've no idea, actually," Ava replied, thinking of Jules. "Luckily though, I know someone who does. Once my roommate wakes up, I'm sure she'll be more than happy to fill us in."

"You were just on your way to breakfast, weren't you?" Lucas asked. "I'm starving!"

"Yes, I was," replied Ava, the lie tasting bitter in her mouth as she took his hand. "Come on, I'll show you the cafeteria."

She bit her lip as they walked together. Ethan had been so helpful to this point. Surely he'd understand that Lucas knew nothing about the fountain. Lucas would think she was crazy.

"So do they have pancakes and sausage?" Lucas asked.

"Of course," confirmed Ava, giving his hand a squeeze.

Disappointment tugged at Ava. She'd really wanted to check in on Courtney today. Homecoming was the perfect day to slip away unnoticed. But it couldn't be helped. She'd be sure to reimburse Ethan for the tickets and rebook them for another time. They'd go another weekend.

"Here we are," said Ava as she steered Lucas toward the cafeteria.

It seemed as if they hadn't been apart at all, Ava marveled as she and Lucas finished up their breakfast. Sure, it had only been a few weeks, but so much had happened since she'd left San Francisco.

"So," said Lucas, looking around, "this place is pretty fancy."

"I guess," replied Ava.

"Did you know Jenna finally got up the nerve to ask Marcus out?" Lucas asked. "They're together just about all the time these days."

"Really?" asked Ava.

She couldn't focus right now on things that were happening back in San Francisco. She'd been so close to seeing Courtney.

"Yeah," Lucas replied. "You should give her a call. She's been asking me about you. She said you haven't returned her emails."

"I've been busy," said Ava, with a pang of guilt.

"Ava," Lucas told her, resting his hand on her arm. "I came because I'm worried about you. If things here are too much, you can always come home, you know."

"I'm fine, really," said Ava, assuring him with a confidence she didn't feel.

Ava flinched as Lucas looked into her eyes. He knew all her secrets. Well, at least he used to know all her secrets. She knew he wouldn't press her. It wasn't his style. Ava imagined what it would be like to fly home to San Francisco tomorrow with Lucas and resume her life there. The thought was tempting, until she remembered that she'd be going back to a very different family than the one she'd known. Her dad. Her house. She had to see Courtney.

"Promise?" he asked her.

"Yeah," replied Ava.

Ava knew she'd missed the bus to Boston by now. Sitting here, having breakfast with Lucas felt all wrong. Why was he so down on her choices? Sure, she hadn't asked to be team captain, but if she had, would that be so bad?

"Ava?"

He'd always been able to read her expression. Could he tell she was holding something back?

"I'm a little homesick, that's all," she answered quickly. "Have you seen my dad at all?'

"Sure," replied Lucas. "We had lunch together this week. Which reminds me, he sent you something."

Ava narrowed her eyes as Lucas fished around in his backpack. Her dad had lunch with Lucas? Sure, they liked each other, but they'd never been pals. Lucas produced a small jeweler's box from his pocket.

"Open it," Lucas urged, holding out the black velvet case.

Ava snapped open the box. Inside was a delicate silver necklace, with a single silver owl charm hanging from the chain.

"It was your mother's," Lucas told her. "Your dad said she wore it to their senior prom. He wanted you to have it."

Ava picked it up and turned it over in her hands. The St. Augustus mascot looked exquisite embossed in silver.

"He'd planned to save it for your prom," Lucas told her. "But he thought maybe you'd like to wear it to the homecoming dance. He's very proud of you for coming here, Ava, but he misses you. He's worried that he pushed you to come to St. Augustus."

Ava felt an electric jolt shoot through her. Her dad had *pushed* her? That wasn't right. Her mind raced. Her dad had never given her anything of her mom's before. She'd thought he hadn't kept anything of hers.

Lucas took the chain from her and fastened it gently around her neck.

Ava looked up from their table to see Jules and Jake approach.

"It's beautiful," Ava told him, touching the charm lightly with her fingertips. "But I hadn't planned to go to the dance. I don't even have anything to wear."

"Oh," said Lucas, sounding disappointed. "I'd hoped I could take you and maybe meet some of your friends."

"Ava!" Jules gushed, taking a seat across from them. "You were up and gone so early this morning, I thought you must have practice. Are you going to introduce us to your friend?"

"This is Lucas, my boyfriend," said Ava. "Lucas, this is Jules, my roommate."

"So nice to finally meet you, Lucas," said Jules, not missing a beat. "I've heard a lot about you. Now Ava, what's this I overheard about you not having anything to wear to the dance? We can take care of that right after breakfast. Lucas, would you mind helping Jake? He has to fold a lot of programs for this afternoon's football game. There's an awful lot to do."

"Sure," replied Lucas.

"Then it's settled," Jules declared, smugly. "You and Ava are coming to the homecoming dance."

"So," said Jules to Ava as she fished through the back of their dorm room closet, "has Lucas met Ethan Roth yet?"

Ava shuddered as she thought of Ethan's cold expression that morning, when she'd introduced him to Lucas.

"Jules," she replied firmly, "Ethan and I are just friends."

"Does he know that?" Jules teased, emerging from the closet holding out two dresses for Ava to try on.

Ava wasn't in the mood for Jules' teasing. She frowned at the sexy dresses Jules held up for her to try. Ava hadn't seen Ethan since they'd parted in the foyer that morning. Still, he *had* said that homecoming wasn't really his thing. Would he come to the game, or the dance? She didn't want to be the reason he missed out, especially since they were no longer going to Boston.

Jules helped Ava wiggle into a silver sequinned dress and zipped up the back, pulling Ava's hair away from the zipper.

"Wow," said Jules, steering Ava toward the mirror. "This dress looks much better on you than it ever did on me."

Ava checked out her own reflection in the tight, shiny dress and stuck out her tongue at Jules to show her distaste.

"What's wrong with it?" Jules asked, grinning. "You'll have Lucas *and* Ethan panting over you if you wear this."

Ava was a few inches taller than Jules, so the dress was indecently short.

"I look like a disco ball," said Ava, turning away from the mirror and choosing to ignore Jules' obvious jibes about Ethan. "Can you unzip me?"

"Fine," replied Jules with a pout and releasing Ava from the dress. "But I still think it looks great."

She handed Ava another dress.

"Here, try this one."

The second dress was black. Ava slipped it over her head and tugged the skirt down over her panties. This dress wasn't much longer than the silver one had been, though at least black wasn't as overwhelming as the sequins had been. Ava turned to admire her reflection in the mirror. The dress clung to her chest and her hips in the right places. She touched the pleated neckline, its soft black fabric folding in a delicate pattern.

"I knew you'd choose that one," said Jules, standing back in an appraising manner. "Although I still think you'd look hot as a disco ball."

Ava took one last look at herself before taking off the dress. She thought she looked passable, or at least not embarrassing.

"I have to tell Bessie I'll be at my gran's tonight," Ava told Jules as she put her clothes back on. "Lucas is staying there tonight and heading home tomorrow afternoon."

"Okay," said Jules, hanging the rejected silver dress up at the back of the closet again. "Is your gran cool? Will she let you two share a room?"

It took Ava a moment to clue in to what Jules meant.

"Uh," replied Ava. "We don't, I mean, we haven't..."

"Really?" Jules asked, incredulously. "Haven't you been together, like forever?"

"Oh, we've talked about it, sure," replied Ava, uncomfortably. "But we wanted to wait."

"Hmm," Jules said, laughing, "it's probably a good thing that you picked the black dress then."

Sitting at a table in the middle of the homecoming barbecue, Ava wondered how she'd ever thought she was going to avoid partaking. Events had taken over the whole campus.

It felt so good to have Lucas here, with her. She reached for his hand across the table. A familiar warmth spread through her. Why had she felt that she couldn't tell Lucas what was happening at school, Ava wondered as she looked into his eyes. She'd always been able to tell Lucas anything.

"Lucas," Ava began, looking at him carefully, "do you believe in wishes?"

"No," Lucas replied flatly. "But you know that."

Ava stared at him across the table.

"What is it, Ava?" Lucas asked. "You look spooked."

"We should get some burgers," she replied, feeling flustered and quickly dismissing any thoughts of telling him about Courtney.

"I could sit here with you all day," said Lucas.

Ava shifted uncomfortably in her seat.

"I thought you came here for homecoming." Ava said, shaking off her moment of weakness and getting to her feet. "Let's go do homecoming!"

"Let's do homecoming," Lucas agreed, as they headed toward the grills.

CHAPTER TWENTY-ONE

The Dance

The football game that afternoon surprised Ava. She and Lucas really had fun. The Owls won in a landslide victory, yet it wasn't just that. Families of all ages, alumni, students, and Evergreen residents practically swam in a sea of school colors and homemade banners in the stands. Ava felt sorry for the opposition. She figured the Owls could've won the game on team spirit alone.

The flow of the crowd pushed and pulled Ava and Lucas down the stands toward the field after the game ended. Ava held Lucas' hand tightly to keep from getting separated.

"Ava! Have you seen Ethan around?"

Ava turned to see a man she'd never seen before come toward her on the field. Something about the man's dark eyebrows seemed eerily familiar.

"Oh, sorry," said the man, catching up to them and walking beside Ava as she and Lucas walked out of the stadium and across the parking lot toward the main campus. "I'm David Roth. Remember, we met at homecoming last year? With your dad?"

Ava looked at him sideways and tripped on the curb, nearly falling into the road.

"Are you okay?" Lucas asked, as he grabbed her arm, stopping her from falling.

Ava stood at the edge of the road, rubbing her arm where Lucas had grabbed her. She stared at Ethan's dad. How could she have been at homecoming last year – and with her dad?

"Anyway," Mr. Roth continued, "I wondered if you've seen Ethan today. He did say he wouldn't be at the game, but I was hoping to see him before I headed back. I thought you might know where he is."

"Me?" Ava asked. Her words were choked. "You think I'd know where he is?"

What had Ethan been telling his dad?

Mr. Roth shrugged, looking from Ava to Lucas and back again.

"Ethan?" Lucas piped up. "Ava, isn't he the guy I met this morning? Didn't he say he had basketball practice or something?"

"Yes," Ava said, clearing her throat. "He did say that, I think."

"Really?" said Mr. Roth, looking perplexed. "Well, if either of you see him, could you ask him to give me a call on my mobile? I was hoping to have dinner with him before I head back to the city. I'll go see if I can find any of his other friends in the stadium, maybe they know where he'll be this afternoon. Oh, and Ava, congratulations on being named team captain. Your mother would've been very proud."

"Thanks," stammered Ava.

This was the man her mother had loved. She watched after him as he walked back toward the stadium.

"That game was really something," said Lucas, taking her hand. They crossed the road toward the main campus.

"Yes, it was," Ava agreed absentmindedly. Her arm still smarted where Lucas had grabbed her.

She and her dad had come to St. Augustus for homecoming last year? Ava's stomach churned. What else didn't she know? She felt a sudden urge to be alone. With a pang of guilt, she stole a sideways glance at Lucas. She needed to think.

"Was it this much fun last year with your dad?" Lucas asked.

I didn't do this last year! She dropped Lucas' hand. It was all she could do to keep from screaming. Slow, steady breaths, she told herself. They were almost to the dorm.

"Maybe I'll even write a song about it," Lucas added, as they walked across the lawn. "I'll call it *'Rocker does Homecoming'.*"

Arriving on the campus lawn after dinner at Gran's, Ava made a beeline for the sports complex. She'd crossed her fingers on both hands. *When had she become superstitious?*

Dinner hadn't gone well. Ava had been so distracted she'd barely participated in the conversation. Lucas had known something was off, but he'd covered for her, keeping the conversation going with Gran at dinner. Ava had seen him stiffen when she'd told him she'd meet him at the gym for the dance. To be fair, she had promised Jules she'd get ready with her in the dorm, but that wasn't where she was headed now.

Wandering the deserted halls of the sports complex, she looked inside the two auxiliary gyms. Seeing no movement, she moved down the hall toward the main gym. It was early still, there was nobody around. A table for tickets and an empty coat rack stood in the hall.

Ava went up to the main gym. Its door was decorated with beautiful flowing green and silver strips of material so that it hardly looked like a door at all, but a gateway to somewhere else.

Tentatively she pulled back the material to expose the door, the silky scarves slipping gently through her fingers. Trying the handle, she found it locked. She peeked through the window in the door, but the lights were out and she couldn't see much. Dropping the silken entrance curtains, she looked down the quiet hallway and walked quickly toward the boys' locker room. Pressing her ear to the door she listened patiently for a minute or more. Ava sighed. Ethan would probably show up at the dance later. Wouldn't he?

Ava headed back across the lawn toward the dorms. The tents and grills from that afternoon's barbecue had been cleared away and the campus lawn looked much as it did every other evening, apart from a slight matting of the grass where the crowd had been. Why had she been so sure Ethan would be at the sports complex? It was hours ago that he'd said he had practice, which she knew he'd made up, anyway. Where had he been all day? She needed to talk to him. She needed to talk to someone who *knew*. Ava pulled her hoodie around her against the chilly night air.

She looked to the right of the main building, where the staff house and the boys' dorm stood. So many windows – and she had no idea which room was his. She realized she didn't even know if Ethan had a roommate. It had just never come up. And how was it that she didn't have his mobile number? They'd spent so much time together these past weeks. She'd never needed to call him, he'd always just been there. With one last look at the boys' dorm, she hurried the rest of the way to her room.

"There you are!" Jules exclaimed, nearly dragging her inside their room when Ava fit her key into the lock. "I'd almost given up on you. Come and sit down! I have a plan for your makeover."

"Makeover?" asked Ava weakly, sinking down onto her bed.

"Wow, Ava," Lucas exclaimed, letting out a low whistle outside the homecoming gym. "You look... amazing. Well worth the wait."

"Sorry I'm so late," said Ava, tugging her skirt down a little.

She'd been so preoccupied with her own thoughts that she'd given Jules free rein on her hair and makeup. After almost an hour, when Ava had slipped the black dress over her head, Jules had pronounced her ready. Relieved, Ava had barely glanced at her own reflection as she'd left the dorm room.

"Oh, don't worry," Jules had scoffed at Ava's nervous twitching. "Nobody shows up to these things on time, although I should be getting over there: I'm supposed to work a shift at the door at eight."

She'd told Lucas she'd meet him at seven o'clock. Ava's heart sank as she thought of him waiting for her all alone outside the dance.

Ava spotted Lucas as soon as she entered the sports complex. He stood by the wall, apart from the St. Augustus students. She still wasn't used to his hair being so long, though he looked sharp in the gray suit his parents had bought the year before for his grandfather's funeral. She had stopped to watch him shift his weight from foot to foot for a moment before letting him know she'd arrived.

"You look great too," she added, smiling in answer to his enthusiastic greeting.

Lucas pulled a clear plastic box out of his inside breast pocket and offered it shyly. Inside sat a single red rose, attached to a silver bracelet.

"Is it cheesy?" Lucas asked her, his voice cracking a little. "I've only seen homecoming dances in movies."

"No," said Ava, slipping the corsage onto her wrist. "It's perfect, Lucas. Thank you."

He held his arm out and she took it, entering the gym by his side. As their eyes adjusted to the dim light, Ava was awash with amazement. She found it hard to believe that this was the same place she'd watched Ethan shooting free throws on her way to swim practice her first week of school.

"Wow," said Lucas. "This place looks awesome."

Ava reached her hand out to touch a tall silver tree that seemed to be growing out of the thick turf they walked on. *Was that real grass under their feet?* A whole forest of wooden trees sat in large, silver flower pots at the entrance, shimmering against a lush, green backdrop.

"The band is playing classic Pearl Jam," said Lucas, leaning in toward Ava and raising his voice above the blaring music. "They sound great."

Overhead, the gym's ceiling glowed like a deep blue night sky, peppered with blinking lights meant to look like twinkling stars. Starlight rained down onto the dance floor at the far end of the gym, which was lit up like the surface of a silver-blue lake.

Many of the girls dancing on the lake's surface wore sleek black dresses not unlike the one Ava had borrowed from Jules. She shuddered to think how the silver disco-ball dress would have looked in this glittering light, although Jules would've had a good laugh.

The kids on the dance floor scarcely resembled the uniformed students Ava knew from class. Had high school dances back home been this elaborate? Maybe she'd been missing out. She scanned the crowd, subconsciously searching for Ethan's dark hair.

Suddenly, Ava gasped. A large stone fountain sat in the middle of the dance floor, spouting water from the top.

"Make a wish?" asked Lucas, nudging Ava.

"What did you just say?" Ava whispered. His words took the wind out of her.

Her skin prickled as she followed Lucas' gaze. She realized he'd been reading the words off of a large silver and green banner above the stage. She breathed a little easier.

"Is that the theme of the dance?" he asked.

Ava just stared at the sign and then back at the fountain. It was large and its stone was darker than the fountain she'd encountered in the woods.

"What do you guys think?"

Jake had appeared out of the crowd. The room turned around

Ava.

"It's incredible," Lucas told him, nearly shouting to be heard above the music this close to the stage. "The band is pretty good, too."

"Care to make a wish, Ava?" Jake asked.

He smiled at her, holding out a coin in his outstretched palm.

Ava shook her head. At least Jake and Lucas could see this fountain. It wasn't a hallucination. The band had started a new song that Ava had heard a lot this fall on the radio.

"Suit yourself," Jake said with a shrug.

He sauntered away, leaving Ava and Lucas standing together at the edge of the dance floor.

"Ava?" asked Lucas, touching her in the middle of her back. "Are you okay? Do you want to dance?"

"I think I need to sit for a minute," Ava replied. She could feel a wave of panic creeping into her chest.

Lucas didn't like to dance.

"Come with me," said Lucas.

Taking her by the arm, he led her to the back of the gym where there was a refreshment table. He picked up a plastic cup and scooped some frothy punch into it, putting it into her hand. Ava noticed that the music had switched to a recorded mix. The band must've finished their set.

"I'm okay, really," Ava insisted.

"Here," he said, handing her the cup. "Take a seat. It's probably all the lights. You just need to get used to them."

Ava nodded, sitting down on a chair against the gym wall. She clasped a hand to her chest. She needed to breathe.

"I just need a minute," she told Lucas, forcing a smile. "Really, I'm fine."

"Sure," he said. "Hey, do you mind if I go meet the band? They're between sets right now. I'll be right back."

"No problem," Ava said, still smiling. "You should go."

"Thanks," replied Lucas.

Ava smiled a genuine smile this time as she watched him make his way along the wall toward the stage. He practically skipped. She was glad he'd found something he was interested in. Otherwise, they wouldn't be staying here long. After she lost sight of Lucas in the crowd, she turned her attention to the dance floor. From where she sat, there were too many dancers in the way to see the fountain. Standing, she walked closer to get a better look.

When she arrived at the fountain's edge, she realized it wasn't made of real stone, but some sort of plastic. Bending down, she picked up a coin from the floor next to the basin and closed her eyes. Taking a deep breath, she tossed it in.

"I wish to undo the wish I made in the woods September 14th", she whispered.

Her coin floated gently through the water, flashing under the lights.

Turning slowly, Ava made her way as if in a daze back across the dance floor toward where she'd parted with Lucas. He'd be back soon to check on her. *Surely that wish wouldn't work, would it?* Suspiciously, she looked around the gym. Nothing seemed to have changed, yet she felt someone watching her. Squinting into the dimly lit gym, her gaze locked with Ethan's. *He'd come.* She moved toward him, but he'd turned his back toward her and walked in the opposite direction. He must have seen her, she thought as she headed toward where he'd gone to stand, near the refreshment table.

"Hi," said Ava, as she approached.

He stood in a group with a few other boys. Judging from their height, they were probably his basketball teammates.

"What do you want?" Ethan asked her, gruffly.

He took a sip from his plastic cup.

"Can I, uh," she stammered, "talk to you for a minute?"

"Why?" Ethan asked, taking another sip of his drink.

His voice was gruffer than she'd ever heard it.

"I, uh," Ava searched for something to say.

She looked around at Ethan's friends. A blond boy standing at Ethan's side gave her a lazy shrug and looked away.

"I need to talk to you," she said to Ethan urgently, reaching across the space between them to grab his arm.

Ethan's dark eyes flashed in the starlit room. He looked away from Ava, toward the stage. The band had started playing again. Ava recognized the song, "Brown Eyed Girl." Lucas had played it for her on her last birthday. He'd be coming back soon, she didn't have much time.

"Ethan," Ava implored.

"Fine," said Ethan, taking her hand without looking her in the eyes. "We can talk on the dance floor. Come on."

Ava followed him onto the starlit lake, while scanning the crowd for Lucas.

"Ethan," said Ava, wriggling her hand free from his grip. "Your dad said I was here for homecoming last year."

"So?" Ethan asked her, moving backwards, closer to the stage, swaying to the music.

"So, I *wasn't*," Ava replied loudly, following him across the dance floor in exasperation.

"Careful what you *wish* for," Ethan said, with an unmistakable slur.

"Ethan," said Ava, taking a step back to look at him. "Have you been *drinking*?"

Ethan swayed a little on his feet before turning from her and walking toward the stage.

"Look," Ava said, going after him, "I'm sorry I couldn't go to Boston today, but don't be mad. We'll go another day."

Was he mad? He didn't seem mad. Hurt, maybe. A little tipsy, definitely. But still him.

"Never mind about that," Ethan said, leaning in toward her.

Swiftly taking her into his arms, he kissed her full on the lips. She gave a small gasp. Ava instinctively melted in toward him even as she knew she should pull away. Ethan gently pulled her closer and kissed her more deeply. Ava's head swam. His mouth against hers tasted sweet, despite the hint of beer on his breath.

She was surprised to find herself kissing him back with urgency. *Why was she not putting a stop to this?* She didn't want to put a stop to it. His hot breath mingled with hers, sending a thrill down her spine. Ethan pressed his whole body against hers until their hips touched. She closed her eyes and the busy dance floor around them faded away. Being so near to him somehow seemed natural. But how could that be?

Something tugged at her mind. Lucas. Lucas was here somewhere, where was Lucas?

"Ethan," she murmured, pushing at his chest lightly with both hands.

Opening her eyes, she found herself staring into the lights on the stage. She blinked and the band came into focus. There, playing bass guitar on the stage just above them, was Lucas. His tie was now gone and his top shirt button undone, but he was still her Lucas, playing the song for her that he'd played on her last birthday. He stared blankly down at her and Ethan on the dance floor as he continued to play.

"Ethan!" Ava shouted, shoving Ethan away from her with two hands.

"Sorry," said Ethan, backing away from her into the crowd, having the grace to look sheepish. "But you could've told me."

CHAPTER TWENTY-TWO

What's in a Kiss?

"And then he just kissed you?" Lucas asked Ava through gritted teeth.

"Yes!" exclaimed Ava. "That's what I've been saying."

Lucas hadn't been angry many times since she'd known him. Not at her, anyway.

Ava's own anger bubbled inside her – though it was Ethan she was pissed at. He'd known Lucas was there, she was sure of it.

Lucas had left the dance right after "Brown Eyed Girl." It was all Ava could do to keep up with him on the walk home to Gran's.

Ava looked at Lucas now as he walked beside her, longing to push his hair out of his eyes. She'd kissed Ethan back and Lucas had seen it. There wasn't much else she could say, and she knew it. Her chest felt tight.

Thin tears streaked down her cheeks as she walked. She'd been careless - careless with Lucas' heart. She'd never done anything like this before. She could hardly blame Lucas for being mad. While she and Ethan had been entwined, her sensibilities had screamed that she should stop, but somehow she couldn't. Somehow, it was exactly what she'd needed in that moment.

Earlier that afternoon, for a brief moment, she had thought she could tell Lucas everything. But it was Ethan who she'd told. And now she'd pushed Lucas even further away.

"I was just as surprised as you were," Ava added. She wasn't sure that was true.

"You didn't look surprised," Lucas muttered, interrupting Ava's thoughts. He knew her well.

"Well, I was," replied Ava defensively. "Believe me, Lucas, he's just a friend. Like I told you, he's been helping me figure out why my English teacher hated my mom. His dad knew my mom. I guess he just got the wrong impression about the time we've spent together."

"He looked right at me on the stage, you know," said Lucas, quietly. His gaze was on the ground in front of him as he walked. "He knew I'd see."

"Lucas," said Ava, stopping on the sidewalk and putting her hands on his shoulders. She had to make him stop. This was not helping. "Whatever he did, I'm *not* interested in him. He's just a friend."

"Some friend," Lucas scoffed, shrugging her hands off him and walking away.

"Lucas!" Ava called, still standing on the sidewalk. "I love *you.*" That, at least, was true. Whatever had happened with Ethan, she loved Lucas. She always had. He'd done nothing to deserve this slap.

Lucas stopped on the sidewalk and turned to face her.

"I know," he said slowly, his eyes still trained on the sidewalk. "And you know that I love you, Ava."

Her Lucas was still in there, after all.

He kicked a pebble off the sidewalk into the grass with his foot.

"It's just I want to punch that Ethan guy right now," he told her, his voice shaking. "I'll probably be able to let that go, but just not tonight."

"Okay," said Ava in a small voice, reaching out to take his hand in hers.

He closed his fingers around hers, giving her hand a squeeze.

Some of the tightness in Ava's chest eased at his touch. Neither one of them spoke as they walked toward Gran's under the street lamps. The sidewalk bordered the West Woods. Ava looked over into the trees, her stomach in knots. She should march Lucas right into the clearing. Tell him everything. Perhaps then he'd understand. Her steps slowed as they came to the edge of the woods.

Lucas looked at her, questioningly.

Ava took one last look at the woods, then shook her head and started back toward Gran's. She still held his hand tightly in hers. Lucas didn't even believe in wishes. He'd think she was off her rocker. Besides, he'd been through too much already tonight. She'd have to hold it together. For him.

The upstairs window was dark at Gran's as they approached.

"Looks like my gran's already gone to bed," said Ava.

She led him silently to the back door and used her key to get in. Ava's heart sank as she saw Theresa at the kitchen table, having a cup of tea. It wasn't that she didn't like the housekeeper. The thought of making small talk at this moment made her stomach churn. Theresa looked up from the magazine spread out in front of her as they entered.

"You two are home early," Theresa said

The bright kitchen was a shock after their chilly walk with the even chillier conversation they'd just had.

"We've had a long day," Ava explained quickly, looking sideways at Lucas, hoping he would follow her lead. "I'm beat."

"Yeah," Lucas agreed, shifting his weight on his feet, "and I have an early morning tomorrow."

"Well," said Theresa, "That sounds sensible. I was just going to put some fresh towels in Ava's room on my way to bed. I'll walk you up."

Theresa closed her magazine and got up from the kitchen table, setting her teacup in the sink.

Ava, cast another sideways glance at Lucas. Their conversation wasn't finished and they didn't need Theresa babysitting them, though Ava wasn't sure what else she could say. Nothing she could think of would make this better. It was bad, and she knew it. Lucas plunged ahead up the back stairs, Theresa following close behind him. Ava fell in behind Theresa with a sigh, her feet feeling heavy as she climbed the stairs.

"Thanks, Theresa," said Ava, her voice cracking slightly.

Her own attempt at sounding chipper echoed vacantly against the stairwell walls. The three of them reached the top of the stairs and stood outside Ava's room.

Ava shuffled her feet a little. It didn't seem appropriate to invite Lucas into her room. Of course, at home, they spent lots of time alone. Even in each other's rooms. Somehow this seemed different.

"Uh, good night, Ava," Lucas said awkwardly.

"Good night," Ava replied, stepping forward to give Lucas a chaste kiss good night. She kept one eye on Theresa.

"Good night, Lucas," Theresa chimed in.

She opened a small door in the hallway, and pulled out two fluffy white towels from the linen closet.

Ava shrugged helplessly at Lucas and followed Theresa into her mother's room. Lucas' footsteps retreated to his room down the hall.

Ava winced as she listened to him go. Any chance of fixing things between them seemed to fade as his door clicked shut down the hall.

"There," Theresa told her, closing the drapes. "Sleep tight, Ava."

"Good night, Theresa," said Ava. "Thanks."

Theresa shut the door behind herself, leaving Ava alone. Ava listened until she heard Theresa's footfalls reach the bottom of the steps. Gran's was a creaky old house, with every sound amplified against its wooden floors. Ava listened carefully as she peeled the black dress she'd worn to the dance off over her head and pulled on the shorts and T-shirt she'd brought to sleep in. She couldn't possibly go to sleep, feeling this way. She still didn't know what she could say to Lucas to make this right. She had to make this right.

Ava shut her eyes and thought back to the time she'd spent with Ethan since she'd arrived. She'd let him hold her hand a few times. She knew exactly how many times, actually. She hadn't realized she'd been keeping track. The first time in the hallway of the West Building had surprised her, but after that, it had seemed normal - comforting, even. Did friends do that? Ava wasn't sure.

Then there was Lucas. She knew that she'd never mentioned Lucas to Ethan. Would he have helped her find the fountain if she had? Ava's stomach churned. She'd known. At some level, she'd known, even if she didn't want to be with Ethan. He'd helped her so much these past weeks. He'd been there. He believed her. And she'd known.

Ava sat on the edge of the bed, listening to the sounds of Lucas getting ready for bed in the bathroom down the hall. She should go to him. She chewed the inside of her cheek, but didn't move - couldn't move.

The bathroom door creaked open down the hall. Ava held her breath as Lucas' soft footsteps came toward her.

"Can I come in?" he whispered, knocking softly on her door.

Ava opened the door to let him in. She stood in front of him, her limbs feeling numb.

Lucas hesitated in the hall, his red plaid pajama bottoms and white T-shirt clinging to his thin frame. He reached out a hand toward her and tucked a strand of hair behind her ear.

Ava's lip trembled as he touched her. Her Lucas. She felt like crying. She was undeserving. Undeserving of him, undeserving of his forgiveness.

Stepping inside the room, he scooped her up into his arms and gripped her in a bear hug.

"Are you okay?" she asked, her small voice foreign to her.

"Yeah," he replied softly, nuzzling her hair. "Are you?"

"Lucas," replied Ava, "I'm really sorry. There's nothing between me and Ethan, I swear."

"Shhh," Lucas said, kissing her lips softly. "It's okay, Ava. *We're* okay. I don't want some jerk to ruin our time together. Let's talk about something else."

Ava bristled, and pulling back slightly.

"He's not a jerk," she said, the words popping out of her mouth before she'd given them any thought. "I mean, he just, uh..."

Why was she defending Ethan? Just when Lucas was about to let it go. But letting Lucas call him a jerk meant that Ava couldn't be friends with Ethan anymore - at least not with Lucas' approval. She wanted Lucas' approval. She had to explain. But explain what?

"I'll talk to him on Monday," she said. "I'm sure he didn't mean anything by it. I'll get it all straightened out."

Should she tell Lucas that Ethan had been drinking? No, that would only make matters worse.

Lucas gave her a hard look.

"Doesn't seem like you have anything to talk about with him," he said hotly. "I mean, he took his shot, I get that. But Ava, you don't need friends like that."

Ava sat down on the bed, feeling drained. She couldn't bring Courtney back without Ethan. She needed his help - wanted it.

"I thought you wanted to talk about something else?" she asked.

"All I'm saying," Lucas continued, sitting next to her on the bed. He looked into her eyes, his face only inches from her own. "Is that it wasn't very cool for him to make a move when he knows you have a boyfriend."

Her mind thought of Ethan, standing unapologetic on the

dance floor. She felt a flash of anger at his arrogance. *What did he know about her and Lucas?* Nothing, she realized.

"You're right," Ava agreed, hoping to end this conversation.

Jules had teased her about Ethan. Was Ava naïve to believe that they could be just friends? Ava thought she might be sick. Had she made this happen?

"I don't blame you, Ava," Lucas told her, the urgency suddenly gone from his voice.

Ava nodded her head, not able to speak. She certainly felt to blame. She looked at Lucas sitting beside her and wished he would just let it go – that things could be as they'd always been. She pushed Ethan from her mind and leaned against Lucas. He wrapped his arms around her and kissed the top of her head, then left a trail of kisses down the side of her face until their lips met. Ava closed her eyes and felt his familiar lips searching hers. She kissed him deeply, looking for the rhythm they'd found so many times before, yet somehow tonight, it wasn't there. Her thoughts swam. Lucas had been her first kiss. They'd been twelve. As Lucas kissed her, she tried to push Ethan's urgent kiss from her mind, but was unsuccessful. His kiss had made her warm to the core. That same feeling crept up on her now - while she kissed Lucas.

The moment lost for her, Ava pulled gently away from his embrace.

"You know I love you, Ava," said Lucas, looking at her.

Ava wanted to answer, but her words stuck in her throat. She thought of how she'd pressed her body against Ethan's. How they had fit together like two halves of a whole.

Lucas flopped back to lie on her bed, staring at the ceiling.

"When I planned this trip," he told her softly, "I thought maybe this weekend would be the right time for us. I feel ready."

Ava's stomach clenched tighter as she looked at Lucas. She didn't want to hear this. She couldn't process this. Not now. Not in Gran's house. Not when she couldn't shake Ethan's kiss.

"Oh, I know it's not the right moment to talk about this now," he continued quickly. "It's just that we've waited so long and I really want to be able to show you how I feel."

"Lucas," Ava replied softly, pangs of guilt tugging at her. "I know how you feel. But we agreed to wait. And this is definitely not how I imagined it…"

Ava knew exactly how he felt, she'd felt it herself. But she certainly wasn't feeling it tonight. Not in this moment.

"Yeah, I know," said Lucas without looking at her. "But San Francisco's so far away. I worry you'll find someone else. I thought tonight for a moment that you had."

"It was just a misunderstanding," Ava told him firmly, willing herself to believe that. "There's nothing to worry about. Nothing's changed."

"Should I go back to my room?" he asked softly.

"Probably," replied Ava, not so much thinking of Gran and Theresa elsewhere in the house, but wanting to be alone. It didn't feel right to have Lucas here, sorting through what had happened with Ethan, when she hadn't had the chance to examine the events herself, yet.

"Well," said Lucas, sitting up on the bed and wrapping his arms around her. "We still have breakfast together before I catch the bus back to Boston."

Ava nuzzled her head into his chest. Where was the connection she usually felt when they were together like this?

"Good night," said Lucas, kissing her quickly on the lips as he got up.

Then he was gone. Ava stared at the door as he softly closed it behind him. Padding over to the light switch, she flipped it off. She climbed into the bed and pulled the heavy quilt over her, tucking it under her chin.

Ava squeezed her eyes shut, feeling a tear roll down her cheek.

She needed to cry. This day had started out so differently. She wondered how she'd be feeling tonight if she and Ethan had gone to Boston as they'd planned. Would they have seen Courtney? Would Ethan have tried to kiss her in Boston? She turned over on her side, trying to get comfortable. She'd been elated to see Lucas sitting on that bench this morning. When had that changed?

She didn't know what she would do if she'd lost Ethan, though she was with Lucas. Ethan knew that now. *Could she still count on him to help her with her wish?*

Alone in her bed, she replayed Ethan's kiss on the dance floor. Her whole body tingled as she lay there, remembering how their mouths had fit together. How he'd tasted. How she couldn't help but kiss him back. How long had she felt that way about Ethan? And how did she feel, exactly?

She loved Lucas. That wasn't in question. But Ethan... even now, it was him she wanted to make things right with. He'd been so angry. So hurt.

It was the second time that day she kicked herself for not having his mobile number. Probably just as well, tonight. He'd been drinking and she didn't really know what she wanted to say, anyway. She wanted to slap him for putting her in this position. She wanted to yell at him. She wanted to...kiss him.

Yes, definitely this conversation would have to wait. Wait until her feelings had passed. They would pass.

CHAPTER TWENTY-THREE

Revived

Ava stared through the dark at the ceiling of her room after another long day. Jules' familiar snores sounded lightly from the other side of the room. Ava hadn't slept much lately, waking impossibly early in the mornings after strange dreams. At first, Coach Laurel had been impressed that Ava had spent so many early mornings at the pool. But even the coach had told her to ease up. Swimming was the only thing that seemed to quiet her mind these days.

Courtney had been banished from St. Augustus forever, to God knew where. And it was Ava's fault.

Ava rolled onto her side. Things with Lucas had been strained since homecoming. On the surface, everything was normal. In fact, they talked and texted more often than they had before his visit, but it felt forced, to Ava. Her secret was big – really big. It loomed between them in every conversation. She'd never lied to him before and it made her feel like she wanted to crawl out of her own skin.

She let out a deep sigh and closed her eyes, willing herself to sleep. As if on cue, the image she saw now whenever she had a quiet moment popped into her mind – she and Ethan intertwined on the dance floor, their breath mixing. She shifted slightly in her bed to dispel the unwelcome tingle spreading across her core.

Had she only imagined their closeness? He hadn't spoken to her since that night.

Ava tried to picture Ethan, her friend, in her mind. Instead she found herself thinking what little progress she'd made in reversing her wish in the past weeks, without him. She knew she had to break the silence with Ethan, and soon.

"Ethan!" Ava called out to him down the hallway of the West Building the next morning.

He'd left class so quickly she practically had to jog behind him to stay within earshot. They didn't walk together to calculus anymore. She'd given up waiting for him to apologize. If *she* had something to be sorry for, she wasn't sure she could put it in words. No, she was going to fix this. She'd make him be her friend again. Whatever it took.

Ethan wheeled around to face her, his face unreadable.

"Ethan, are you ever going to talk to me?" Ava demanded once she'd caught up to him, her voice breathy from having to run.

"About what?" Ethan asked, clearly a challenge.

It was a loaded question. She hadn't really planned out what she was going to say. Conversation had always been so easy between them - until now. Ava's lower lip quivered just a touch. Where should she start? Taking a deep breath, she plunged ahead.

"About the fountain. About Courtney. The rest – well, if you want to," Ava answered, watching his blank face hopefully.

"Are you still trying to find your fountain?" Ethan asked, his voice light.

Ava felt as if he'd kicked her in the stomach. He didn't believe her anymore, she realized. Had he ever? Or had that all been an act to get to know her? Their whole friendship suddenly felt like it was sinking in quicksand.

Her phone – which she'd been holding – jingled to life. Glancing down, her cheeks reddened as a picture of Lucas and her smiling popped up on the screen.

"Why don't you get your *boyfriend* to help you find it?" Ethan scoffed. He turned and walked away from her, toward their next class.

Ava stood in the crowded hall and stared at her phone just a moment more before she answered.

Lucas checked in often these days. She had to answer.

"Hey, Lucas," she said into the phone as she watched Ethan's back disappear into the crowd. Her voice was tight.

Ava slowly put one foot in front of the other as she listened to Lucas recount his day, following Ethan toward their class.

Courtney's shadow seemed everywhere as Ava threw herself into preparations for the swim meet. Every morning she expectantly looked for Courtney in the halls or in her seat in class. But Courtney stayed gone and the shadows disappeared when Ava looked too hard.

Short sentences scrawled in the notebook Ethan had lent her on her first day of classes kept track of the days Courtney had been gone. She tried to record anything that might be affected by Courtney's reappearance, but the paragraphs in the first weeks dwindled to a few words as the days wore on.

Ava read Isaac Young's journals front to back until they wouldn't close flat anymore. Nothing else seemed to be a clue. There were a lot of ramblings about the success and importance of St. Augustus students. It seemed a noble cause, but not helpful where undoing Ava's wish was concerned. Had he even known about the fountain?

The Fountain

The silent wall between her and Ethan left an aching hole in Ava's campus life. After class, he'd bolt out into the hallway without even looking in her direction. Had he been for real at the dance? Ava lingered longer in the cafeteria, hoping to see him, but he never showed. He'd have to talk to her eventually, wouldn't he?

She reached for wisps from the short time she'd known Courtney. Jules and her friends had said Rhoda hadn't returned to school this year because of something Courtney had done. That must have been true, because now – with Courtney gone – here she was, living in the lucky room. Courtney's room. It was hard not to smile around Rhoda – she nearly bubbled over when she talked. Ava couldn't imagine anyone not liking Rhoda. More than once, Ava found herself staring at Rhoda as she talked. If Ava was successful in bringing Courtney back, Rhoda would be wherever Rhoda had gone to school this year. Rhoda had no idea. She would think Ava was nuts.

After Ava and her teammates had hung the posters, put together the welcome packages, and scheduled all the heats, the day of the swim meet arrived. Maybe team captain Courtney would have done better, but this would have to do.

The line waiting to pay admission snaked out the doors of the sports complex as Ava approached. She relaxed a little. At least there would be spectators. In less than an hour, she'd be in the water competing.

She'd given the planning a lot of her time. Time she could have spent looking for the fountain. She'd be able to focus again on that tomorrow.

Ava entered the sports complex, giving the ticket line a wide berth. She found herself standing in front of the main gym - the gym where she'd first seen Ethan. She realized with surprise that the boys' basketball team practiced inside. Of course, the whole campus wasn't about to shut down because of her meet. Edging closer to the open doors, Ava strained to see if Ethan was there. She drew in her breath as she spotted him, his back to her.

Ava watched him longer than she'd meant to, his arms flexing and relaxing every time he passed the ball to his teammate. She ached to call out to him. He knew her secret. She couldn't replace that. He didn't turn around. Ava bit back her words, toying with the idea of yelling out to ask him if he was coming to the meet. A frown crept across her forehead. What was the point? He wouldn't come. He'd made it very clear by his silence that they were no longer friends. Worse, that he no longer believed her.

Just as she turned to go, she caught sight of Ethan turning her way. His gaze locked on her standing in the doorway and he stood in the middle of the court for a moment, looking her way.

Gone was his hardened expression she'd come to know these past weeks. Her friend stood in the middle of the gym, looking at her. His eyes were sad, but not with pity. He missed her, too - Ava could feel it. She held her breath as she took him in. It was all she could do to stop herself from running into his arms.

The teammate Ethan had been passing with took careful aim and beaned the ball off the side of Ethan's head. Shouts of laughter filled the gym, breaking the moment they'd shared. With one last look her way, Ethan turned away.

Tearing herself away from the doorway, Ava scuffed the floor with her feet as she made her way toward the locker room. Minutes ago, she'd hoped he'd come to the meet to cheer her on. Now she was glad he probably wouldn't – that moment they'd just shared had been so charged, his presence would throw her off her game.

Ava shook out her hands as she walked. No, it was better that he wasn't coming, though this would also be the first meet she'd ever swum in that her dad wouldn't be in the stands. Nobody would be there cheering for her. Ava pushed open the locker room door. It felt heavy.

She'd have to snap out of it. This meet was important. She'd trained hard. She was expected to win. Ethan would have to wait. Ava pushed the moment they'd just shared as far down in her mind as she could.

The locker room teemed with girls – teams from four schools plus a handful of individual entries had come to swim. Excited chatter filled the air.

Ava slung her backpack down onto a bench – she hadn't used a locker since that first practice.

Tugging her hoodie off over her head and slipping off her sweatpants, Ava turned to face a wall. She felt anonymous. Slipping on her Owls swimsuit, Ava tried to shut out the noise of the room. She had to focus. Winning was something she knew. Winning would make everything feel right.

Several hours later, Ava's hand stretched through the water to touch the pool wall. Popping her head up and taking a quick look, she knew she'd won – and by a good measure. She smiled broadly. Her heart pounded from exertion. Only the relay left to go now.

Feeling lighter than she had in weeks, she hoisted herself out of the pool and pulled off her goggles and cap. Heat rose to her cheeks as Jules' squad launched into an Ava cheer they'd made up on one of her earlier heats. To think she'd been worried nobody would be cheering her on. She'd forgotten about Jules. She made a playful face at her roommate.

The squad chanted A-V-A!

Ava made her way over to the podium, where she'd been several times already that day. The second-place swimmer was already there, clad in the suit of the biggest rival school there.

"Congrats," the girl said to Ava, extending her hand to shake.

"Thanks," Ava replied, shaking her hand, "congrats to you too!"

Ava climbed up onto the first place spot on the podium and looked around. A girl walked their way, wearing a swimsuit Ava didn't recognize. She wasn't from one of the four main schools.

The girl pulled off her goggles and cap, shaking out her long, bushy red hair as she approached.

Ava felt her knees go weak and the blood drain from her face. She fought to stand up straight – and grabbed the second-place girl's shoulder just in time to stop herself from falling onto the pool deck.

The girl was Courtney.

CHAPTER TWENTY-FOUR

Courtney 2.0

"Hi, I'm Courtney," Courtney informed Ava as she climbed to the lowest medal step.

"I, uh... I know," Ava stammered. She looked at Courtney, stricken.

How had she returned, and why wasn't she wearing the Owls' uniform?

"You're Ava, right?" Courtney asked. "I've been watching you all day. I knew you were the one to beat."

"Uh, thanks..." Ava stammered. She couldn't help but stare at Courtney, whose green eyes looked so much friendlier than she'd remembered. "Congratulations, yourself."

A million questions ran through Ava's head. Her hands trembled. What was Courtney doing here? Where had she been all this time? *What was she doing here?*

"I'm just happy I placed," Courtney answered with a shrug. "It's the only heat I placed in all day. My high school doesn't have a pool, so our practices are only once a week. If I practiced more, I'd probably be faster."

What high school was she talking about? Courtney wasn't at St. Augustus. Courtney had another life. What life did she have? Was it better? Worse? Ava's heart pounded in her chest. Courtney was not a mediocre swimmer. She was fast. Maybe even faster than

Ava. They'd never raced. Before.

"We have a couple of dads that coach us - not my dad, though," Courtney continued. Ava thought Courtney's expression changed slightly at this confession. "They do all right, but I'd like to have a coach that can actually challenge me."

Ava looked up into the stands, desperate to see Ethan's face in the crowd. If he saw Courtney now, he'd have to believe her – right? She scanned the rows of unfamiliar faces. No Ethan.

"I've been trying to get into St. Augustus for over a year," Courtney rambled on over her shoulder toward Ava as the bronze medal was placed around her neck by one of the officials. "Last year, my application was returned, unopened after three months. Something happened with the mail, can you believe it?"

Courtney let out a heavy sigh.

Ava choked back the bile that rose in the back of her throat.

"So this year I took no chances," Courtney went on. "I hand delivered my application today to the headmistress. Hopefully I'll get in for next semester – do you like the swim program here?"

Ava's head felt light as she bent her neck down to accept her third gold medal of the day.

I wish that St. Augustus had never heard of Courtney, or her family.

Courtney's application had been returned. The fountain had made sure. It had never reached St. Augustus. They'd never heard of her.

Coach Laurel was nearby, and tossed Ava a towel. She wrapped it tightly around her shoulders, trying to control her shaking. If only it were from the cold.

Courtney had been in the headmistresses' office today, where Ava had last seen her. Ava took a sideways glance at Courtney. The medal presentation was over, the clapping had died down. They were free to go.

"Good luck, maybe see you on the team, then," Ava managed to choke out, stepping down from the podium. She couldn't get away fast enough.

Slamming her way into the locker room, Ava barely made it into one of the restroom stalls before her stomach lurched violently. She crouched in front of the toilet as her spaghetti lunch splashed into the bowl. Reaching out, Ava pushed hard on the flush handle to cover the sound of her retching. She cringed against spots of cold water splashing her face, but she didn't have the energy to move away. Slumping down onto the tile floor, Ava used the towel slung around her shoulders to wipe her mouth.

Courtney couldn't come to St. Augustus. Not like this. Ava ran her tongue around the inside of her mouth, tasting sour. She spat remnants of her lunch into the toilet. If Courtney came as a new student, everything would be wrong. Courtney wouldn't take back team captain. She wasn't even a fast swimmer. Not fast enough, anyway. Ava hadn't made the wish to be handed Courtney's position. She had to find the fountain.

Later that night, the door to her dorm room clicked and Jules bounded in.

"I thought I might've seen Ethan Roth in the stands today, was he there?" Jules asked Ava.

Ava shook her head and busied herself getting ready for bed. She'd brushed her teeth at least five times since that afternoon, but the bitterness lingered.

She'd thrown on her tracksuit over her wet swimsuit and gotten out of the locker room before the other girls had come in from the deck. She couldn't risk running into Courtney again.

Courtney was on the St. Augustus campus. She hadn't known who Ava was. Ava's skin prickled as she remembered Courtney's cheerful smile. Courtney had been a whole new person – a different person than Ava had seen before. Had she missed something?

Though her stomach had been still upside down, she'd gathered herself up off the bathroom floor of the locker room after the meet and pulled on her track suit. She'd left the locker room determined to find Ethan. She'd scoured the gym hallway, but basketball practice had been long over. Ethan was the only one who could possibly understand. He could help her feel normal – but he was nowhere to be found.

"So, are you *ever* going to tell me what happened with Ethan at the dance?" Jules asked, sounding exasperated as she flopped onto her bed in their dorm room. "You two spent every waking minute together at the beginning of the semester and then Mr. San Francisco shows up and now you and Ethan don't even speak? C'mon, Ava, I'm not blind. Something happened."

"I guess you'll have to ask him," Ava said, avoiding Jules' gaze and tugging on her pajama bottoms.

Courtney could be just the reason she'd need to convince Ethan to start talking with her again. He should grow up. There was no reason they couldn't be friends. This was not something she was about to discuss with Jules.

"Oh, come on, don't be like that," said Jules, fishing under her pillow for her silk pajamas. "I only thought you might want to talk about it."

"Well, I don't," Ava answered flatly, crawling under her covers. A dull ache nagged at her chest - the same ache she always felt these days when she thought about Ethan. And Lucas.

The moment she'd shared with Ethan when she'd seen him in the gym before the swim meet that afternoon had given her hope. She needed him, whether he believed her or not.

"I think I held my breath your whole last lap of the relay," Jules told her as she got changed, apparently dropping the subject of Ethan. "I wasn't even cheering with the squad, I just stood and watched. We were so far behind I thought there was no way you could win, but I've never been so glad to be wrong. I'm going to start coming to all your meets."

"Sure," said Ava, softening her tone. "That'd be great, Jules."

Ava closed her eyes, trying to signal to Jules that she was ready for bed. She needed to think. She needed to find a way to make Courtney's appearance today seem less crazy in her mind.

"Lights out, girls!" Bessie's booming voice rang through the hall.

"You know, Ava," Jules said quietly into the darkened room after turning off her bedside lamp. "I think it's okay if you like them both."

Ava rolled away from Jules toward the wall without answering. Courtney's bright voice played through her mind. Ava tried to recall how horrible she'd been at the start of the year, but the memory blurred. Despite weeks of spending time that she should have been sleeping thinking about it, she was no closer to finding the fountain. It just seemed gone. She was beginning to think it'd never been there at all. She tried to focus on the glimmer of hope she'd seen with Ethan. She could build on that.

CHAPTER TWENTY-FIVE

Caught

Ava got to English class early Monday morning, a nervous energy turning the oatmeal she'd eaten for breakfast into rolling waves inside her stomach. As students filed into the classroom, she got pats on the back and cheers to congratulate her on her win at the swim meet - though Ethan wasn't among them.

She sensed a familiar dread as Ms. Krick appeared in the doorway just as the bell rang. Ava looked quickly down at her desk, avoiding Ms. Krick's gaze. Ava swiveled around to see Ethan's chair empty in the back row.

Creak.

The squeaky classroom door announced his late arrival. Ethan hesitated on the threshold then walked quickly toward his seat, eyes down. Ava thought he looked less confident than usual.

"Mr. Roth," Ms. Krick announced just as he reached his seat. "It's so nice of you to join us this morning. I'm so looking forward to spending extra time together after school in detention."

Ava swiveled around in her seat to look at Ethan, who'd slipped quietly into his desk. Detention? What had he done?

"Let me tell you," continued Ms. Krick, "that if I were headmistress, you'd surely have been suspended. If I ever see you near the West Woods again, that is exactly what will happen."

Ava let out an involuntary gasp, attracting Ms. Krick's watchful gaze. Looking down at her books on her desk, Ava's heart raced. Ethan had been in the West Woods. Had he seen the fountain? What had he wished for? She took a furtive look to the back of the classroom, half expecting to see Courtney's smug smile – but someone else sat there.

"Ava, perhaps you could share with us which perspective this story was written in?" Ms. Krick's question interrupted her thoughts.

"Uh," Ava stammered. "Sorry, Ms. Krick, which story was that?"

"Mmm," Ms. Krick murmured with a critical tone. "As I thought. Could someone give Ava the correct answer?"

Ava didn't hear who answered. In fact, she didn't hear much for the rest of the class. *Ethan was still looking for the fountain.* Wasn't he? Why else would he be in the West Woods? He'd said he'd never been there before. She felt a pang of guilt that she'd ever doubted him. Warmth spread through her core. Of course he was still looking. He believed her. He'd know for sure once she told him that Courtney had been here for the meet. Wouldn't he?

She turned her head slightly to steal a glance at Ethan. She willed him to look up but couldn't catch his eye. Her thoughts continued to spin until the bell signalled the end of class.

Snapping up her books, Ava hurried to the hall ahead of the other students, waiting in ambush by the door for Ethan to leave the room.

"Ethan," she addressed him as he came out of the classroom door.

She bristled as Ethan brushed past her without acknowledgement, bumping her shoulder roughly.

"Ethan?" Ava called urgently as she hurried to follow him through the crowded hallway.

"What?" Ethan said as he wheeled around, his eyes flashing.

Ava stopped and stared at this boy, who had been her friend. She wasn't sure what she wanted to say. Her heart raced. He looked pissed off.

Ethan turned his back on her again and joined the throng of students going down the stairs.

Ava took a deep breath and steeled her nerves.

"Ethan!" Ava called, hopping down two steps at a time to catch him and tugging the back of his school sweater.

"Hey!" He exclaimed, turning to face her. "What do you want?" His cheeks were red.

She squared off against him. There was less than a foot separating them in the crowded hallway.

"What were you doing in the West Woods?" Ava blurted.

"What do you care?" Ethan asked, turning away from her and continuing down the stairs.

Ava stood and watched him go for a moment before barreling down the stairs after him toward their calculus class, fighting her way through the crowded stairwell. When she got to the classroom, Ethan was already seated at the back. She plopped herself into the desk in front of him and leaned closer so that nobody would overhear what she had to say.

"Did you see it?" she whispered. "Did you see the fountain?"

"No," Ethan answered her flatly. He sat back in his desk and opened his book in front of her on his desk with a bang.

"She was here at the meet this weekend – Courtney," she blurted, a little louder. "She was here. And she's coming back. She's going to be a student."

Ethan sat back in his seat, his eyes wide. Ava let her guard down a notch. It looked like she'd gotten his attention.

"Ava," Chloe said, cheerily, from the desk beside Ethan, "I didn't get the chance to congratulate you yesterday - but great swim."

Ava blinked – surprised at Chloe's interruption.

The late bell rang for class.

"Thanks," Ava mumbled to Chloe, trying to muster a small smile. She made her way to her own desk in the front row.

After calculus, Ethan was off and out the door before Ava had even packed up her books. The ache in her chest returned. Had she misread his interest in Courtney's return?

Ava found herself walking through the dorm hallway at loose ends after school that day with no swim meet planning to fill her time. She'd almost forgotten what it was like to have a free afternoon. She wandered the campus, trying to look casual. Really, she was looking for Ethan. After her third lap past the same group of seniors in the foyer, she headed back to the girls' dorm. They'd been giving her dirty looks. She'd told Ethan her news about Courtney and he still didn't want to talk to her. She knew she should take a step back – give him some space. But she didn't know how. Noticing Rhoda and Amy's door was ajar, Ava peeked in.

"I miss you so much," Ava overheard Rhoda say into her phone.

Ava turned from the door instinctively, not wanting to interrupt.

"Ava!" Rhoda called to her. "Come in!"

"Oh, I don't want to intrude," Ava replied, standing in the hallway outside the door. "I just wanted to say hello."

"Not at all, I'm just saying goodbye to Mark," Rhoda was on her feet now, opening the door wide for Ava to enter. "Goodbye, Mark!" She laughed cheerily into the phone.

Ava stepped into the room tentatively and sat on the edge of Amy's bed. She still didn't see anything "lucky" or out of the ordinary about this room. She looked around again now, noting the extra few feet near the closet where Rhoda's fish tank sat. Other than that, the room was identical to hers.

"Love you too," Rhoda said into her phone.

After hanging up, Rhoda smiled broadly at Ava.

"I was just recounting your epic swim to Mark," said Rhoda. "He says congratulations. We would never have won the relay without you."

Rhoda had been really helpful planning the swim meet. She'd even placed in a few heats herself. The two girls had bonded during the planning sessions over their shared experience of being away at school and leaving a boyfriend home, though Rhoda seemed to spend every spare moment on the phone talking to hers.

"Thanks," said Ava.

"I can't believe Thanksgiving is coming up so quickly," said Rhoda. "The semester is flying by."

She leaned over the aquarium, scooping some frozen sludge into the water.

Ava watched Rhoda's pet shark's gray body glide to the surface of the tank, greedily gulping the food floating on surface tension of the water.

"Are you and Amy both heading home for the break?" Ava asked, looking around the small room.

"Yes, and I can't wait," said Rhoda, flopping down on her bed with a giggle. "I don't know how much time I'll spend with my parents, though. I hope to spend the whole five days with Mark. I know I don't have to tell you what carrying on a long-distance relationship is like!"

Ava couldn't help but smile. Rhoda was positively giddy over Mark.

"So, who feeds Gus when you're away?' Ava asked, a plan creeping its way into her consciousness.

"Oh, usually Bessie," Rhoda said, propping herself up on her side on her elbow and scowling slightly. "Though, when I asked her yesterday, she said she's going to her sister's for the weekend. I guess I'll have to find another lonely staff member who has nothing better to do than stay and watch the kids who don't leave for break. I know Krick usually stays, though the thought of her in my room gives me the creeps. She always asks such strange questions. Did you know she has a weird obsession with this room's 'luckiness?' What a load of crap that is."

"Oh?" asked Ava. This was the first time the subject of the room being lucky had come up with Rhoda. "You don't think it's lucky?"

"No," answered Rhoda with a laugh. "This is my second year rooming here and so far, no luck."

"I'll feed Gus over Thanksgiving weekend," Ava told her in a rush.

"Really?" Rhoda asked, looking at her sideways. "I thought you were going home to San Fran?"

"No," replied Ava, feeling reckless. "My plans changed. I'm spending it at my gran's, but it would be no problem to come back to campus to feed him. It's just a short walk."

Ava felt her heart thud in her chest as the lies came out of her mouth. *What was she saying?*

"Okay, then," Rhoda said to her, clapping her hands. "Thanks a bunch. I'll get you an extra key from Bessie."

"Great," Ava agreed.

"So, this food, he needs just a couple of pinches per day," Rhoda said, holding up a vial, "but he also likes bloodworms, I keep them here in this little mini-freezer. Simple."

Rhoda opened the freezer, which looked just like a mini-fridge. It sat on the floor next to the fish tank. She showed Ava the little packages of food.

"No problem," Ava said, scrunching up her nose at the thought of touching worms.

She took a good look around room 65. She'd have a whole weekend to discover its secrets.

CHAPTER TWENTY-SIX

The Dream

Ava sat on Rhoda's bed on the Saturday of Thanksgiving break, watching Gus flick his tail gracefully each time he changed direction in his tank. Concentrating, she twitched her own feet a little, imagining moving like that in the pool. She hadn't swum all weekend.

Leaning back onto the bed and closing her eyes, she replayed the disappointment she'd heard in her dad's voice. He'd even offered to come to Evergreen for Thanksgiving instead, but Ava could tell he couldn't afford it last minute. Ava sighed. He'd called twice so far over the weekend. He hadn't been pleased that she'd canceled her flight home. The flight Mia and Chuck had paid for. Ava still couldn't get used to her dad being dependent on them.

She felt genuinely bad for lying to her dad and Lucas about being sick, but even talking to them on the phone had been strained, she couldn't imagine being there in person. Rhoda would return the next day and Ava still hadn't found anything unusual in the room.

Thanksgiving had been Ava's favorite holiday as a kid. Her mom had been a fabulous cook. Mia and Chuck had always come to their house for the feast – the house that apparently was no longer theirs. Ava's job on holidays had been setting the table and making place-cards telling people where to sit. Her dad built the fire in the fireplace of their big, draughty house to keep out the November chill. Of course, November in San Francisco was still warm compared to New England. She'd always carefully positioned her own place-card next to her mother's seat, her own little chest swelling with pride as the meal progressed, as if she'd prepared it herself. *What would holidays have been like if her family had always lived with Mia and Chuck?* Ava shook her head, not willing to find out. She'd stayed on campus with only a smidgen of regret.

Thanksgivings had been different without her mom. Mia's turkey was dry and her stuffing often burnt. Last year, Ava's dad had let Ava have a glass of red wine with the adults. She'd sipped its bitterness feeling very grown up, though there was still some left in the bottom of her glass when she'd cleared the table. She clenched her teeth in frustration. This weekend had been a waste. Perhaps being in San Francisco with everything still upside down would have been better. At least she'd have had Lucas.

Opening her eyes, she studied the ceiling of the lucky room, which was smooth and painted white, just like the ceiling in her own room. She traced the lines with her gaze where the ceiling met the walls for the millionth time, looking for something amiss.

Why had it been so important to Courtney to have this room? *What was here?* Would she try to get the room back? Ava's thoughts got muddled when she tried to trace the possibilities of this alternate timeline. Because of Ava's wish, Jim Wallis had no longer gone to St. Augustus. Even if she came now, Courtney would no longer be an alumni kid. The secrets of the room couldn't be passed on to her.

Ava's search of room 65 had been tentative the first morning she'd come, though as each day passed, she'd become bolder, knocking on walls and doors, looking for loose floorboards. She'd even gone through Amy and Rhoda's drawers and belongings, always careful to replace everything just as she'd found it.

There had been letters from Mark in Rhoda's desk. Ava had told herself she was looking for clues, though truthfully she couldn't put them down once she'd started reading. Mark's simple words were so genuine. Lucas had never written to her like that. Even when she'd been able to tell him everything.

Rhoda,

There is nothing that I couldn't share with you. Nothing that ever goes unsaid...

That was the letter that had tugged at her most of all. She couldn't say those things anymore to Lucas. She'd expected disappointment in his voice when she'd called to tell him she couldn't make it home for Thanksgiving, though she thought she'd heard something else. Had he known she was lying about having an ear infection? If she'd really had one, flying wasn't recommended. She knew that from a girl in grade school who'd had to miss a family ski trip once. That had always stuck with Ava because it had seemed so unfair. It was the perfect excuse – but it was an excuse.

Ava had been genuine in her apology to Lucas, but he knew her well.

Thanksgiving dinner at Gran's this weekend had been delicious. Theresa was a much better cook than the other housekeepers Ava remembered.

Rhoda's soft pillow felt great. Ava had been plagued with insomnia for months now. She lay awake nights, thinking about what she'd done. What should be happening next. What was happening next, instead - because of the fountain. Because of Ava. As many thoughts ran through her tired psyche, she couldn't resist the pull of her eyelids as they sank themselves closed and she drifted off to sleep in room 65.

Ava woke with a start, her dream as vivid in her wakened state as it was while she'd slept. Rhoda's room felt darker than it had been before she'd closed her eyes. *How long had she been asleep?*

In her dream, she'd seen the fountain. It had seemed more real, more detailed than she remembered. She checked her phone for the time and scrambled off Rhoda's bed. Gran was expecting her for supper. She had to get back. Grabbing the pillow, she fluffed it up and set it gently at the head of the bed.

Had it been just a dream? The markings on the fountain were so clear - like a snapshot, letting Ava explore each small detail as she slept. Hurriedly, she smoothed out the creases she'd left on Rhoda's bedspread.

Were there really arrows pointing from every image on the fountain? Ava squeezed her eyes shut and found she could still see the dream. Very strange. No matter which direction Ava faced the fountain, the arrows pointed the same way. Ava turned her body toward the west – the direction of the clearing. She stared at the closed door of room 65. Would the arrows have pointed north? Or maybe they pointed northwest. Was there something else to find? Energy radiated to the tips of Ava's fingertips. She had to get to the clearing. She could go today. Technically, she wasn't a ward of the campus on this break. Ms. Krick probably didn't even know Ava was here. She wouldn't be watching.

Ava opened the door to the hall and stepped out. She felt she was there before she even saw her. Ms. Krick stood in the hallway, waiting.

"Ms. Marshall, do you mind explaining what you are doing here?" asked Ms. Krick in an icy tone. "You are not on the roster of students that is registered to stay at school over the break."

"I uh, no..." Ava stammered. Her stomach reeled. "I am staying at my Gran's."

"I see," said Ms. Krick. "Your gran lives on the other side of the

West Woods, does she not?"

Ava nodded, looking at the floor. *Let me go*, she willed.

"Room 65," said Ms. Krick in a low voice, staring at the door that Ava had just come from. "Where your father roomed."

"Uh, I think so," Ava volunteered, happy to avoid the discussion of the woods. "He was roommates with David Roth."

"Ah, yes, I had forgotten," said Ms. Krick, her stony face suddenly displaying a half-smile. "Of course, that explains Mr. Roth's recent interest in the woods."

Ava could hardly breathe. She hadn't meant to give Ms. Krick new information.

"Tell me," hissed Ms. Krick, seizing Ava's forearm tightly. "What have you learned?"

"I, uh, we..." Ava stammered, not daring to move. Ms. Krick's grip hurt. Ava stared at Ms. Krick's hand on her arm. "I don't know what you're suggesting, Ms. Krick, I only came to feed Gus, um, Rhoda's shark."

"Ah, yes," said Ms. Krick, still holding Ava's arm tightly. "The *shark*." She nearly spit the word.

"Right, well," said Ava, summoning all of her courage as she gently tugged her arm out of Ms. Krick's grasp, "you needn't worry about me, Ms. Krick, I'll be at my gran's for the night, then back to campus Monday morning."

"Mind you take the road to your Gran's," said Ms. Krick frostily. "We wouldn't want you to end up with detention like your *friend* Mr. Roth."

"Of course, Ms. Krick," Ava said, giving a nod and an uncharacteristic half-curtsy.

Not waiting to hear more, Ava walked as quickly as she thought was proper toward the door at the end of the hall. Once outside in the twilight, she kept going all the way to the road and then to Gran's. There was no way she'd try for the woods tonight. Ms. Krick was watching.

The details she'd been shown in the dream did not fade, no matter how many times she turned them over in her mind that evening. With each passing hour she felt more certain that there was something else in the clearing to find. She'd looked longingly at the edge of the woods from Gran's yard in the gathering darkness. Ethan wasn't caught in the woods by chance. Ms. Krick was watching. Watching Ethan and now, watching her.

She found herself walking very slowly toward English class on Monday morning. Between Ms. Krick's suspicious hovering, Ethan still giving her the cold shoulder, and barely scraping together a pass in the class, nothing good awaited her.

Deciding there was no reason to be even one minute early, Ava stopped by her dorm room instead of heading straight to the West Building. She had time to drop off her overnight bag. Jules was back from New York and sat on her bed, frantically brushing her hair.

"Oh, Ava, hi," said Jules, looking up as the door opened. "My bus from the airport was late last night due to the storm and I slept in. How do I look?"

"Great," Ava replied. Jules always looked great. "What storm?" asked Ava, tossing her bag on her bed.

"Don't you watch the news?" replied Jules, grabbing her backpack and leaving the room.

Ava followed closely behind.

"The roads were terrible the first half of our drive," Jules continued as they walked toward the West Building. "Snow. Lots of it. The Weather Channel says it's moving toward us. I hate snow, but especially in November. Yuck."

Ava thought back to the only time she remembered it snowing in San Francisco. She'd been ten, just before her mother died.

"How was San Fran?" Jules asked her, linking her arm in Ava's. "Or more importantly, how is Mr. San Francisco? And didn't you come back yesterday? Where were you last night?"

"Uh," Ava stammered. Jules believed she'd gone home for Thanksgiving. "My Thanksgiving was good, thanks."

She hadn't exactly lied.

They parted ways in the busy hallway of the West Building. Jules gave her a quick wave as she skipped into a classroom across the hall. Ava entered Ms. Krick's room just as the bell rang. Ethan sat in his customary back seat row. Ava sat in her seat near the front and cleared her throat, trying to catch Ethan's eye. He didn't look up. Ava stared for a moment at Ms. Krick's back as she wrote on the blackboard. It wouldn't be good if Ms. Krick turned and saw Ava at Ethan's desk. Class had already started, even if Ms. Krick hadn't acknowledged the class yet.

Ava hurriedly scribbled out a note on a sheet of paper she'd torn from her notebook – the notebook that Ethan had lent her on her first day. He'd insisted she keep it.

ETHAN,
PLEASE DON'T BE LIKE THIS. I NEED TO SPEAK WITH
YOU, IT'S URGENT. MEET ME AT LUNCHTIME IN THE
STUDENT LOUNGE.
YOURS,
AVA.

She folded the note into a neat rectangle and pushed it in her sweater pocket. After class, she waited for him at the door and pressed the note into his palm as he left the classroom.

"Please read it at least," she pleaded, trailing after him as he kept walking toward calculus.

"Fine," he answered, not looking back. "I will."

CHAPTER TWENTY-SEVEN

Olive Branch

Sitting in the student lounge at lunchtime, Ava shrugged her shoulders back a few times. They were stiff from practicing the butterfly before the break. She'd shaved a few seconds off her laps, but the days off she'd taken for the Thanksgiving break had been necessary. The last thing she needed right now was an injury. Swimming took her mind off things.

She'd been so sure he would come. The round clock on the wall ticked the seconds away loudly. Jules and the girls would be just finishing up in the cafeteria about now. Ava looked back toward the entrance and let out her breath. Ethan looked her way. Their eyes met and he came toward her.

"Hey," he said as he approached, his voice void of the hostility she'd come to expect.

"Hey," Ava replied, giving him a tentative smile. "Thanks for coming."

"So," Ethan said, sitting in the armchair across from her and placing his backpack on the low table between them. "You said it was urgent. Is this about Courtney again?"

"No. Um... sort of," replied Ava, feeling color flood into her cheeks.

He'd been very clear that he wasn't interested in Courtney. She looked at him now, watching her with a passive interest. Why had she thought he was going to listen today? He didn't care. She took a few short breaths. She had nothing to lose anyway. She needed to talk to someone – she needed to talk to Ethan. She was ready to burst. If he thought she was crazy, she'd just be piling more crazy on top. At least their friendship had been real, right?

"I found the secret of the lucky room," Ava said, plunging ahead.

"Oh?" replied Ethan, raising his eyebrows.

His reaction was promising. Or at least, not a complete shutout. Ava watched his furrowed brow carefully, wishing she knew what he was thinking. The kiss hung in the air between them, but Ava didn't want to spook him. The cloud that had followed her since the dance seemed to lift as they talked and she didn't want it back.

"I stayed here over the break and offered to feed Gus, Rhoda's shark," Ava continued. "At first I didn't find anything, but then I fell asleep..."

"You fed Rhoda's shark?" asked Ethan, a strange expression coming over his face. "Wait - you stayed here for break?"

"I, uh," Ava stammered. She'd told him she'd seen Courtney. She'd told him she'd solved the secret of the lucky room. But he was interested in what her plans had been for Thanksgiving? She gave her head a slight shake before explaining. "It was a chance to spend time in room 65 to find out how to undo my wish."

"Oh," Ethan replied, frowning a little.

"Well, why were you in the West Woods?" Ava demanded. Two could play at this. She'd played through all the scenarios that would put him in the West Woods. Only one fit.

"I was looking for the fountain," Ethan said with a shrug as if the answer should be obvious.

"Oh," Ava replied. That had been the answer that fit. "Have you seen it?"

"No," Ethan replied. "I've told you that."

"Right," Ava replied, having lost her train of thought momentarily. "Anyway, when I fell asleep in Rhoda's room, I had a dream…"

Ava looked around the deserted lounge as if Ms. Krick might be there listening.

"Ethan," Ava continued, almost in a whisper. "The room, I think it *showed* me the fountain, in my dream."

She sat back and studied Ethan, waiting for a reaction. She hadn't told him the best part yet. She thought he looked slightly amused. That was better than disgust.

"Don't you see?" asked Ava, triumphant. "That's what makes the room lucky. Kids that stay there are shown the fountain, and if they seek it out, they get their wish."

"But you've already been to the fountain," said Ethan, scowling slightly. "So, what does it prove? You dreamed about something you've already seen."

"The carvings," Ava replied quickly. "When I was at the fountain before, I didn't notice the arrows on the carvings. They're all pointing the same way. Ethan, we have to go back, there's something else there to find. I'm sure of it."

"Carvings?" Ethan asked, tilting his head to the side and looking thoughtful. "I don't know, Ava, Ms. Krick is watching pretty closely these days. She's monitoring the woods."

"Yeah," Ava answered. "She was poking around the dorm this weekend, she saw me coming out of Rhoda's room and seemed pretty mad."

"I don't see how we'd get there unnoticed. Besides, there's supposed to be a storm coming tonight," Ethan said. "Maybe if we waited a few weeks, Ms. Krick will lay off a little."

"She's not likely to be out tonight in a storm, is she?" Ava asked.

"No, she isn't," Ethan answered. "If it snows hard enough, it might actually hide us."

"So, we'll go tonight?" breathed Ava.

"We need to dress warmly," replied Ethan. "It's supposed to get windy."

Ava nodded her head. He'd said he'd come with her.

"And we probably can't leave the windows open like we did the last time to get back in, because of the storm," he continued, his tone suggesting he was taking charge. "Which means we'd have to use doors and hallways. Do you think you can handle that?"

"Yes," replied Ava without hesitation. She would rather use doors than climb from the window any day, but especially in a storm. She'd heard of girls visiting other girls' rooms after lights out. If they could be in the hallway without getting caught, she should be able to leave by the outside door.

"Ava," Ethan said, looking at her suddenly, "have you actually ever *been* in a snowstorm?"

"Not exactly," Ava answered sheepishly. "But I do have boots and a hat. I'll be fine."

"I have an extra set of gloves, I'll bring them for you," he said, not looking convinced. "Or maybe we should go another time."

"No, I'll manage," Ava answered quickly.

"Okay, then," Ethan agreed, in a business-like tone as he got up to leave. "Let's meet in the trees by your window at midnight and we'll go from there. The storm is supposed to hit around suppertime, maybe the wind will have died down a bit by then."

"Before you go," Ava said, putting her hand on his arm to stop him from walking away, "I should get your mobile number. I realized I don't have it."

"Ava Marshall," he said, flashing her a grin that she'd missed these past weeks. "Are you asking me for my phone number?"

Ava laughed, happy to see some semblance of her friend return.

She handed him her phone for him to add his contact details.

"I'll text you this afternoon so you have my number," Ava told him.

"Don't bother," he replied, handing her back her phone. "I have it."

Ava could only stare at him as he walked away, wondering what she'd gotten herself into.

By the time the last bell of the afternoon had rung, large fluffy snowflakes had begun to appear in the sky, melting as they hit the ground. Ava held out her palm to catch a flake, watching it fade away as she walked from the West Building toward the dorm with Jules. This kind of snow wasn't going to hide them from Ms. Krick.

She needn't have worried. By the time she and Jules got ready for bed that night, she could barely see the ground from the dorm room window. Ava watched as swirling snow hit the pane with stinging pelts. Standing near the window, she felt cold right through, as if the storm could pull all the warmth out of her.

"It's not fair," Jules whined, peeking out the window next to Ava. "Back home, if it snows this much, school gets canceled. But since we're already here, I suppose they won't bother."

Ava got ready for bed slowly, knowing she wouldn't let herself sleep.

"Yet another disadvantage to living on campus," Jules grumbled, climbing into bed. "If you need to borrow a jacket tomorrow, Ava, I have an extra. Remind me in the morning."

"Uh, thanks," replied Ava, thinking of the small stack of clothes she'd stashed under the bed for her midnight trek.

She'd planned to get dressed after Jules fell asleep, picking out the warmest clothing she had. She'd wear two sets of sweat pants, one on top of the other and her school sweater under the fall coat Mia had sent her in October. There was no way she'd find Jules' extra coat tonight; the closet was still overstuffed. Ava did have a wool hat she wore after swim practice sometimes when her hair was wet in the early mornings. The one thing she was lacking was a pair of winter boots. Her rubber rain boots, worn with two pairs of socks, would have to do.

"Have you ever made a snow angel?" Jules asked with a giggle, turning out the lights.

"No," Ava admitted.

"Well," Jules told her, "I'll teach you tomorrow."

"Okay," replied Ava. "Good night Jules."

"Good night."

Ava rolled over toward the wall, listening to Jules' breathing slow down as she prepared to sleep. Even though she knew Ethan wouldn't be at the trees for nearly two hours, Ava was already waiting.

CHAPTER TWENTY-EIGHT

Blizzard

Swirling snow swept up under the branches of the tree Ava huddled near, stinging her face. It fell so thickly she could barely see the tree beside her. Squinting into the white mess, she wondered how this journey had seemed so urgent a few short hours ago. *Why on earth would people choose to live in a climate like this?*

Ava's eyes played tricks on her with distances. The flakes could be an inch from her nose or a foot, it was impossible to tell in the dim light. The swirl of snow was disorienting. She brought her phone up to her face to check the time, her cold fingers trying to unlock the touch screen. Her breath hung in an eerie cloud between her and the phone. She tucked her hands up against her frozen cheeks, which didn't offer much warmth.

"Ava?" Ethan's voice rang out from the direction of the dorm wall.

"Over here!" Ava called, through chattering teeth.

"Ava, what on earth..." Ethan said as he appeared as if from a dream out of the snow, huge flakes clinging to his woolen hat. "How long have you been out here?"

Ava shrugged and Ethan sprang into action, putting his own scarf around her neck. He stood back and looked at her warily, as if she might collapse at any moment. She noticed with envy that he wore a thick down coat and sturdy winter boots. His hat had flaps that covered his ears. She stood with her arms crossed over her chest.

"Here," Ethan said, pulling off his gloves and handing them to her. "Take mine, they're warm."

Ava tugged them on as he produced a second pair out of his coat pocket and slid them onto his hands.

"Don't you own a winter jacket?" he asked incredulously, eyeing her corduroy fall coat.

"I've never needed one before," Ava replied, her voice trembling with cold. "But I'm fine, really. Let's go."

Ava couldn't wait another moment to get to the fountain. She tried to stop her knees from shaking. She wasn't turning back.

"I dunno if we should," said Ethan, looking her up and down. "Ava, are those *rain* boots?"

"Really," Ava insisted, hoping her brave tone sounded convincing. "I'll be fine once we start walking."

"We should probably jog to warm you up," said Ethan, still looking apprehensive. "Well, c'mon if we're going."

He took off across the lawn at a light jog, waving for her to follow. Ava looked at the hollows his footsteps left in the snow for a long moment. Far from the snow hiding them, Ava had just realized their footsteps would be obvious to anyone who wanted to follow. Taking another brief look around the deserted, snowy campus, she felt comforted by the curtain of white hiding anything further than two feet from her view. She hurried in the direction that Ethan had gone, using his footsteps in the snow as a guide. He'd been swallowed whole by the white cloud ahead. Ethan seemed pretty sure of where he was going, despite the poor visibility. Ava wondered just how many times he'd been to the clearing since she'd shown it to him in September. Circulation tried to return to her fingers as she jogged to keep up. Her feet seemed to have gone numb in her floppy boots.

Ethan stopped just inside the trees of the woods to let her catch up. Ava was glad for the chance to catch her breath. It was still cold, but the wind didn't bite here and the snow was lighter, though fog filled the spaces between the flakes, still making it difficult to see.

"You sure you're okay?" asked Ethan, searching her face.

"I'm fine," she answered, though her feet shot pins and needles of numbness with each step.

The canopy of trees in the woods kept out any moonlight that might have gotten past the snow. Ethan pulled his flashlight out of his coat pocket and shone its beam on the path. Its eerie glow shot out in all directions, dispersed into the wall of falling snow. They walked in silence, Ava concentrating on controlling her shivers. When they reached the clearing, Ethan swung the light in a wide arc. The beam magnified itself on each snowflake and bounced back, bathing them in its glow.

She almost felt her cheeks shrink at the thought of stepping out from under the trees and into the heavy snow once again, though it did look beautiful. The light cast a virtual snow globe around them, each flake sparkling in its wake. Tilting her head, she thought maybe the beauty of the snow was what made people live here.

Ethan had already stepped into the clearing, a white layer forming on top of his toque.

"I don't expect the fountain to be here," said Ethan in a matter of fact tone. "But we should make sure."

She nodded and stepped out beside him, her boots sinking into the snow up to her ankles. The deep white threatened to suck her rain boots right off her feet. Ava curled her sore toes to keep the boots in place. She knew about frostbite. Your toes turned white. Or was it black? Ava tried not to think about it. It wasn't going to help.

They walked together slowly toward the center of the clearing, hands outstretched in front of them. Ava tried to orient herself, not sure how far they'd gone.

"Hey!" Exclaimed Ethan, as Ava saw him reach for something beyond the span of the light, which turned out to be a tree. "We're all the way to the other side of the clearing. Guess it's not here."

With a start, she realized that she had somehow expected the fountain to be there tonight. Once again they stood under the shelter of trees.

"What now?" Ethan asked, shining the flashlight back at her.

"Well," Ava said, squinting and holding a glove-clad hand up to avoid the glare, "the symbols all pointed the same direction."

"Okay, so we follow them?" Ethan asked. He shone the flashlight back toward what Ava thought would be the center of the clearing. "Do you know which direction?"

"Um," started Ava, looking helplessly at the snow, which looked the same all around her. She closed her eyes and explored the image from her dream. "I think north, maybe northwest?"

"I don't think we'll find much in this snow," said Ethan, staring out into the white.

"Maybe," said Ava, reaching into her coat pocket, "this might work."

She tugged off her glove with her teeth, breathed on her frozen fingers and pulled up a compass on her smartphone.

"Voilà," said Ava, holding up the phone for Ethan to see the compass and pointing her arm. "North is that way."

"Nice," Ethan said in an approving tone and shining the flashlight in her path. "You lead."

Ava held one hand over the screen to keep snow from falling on her phone as she trudged through the middle of the clearing toward North. Ethan followed closely behind her. Looking around, Ava saw only snow and more snow as she squinted into the night.

"Do we know what we're looking for?" Ethan called from just behind her.

"No," was Ava's honest answer.

They'd reached another edge of the clearing. Ava felt her stomach drop. She'd brought Ethan out in this weather. *What was it that they were supposed to find?*

Ethan swept the flashlight slowly from side to side.

"Can you see anything?" Ethan asked.

Ava thought she could hear impatience creeping into his voice. Maybe he wasn't as warm as she'd thought. As for her, she could never have prepared herself for how underdressed she was out in the cold. She looked up into the sky, blinking back tears. There were evergreens in front of them. Ava recognized them as the clump of trees beside the path that led to Gran's - Gran's warm, dry house.

Taking a closer look, she tilted her head to one side, studying the trees.

"I think there was a hollow under here," Ava said to him. "I played there as a kid. Let's duck underneath and sit for a minute until we come up with a plan."

Her teeth chattered as she spoke. Ethan nodded his head. Ava prodded with a gloved hand to shake snow from the branches, uncovering a slight gap. Crouching down on all fours, she crawled underneath, pine needles sticking into her from all sides. She brushed at the needles with her gloved hands, but continued on. Ethan followed close behind her.

"Whoa," Ethan said, giving a low whistle, "it's like a little cave in here."

Ava remembered it being a much larger space, though looking around, it was only about the size of a back seat of a car. It did feel warmer in here, the smell of Christmas tree inviting. The crawlspace was too low to stand up fully, so Ava sat, pushing her back up against the far side of the little room to give Ethan as much space as possible. He sat beside her with a heavy thud.

"You've been here before?" Ethan asked her, looking around.

"My mom and I played a fairy game under here when I was small," Ava said, rubbing her cold hands together. "It seemed bigger when I was eight."

"So, what now?" Ethan asked.

"I dunno," Ava answered, slumping back against the tree branches. "I just need to warm up. I thought it'd be obvious once we got to the clearing, but all this snow... I forget, are you supposed to keep moving, or stay still when you're about to get hypothermia?" "

"Actually," Ethan replied in a teasing tone. "You're supposed to get naked and huddle together under a blanket."

"What?" Ava asked. She knew maybe she was being dramatic, but she had never felt this cold.

"Here," said Ethan, placing the flashlight on a flat rock between them and breaking off a few dead branches from the tree that Ava leaned against. "Sit on these instead of the snow. They will insulate you a bit. Do you think you can handle jogging back to the dorm? It's a little warmer in here out of the wind, but the sooner we get you home the better. I don't think we're going to find anything out here tonight."

"You're probably right," Ava agreed with a sigh.

"Wait," said Ethan. "What is *that*?"

Ava followed his gaze, to where the beam of his flashlight shone. A strange, flat surface peeked out from where he'd broken off the branches. The pair exchanged a quick look then started pulling away at the evergreen. The brush was thick, but there was definitely something solid behind it.

"Whoa," said Ethan, picking up the flashlight and shining it over what appeared to be a low stone wall. "Why is there a wall here?"

Ava wiped some snow away from the stone with her glove,

revealing markings on the wall. Ethan produced a small pocket knife from his coat pocket and hacked away at the last small branches that obscured the wall. They found themselves staring at some kind of list, carved into the stone - the same white-gray stone that the fountain was made from.

Crouched side by side, they studied the wall by the light of the flashlight.

"These are people's wishes," said Ava in a whisper. "Lots of them."

"You think they're wishes from the fountain?" asked Ethan.

Ava nodded, pointing to the wish at the bottom of the list.

"*I wish St. Augustus had never heard of Courtney or her family,*" Ethan read out loud, pointing his flashlight at the words. "That was your wish?"

"Yes," Ava answered. "Look, there are dates."

"There sure are a lot of them," Ethan said, running the beam of the flashlight along the wall. "It looks like the earliest wish is 1935, the year the school opened. *I wish for my scholarship to be renewed next year.*"

"He wished for money," said Ava quietly. "I guess some things are timeless. Can you look at the wishes in the 80's? What year did my mom break up with your dad?"

She held her breath. Had her mother really wished for her dad to fall in love with her? Why would she do that, when she'd been with David?

"They were the class of '88," answered Ethan, scanning the wall with the flashlight.

"I, uh... I think my mother made a wish," said Ava. "I've read her diaries. I think that her breaking up with your dad had something to do with whatever wish she made."

Ava read the wishes Ethan shone the flashlight on out loud.

"*Please let me pass the test tomorrow,* December 10, 1986. *I wish my acne would clear up in time for prom,* May 1, 1988, *I wish*

The Fountain

for Mariam and me to fall madly, deeply in love."

The wish was dated June 12, 1988. Ava sat back in the snow, stunned into silence.

"Wow, your dad *wished* for your mom," said Ethan with a low whistle. "No wonder my pops didn't stand a chance."

Ava's shoulders slumped. She'd been so sure that it had been her mother who'd used the fountain. In all her life, she'd not once seen her dad throw a coin into a wishing well.

Tears pricked at her eyelids. Her dad had *made* her mother fall in love with him, when she'd loved David Roth. Of course now the diary entries fit. Why hadn't she considered that it could have been her dad that had used the fountain? Everything felt upside down again, like she'd felt when she realized Courtney was really gone.

Ethan had started reading from the wall again, working backward from her father's wish.

"These are fascinating," he said. "I wonder how many of these people realized that the fountain actually granted their wish."

"Wait," said Ava, "what was that last one you read?"

"*I wish for my mother to get over her illness*".

"What was the date on that?" Ava asked, leaning in toward the wall.

Ava's heart pounded. Her mother had always referred to Gran as having an "illness" when she'd been in high school. She'd been confounding doctors for decades with her lack of decline. It had to be her.

"*September 14th, 1984*," Ethan read.

Ava gave a small gasp. September 14th, the same day that she'd made her wish. Her mother would have just started school at St. Augustus. She would have been in the ninth grade. Of course she would have seen the fountain, having used the path every day to and from school.

Out of the corner of her eye, she saw a flicker of light near where her own wish was listed. Ethan quickly moved the flashlight away from the wall. He must have seen it too.

"Ethan," said Ava. "Can you shine the light at the end of the list?"

Ethan shone the flashlight back to the wall. Ava studied the words, the last wish etched lighter than the others, as if it could be rubbed away by hand. It hadn't been there moments before. Her eyes grew wide as she read the faint message.

I wish for Ava.

CHAPTER TWENTY-NINE

Wish

Ava stared at the wall where the last wish had appeared. It glowed faintly on the wall, the only wish listed without a date beside it.

"Ava," whispered Ethan, "I, I can explain."

Ava could feel him looking at her, though she couldn't take her eyes off the words.

"I don't understand," said Ava slowly, frowning at the wall. "I thought...and undoing my wish?"

"Ava," said Ethan urgently, "I didn't make that wish."

"Well if you didn't," replied Ava impatiently, gesturing at the wall, "then who did?"

The thought of someone wishing for her, as her dad had done for her mother, left her cold. She leaned as far away from Ethan as she could, given the small space they were in.

"Well," Ethan said slowly rubbing more snow off of the words with his gloved hand, "the thing is, it *is* my wish. But I didn't make it."

The words seemed to glow brighter on the wall under his touch.

"But you've never even *seen* the fountain!" Ava exclaimed.

"Well I, uh..." Ethan trailed off, looking at Ava.

"Oh," said Ava, the pit of her stomach falling out from under her, "I see."

He'd lied.

"I've seen the fountain every time I've been to the clearing alone," Ethan explained in a rush of words. "I keep coming back and it's still there. I planned to undo your wish, really I did. But every time I stand next to the fountain and try to throw my coin, I feel overwhelmed with another wish - *that wish*." He swept his hand toward the glowing words on the wall. "Somehow I just know that if I throw that coin, the fountain will know what is really in my heart, no matter what my words ask. Looks like I was right."

"And you didn't think to tell me this?" Ava asked hotly. "You just thought you'd let me think I was crazy, and that the fountain didn't exist at all? I would have understood."

But even as she said the words, she knew that probably wasn't true.

"Ava, I said I believed you. But to see these words in stone," he replied, gesturing toward the wall. "Ava, I would never make that wish."

Ava said nothing. She felt unbearably cold. The tears that had welled up a few times that night threatened to fall. He'd known that the fountain was real. The betrayal tugged at her. "I've tried to keep my distance these past weeks, Ava," Ethan explained, his voice sounding pained. "I hoped my feelings would fade. I thought that if my mind were clearer, I'd be able to undo your wish when I visited the fountain. But..."

Ava looked at him where he sat slumped against the wall. His feelings hadn't changed. He'd lied to hide them. Her resolve softened and she reached a hand out to touch his knee.

"That's why you've been such a jerk?" she asked, with more levity than she felt. "Man, Ethan, you need some lessons on how to show a girl that you like her."

Ethan met her gaze, looking as miserable as she felt. She

slipped her gloved hand into his and gave it a squeeze. He'd been trying to help her all along.

"Ava, I'm so sorry." Ethan said, his eyes pleading with her. "I *was* a jerk. I had no right to kiss you at the dance. I just – meeting Lucas like that was such a slap. I know you and I, it wasn't like that, but I thought that it could be. I wanted it to be. I..."

Ethan withdrew his hand from hers and looked away, staring into his lap.

"It's just that my feelings for you are so strong," he continued. "I didn't know what to do. They haven't changed. And I know that isn't fair. I want you to be happy. I want to help you undo the wish, but I don't know how. It's all such a mess."

The words he'd just spoken rang in her ears and she needed a moment to think. What could she say to him that would make things all right between them? He seemed so broken. She'd wanted that kiss - though she hadn't realized it at the time. She'd never felt that kind of passion with Lucas. "These wishes," said Ava, choosing to focus on the last part of his confession, "each one has changed so much. But in this whole list, I don't see where anyone has ever undone their wish."

"Is it really so bad if things stay the way they are?" Ethan asked. "Do you really want to give up being team captain and maybe get expelled?"

"I don't know what to think anymore," admitted Ava. She'd thought about the wish upside down and backwards and had never arrived at a solution. "At first I worried about my dad and everything being different with my family since he didn't go to college. Yet he actually seems pretty happy. He even talks about my mom now and seems much more at peace with everything."

"See," said Ethan, taking her hand again and nodding encouragingly, "that sounds good. Ava, it's okay to be happy. It's okay to get what you wish for sometimes."

"But, Courtney," Ava said, her voice strained. "I still don't know that she's okay. Ethan, she was supposed to go to this school and be captain of the swim team. I took that away from her. Even if she comes to the school next semester, nothing will ever be the way it was supposed to be."

Ava felt the familiar stirring in her stomach she felt whenever she thought about the wish.

"Yes, and she picked on you and everyone else around her," replied Ethan. "Courtney's better off this way. And so are you."

"You didn't meet her, Ethan," said Ava, looking at him. "She really wants to swim at St. Augustus. Her life is different."

"Trust me, Ava," Ethan said, averting his eyes again, but still holding her hand. "Courtney's fine."

"How do you know that?" Ava asked.

Something in his voice told her that he did.

"I uh, I did meet her," Ethan admitted. "I went to Boston."

"What?" Ava asked, pulling her hand away from his. "When?"

"The day of homecoming," he explained, drawing a breath in. "I went to Boston like we'd planned. I found the Wallis' house, she was outside. I went over and said I needed directions first of all, but then we sat on her lawn and talked for a bit. It felt strange, like I'd known her all along. I suppose I did."

"Even Courtney can't resist your charm," muttered Ava.

How much more had he hidden from her? She'd never been one for surprises. A shiver ran through her. Wet cold had soaked through her two pairs of sweat pants. She looked at him expectantly. She wanted him to finish. She needed to know.

"Well," Ethan said, looking embarrassed, "Actually, after we talked, she gave me her phone number. Come to think of it, she probably wondered why I never called."

Ava stiffened at his attempt to joke. She wasn't ready to laugh about this. She might never be able to laugh at this. It felt too raw.

"What makes you think she's okay?" Ava asked.

"I don't know," replied Ethan. "I didn't really learn anything more than you did. She goes to a local school in Boston, swims there. She mentioned last year she went to state finals. I was thinking you might even swim against her this year, but I guess you already have."

"Yes," Ava replied, reeling. He'd gone to Boston, seen Courtney, then returned to the dance. She'd had no idea.

"She seemed – nice," Ethan finished. "Much nicer than the girl you described. Maybe it's good for her that she isn't here."

Ava let his news sink in as they sat in silence for a moment. Thinking back, Courtney had certainly seemed nicer when she'd met her at the swim meet, though Ava hadn't really noticed at the time. Is it possible that being at St. Augustus had somehow changed Courtney?

"I know it's a lot to take in," he said quietly. "And I am so sorry I didn't tell you all this before. I just didn't know how."

The wind whistled through the branches of the trees they sat beneath. The storm hadn't let up, but the canopy over them slowed the snowflakes hitting their space so that they fell slowly.

Ava searched for the anger she thought she should feel, but there was none. She brushed a snowflake from her eyelashes. He hadn't told her what he knew. He'd gone behind her back. He'd made her think she was alone. And he'd done it all for her. He knew she'd have an impossible choice. Suddenly it didn't seem so impossible.

"And I'd had a few beers with the guys before the dance," Ethan rambled on. "It had been a really crazy day and it probably was a bad idea. But I just had to show you how I was feeling. It didn't happen the way I would have liked. I know it isn't what you want. I'm sorry if I made things difficult with Lucas. I'll talk to him if you think it would help."

Ava shook her head. He should definitely not talk to Lucas. But she was going to have to. She was acutely aware that she and Ethan had narrowed the gap between them as he talked. Their foreheads almost touched. She searched his eyes in the dim light. She saw a tenderness there that she hadn't noticed before. He looked at her now. Really looked at her. Ava's heart pounded as she caught her breath.

Courtney was okay. Ethan had made sure. He'd known it was important to her. He wasn't asking for anything in return. He'd never stopped trying to help her.

"Ethan," Ava said slowly, trying to think faster than she spoke. Every part of her body felt electric at his words, pushing aside the cold. She reached her gloved hands across the small space between them now and rested them on his hips." You don't need to wish for me."

A beat of silence passed as she tried to organize her next words carefully. She knew what she wanted to say. What she needed to say. What she wanted to do - who she wanted to be with.

Ethan pulled his gloves off as he leaned in to close the remaining space between their lips and kissed her. Not the rushed kiss they'd shared on the dance floor, but a long, soft kiss that seemed to last longer than the moment it did.

"Ava, what about..." Ethan said, pulling back a little and asking his question with his eyes. He gently stroked her cheek with his right hand. Ava leaned into his warmth.

"I don't know what will happen with Lucas and me," Ava answered honestly, though feeling surer of herself than she had in a while. "But I do know that when you and I have been apart these past weeks, I missed feeling as alive as I do when I'm with you."

"Well," replied Ethan, smiling and kissing her again, "there's nothing like a midnight stroll in a blizzard to make you feel alive!"

Ava rested her head on his shoulder, closing her eyes. Ethan put his arms around her and held her tightly.

"I could sit here all night," whispered Ethan.

"Well, it's a little cold," Ava admitted.

"And late," Ethan added, kissing her on the forehead. "I feel like we should cover this wall up before we go. It holds so many people's secrets."

"Yes," Ava agreed. "It should definitely stay hidden."

She shuddered as she thought what might happen if Ms. Krick discovered the wall, though she felt certain that she hadn't. Ethan pulled his winter gloves back on and set to work. Ava busied herself helping him replace the branches they'd broken off. She'd learned the truth about her parents. Gran might have died from her poor health if it hadn't been for the fountain. And then there was Ethan.

"You okay?" Ethan asked, reaching over and touching Ava lightly on the arm.

"Yes," she replied, "better than okay."

Ava really did feel better, though she didn't look forward to the conversation she was going to have with Lucas. She'd known for a while that she'd moved on, but it had been easier to ignore the facts. She couldn't ignore them any longer. Not telling him about the fountain had spelled it out for her. How could she ever explain?

She looked over at Ethan, thinking how disorienting it would have been to wake up one morning and suddenly have feelings for someone. Like her mother had. What Ava felt for Ethan now she knew had not been sudden. What would her mother have thought if she'd known what her father had done?

"I think it's good now, Ethan," Ava said, looking at the branches they'd just replaced.

The wall was no longer visible.

With Ethan in the lead, they crawled back through the gap in the trees and stood in the shelter of its branches for a moment. Ethan offered Ava his hand and together they headed back into the storm.

ACKNOWLEDGMENTS

Phew! What a journey this book has had so far.

The beginnings of this boarding school novel I've carried with me since my tweens. On maternity leave with my third child, I finally sat down to weave these stories into The Fountain.

A project like this takes a village to make it happen – or in this case - several villages. I feel very blessed to have such an incredible network of support.

Thank you to all my Villages! A Village of Family - Many thanks to my amazing husband, who never questioned whether this book would be published. Jamie - thank you for the umpteen Saturdays you took the kids to the science centre so I could write all day, for reading and giving feedback on the book in the beginning, and then in the end, and for your unwavering belief that this project would see the light of day. Thank you to my three beautiful kids, who ask me relentless questions about characters, help me come up with names for them, pranks to play on them , and wishes for them to make. Thank you also to Grannie, Gramma and Papa for spending time with the kids to give me time to finish my chapters.

A Village of Early Readers - Thank you to the kindergarten mommies book club, my Aunt Jane, Karen M, Yama, Susan C, Naomi S., Jen D., Tanya S. and my mom, for reading early drafts of the book and providing feedback.

A Village of Writers - I've been amazed at how supportive Canadian writers have been throughout this process. Thank you to Simon Rose, who was a terrific mentor, sounding board and editor through the first draft of The Fountain. Thank you to John Lawrence Reynolds, Tyler Trafford, Avery Olive, Nicole Kriaski and Susan Forest, who took the time to read sections of this manuscript and provide feedback, introductions and thoughtful advice that was incredibly encouraging and helpful. Thank you also to Robert Runte, whose comments and suggestions to improve this manuscript helped shape it into what it is today. Thank you especially to Randy McCharles and the whole When

Words Collide gang for taking me into your ranks and providing me with incredible opportunities to meet other amazing writers.

A Village of Friends – Thank you to all of you for asking for updates, sharing my excitement and for supporting my dreams. I appreciate you all and couldn't possibly name everyone without leaving someone out. You know who you are, and so do I. THANK YOU!

An Evil Alter Ego Press Village - I can't say enough how lucky I am to have found the perfect publisher for The Fountain. Michell Plested, thank you so much for believing in me as a writer and for tirelessly answering my new author questions. And to my editor, Jeff Hite, who wasn't afraid to tackle the tough issues and made this manuscript great.

Thanks to everyone for sharing this journey with me. I can't wait to see where it leads.

ABOUT THE AUTHOR

Suzy Vadori is an Operations Executive by day, Writer by night. The Fountain is her debut novel for Young Adults. Suzy is an involved member of the Calgary Writers' community, serving as When Words Collide (a Calgary Festival for Readers and Writers) Program Manager for Middle Grade and Young Adult since 2013. Suzy lives in Calgary, Alberta with her husband and three kids.

OTHER EVIL ALTER EGO PRESS BOOKS

Dimensional Abscesses
(edited by Jeffrey Hite & Michell Plested)

Scouts of the Apocalypse: Zombie Plague
By Michell Plested

Mik Murdoch, Boy Superhero
By Michell Plested

Mik Murdoch: The Power Within
By Michell Plested

Mik Murdoch: Crisis of Conscience
By Michell Plested